Copy Desk Murders

Minneapolis

Second Edition December 2022

10 9 8 7 6 5 4 3 2

ISBN: 978-1-959770-44-2

Cover and book design by Gary Lindberg

To Mary —
Welcome to Featherstone!
Newell Searle
4/20/24

Copy Desk Murders

Newell Searle

Minneapolis

“Home—your heart. It’s the place you ran from. You’ll return to it when you’re ready to resolve the contradictions in your life. When you’re ready to be the person you’re meant to be.”

–Father Frank Carson

To Jane Searle, mother and librarian, who nurtured my love of reading—a gift beyond price.

Also by Newell Searle

Saving Quetico-Superior, A Land Set Apart

CHAPTER 1

Boston Meade mentally kicked himself in the ass for today's editorial in the *Statesman*, his last as its interim editor. "Dad would have scorched you for this," he muttered. The late London Meade was an editor's editor, a man of carefully chosen words who had long shaped public thoughts and actions in Alton County. He recalled his father telling him words were like gyros that guided people's thoughts. "So, use words with care," he said often. "You're responsible for what happens. Careless choices have consequences." Staring at his editorial, in his head, he heard the old man's voice saying, *I taught you better than that*.

Seated in an Adirondack chair on the wrap-around veranda, he listened to the drowsy buzz of a katydid among the clematis vines. Then he turned to pick apart his work as if that could amend the mistake. You wrote a shitty editorial, he thought. You were in a hurry. You should've read it one more time. Better yet, you should've written it last week and then slept on it. Now it's too late.

> *The Alton County Statesman*, September 1, 1984
>
> Today, I step down as the *Statesman*'s interim editor after the privilege of briefly succeeding my father. I am grateful to the staff and the readers who helped me uphold his standards.

"I meant that," he whispered. He meant it because his white-maned father had received many awards for the erudite editorials he drafted with a fountain pen. His vision and drive had turned the family's bi-weekly newspaper into a daily that was read throughout southeast Minnesota. Now you own it, free and clear. As the owner and publisher, you inherited the coin of your father's fame and the weight of the subscribers' expectations. He reread the second paragraph:

> I learned anew how this community newspaper helps us understand the world we inhabit. Its series about the Midwest farm crisis—foreclosures, business failures, suicides—reported on the people you know who were affected by foreign trade, interest rates and grain prices. The farm crisis is national in its scope, abstract in its complexity but intensely personal in its reality. I am proud to have had a hand in these stories.

That sounded like Dad, he thought. Then he scowled at the paragraph that haunted him:

> It gave me great pleasure to mentor Peder Norgaard, our summer intern. After many years in Chicago, I saw my hometown afresh through his eyes. At seventeen, Peder is a natural reporter—

"I should've put a period after 'reporter' and cut the rest," he muttered and continued reading:

> At seventeen, Peder is a natural reporter, a rookie who became a veteran overnight with the discovery of Max Kaplan's bones. We may never know what the Minneapolis detective was doing here long ago or who hid his body in the abandoned farmhouse, but this unfinished story with its unanswered questions may yet propel Peder to become a fine journalist someday. Let us hope so.

That's where you fucked up. He struck out all the words after "Peder is a natural." The Kaplan reference will piss off those who were pissed off before, he thought. He removed the tortoise-shell glasses and rubbed the scar beneath the right brow. "Too late now," he mumbled and replaced the glasses to read the conclusion:

> Tomorrow, I will return to Chicago as the new editor-in-chief of *American Outlook*. Though I remain the *Statesman*'s owner, your newspaper is in the capable hands of Ginger O'Meara, a Featherstone native whose editorial skill equals my father's. With gratitude for your many kindnesses during the summer, I say thank you and farewell.

He slumped in the chair, rueing his flawed valedictory, wishing he could reel in the words like a fishing line and cast them anew. After three months, they still treat you like an outsider. "They'll be glad when you go tomorrow," he whispered to the katydids. "Glad but not as happy as you will be. You never could be yourself here, he thought. Not as long as everyone assumed you were Dad's clone. Sure, you've got his build, patrician features and Roman nose. But that's not who you are. But they didn't accept that. Instead of Dad's gregarious persona, you're reserved like Mom was. You had to get out and go to Chicago as the only way to be yourself. For that, they criticized you for acting as if Featherstone and the *Statesman* weren't good enough. Well, people see what they want to see, he thought. Being myself and outdoing Dad's success, that's what mattered the most. That's what drove Vicky into her affair. That's what led to the divorce. He shook his head as he recollected the June morning when *American Outlook* promoted him to its top job. And then learning of Dad's death right after that. In less than an hour, he advanced to the career post he coveted as he inherited the job he had despised. "Jesus," he whispered to the katydid. "The cosmos has an ironic sense of humor."

He stood, arched his back, windmilled his arms and then walked across the yard to the carriage barn. What a pleasure to drive the BMW cabriolet out of storage. He had driven it from Chicago and then garaged it all summer. Driving it around Featherstone would have reinforced the snooty outsider image. To blend in, he drove Dad's Wagoneer, the black Jeep of the family.

The cobalt Beemer was dusty, and he began wiping it clean with a soft rag. The circular polishing stirred memories of summer jobs at the *Statesman*. At thirteen, you swept the floors. At fourteen, you worked at the presses and liked it. The press was better than working in circulation at fifteen and layout at sixteen. But the best was last, as an intern reporter during the summer before your senior year. Experience at the *Statesman* gave you a foundation for Columbia University, a stringer's job, then a reporter's beat with *American Outlook*.

He paused, rag in hand, regretting the way his success had come between his father and him. "You never understood why I couldn't give up my career to succeed you," he whispered as if talking to the old man. "I guess I never told you, either. We were both wrong. You made the paper what it is. I worked just as hard to rise within the *Outlook*... it's my fault we stopped talking."

Then he snapped dust from the rag as if to shake off his regrets. Turning his thoughts to Peder put a shine on his mood like the one on the car's hood. He wagged his head in amazement. You didn't know what to do with an intern. Not when you faced settling the estate, paying bills, managing the *Statesman* and hiring a permanent editor. An intern took time, something you didn't have. So, you assigned Peder to write about Joachim Breuer's alleged bootlegging. That stop-gap should have kept him busy for a couple weeks. It lasted three days. He grinned at the memory of Peder's breathless phone call, "I'm at the St. Ansgar store... a twister wrecked Breuer's place... I'm okay... there's a chest in the wreckage... it's got a man's body! Can I have an exclusive?"

You couldn't say no to that. So, you said yes, thinking it would divert him for a couple weeks. The next morning, Peder turned in a story that wove Breuer, the tornado and the chest into a narrative. After that, you made the time to mentor him the way Dad mentored you—because he was a natural.

The man in the trunk had been dead for decades, and the coroner said he was murdered. A week later, he was identified as Max Kaplan, a Minneapolis detective missing since 1949. Boston thought of his brother Jack, the Alton County sheriff who, for reasons he couldn't fathom, refused to investigate Kaplan's death. Unanswered were the questions of what he was investigating outside Minneapolis or who might have killed him and left his body at a derelict farmhouse. Jack didn't like the editorial he wrote demanding an investigation. He said Kaplan's death was a Minneapolis problem, not his. The editorial upset the Chamber of Commerce leaders, too. They said bad press might scare off new business investment. What a lame excuse. That's when you asked Peder to look into Kaplan's past for anything Jack could use.

To his surprise, he took pleasure in editing the *Statesman* because he enjoyed Peder's company. Despite Jack's irritation, he spent time with his brother and his growing family. Their daily presence gave him solace as he grieved his father and his divorce. Though he felt loved, life in Featherstone passed like a state of suspended animation. He gave the fender a final swipe, satisfied the car was ready for tomorrow's six-hour run to Chicago. He returned to the veranda and reviewed the last to-do items in a notebook. Running a finger down the list, he saw each task had a double check. "Good. I can leave now," he said under his breath.

The eagerness to go was matched by sadness over selling the three-story Queen Anne house with its hexagonal corner turret and conical roof. From attic to cellar, it sparked memories of his mother at the piano, the family caroling by the tree, Jack cheating him at Monopoly, Sunday dinners on the Havilland China and grandfather's tales of soldiering in Cuba with Teddy Roosevelt. All of it would vanish when the realtor sold the house. If only you could take the baby Steinway with him. He found consolation during the summer playing the pieces she had taught him. The piano was more than furniture, and parting with it felt like one of many small and unavoidable amputations. Going and letting go were conflicting actions.

Grandfather Meade built the house among the bur oaks at the end of a low limestone ridge he dubbed San Juan Hill. From there, he saw most of Featherstone a mile to the east, where the late afternoon sunlight gleamed from the water tower, courthouse dome, church spires and grain elevators. From east to west, his gaze took in the fencerows that divided southeastern Minnesota into fields of corn and soybeans, oats and pastures interspersed with groves and farmsteads. He could see for miles until the countryside dissolved into the haze at the horizon. At this evening hour, long shadows stretched from behind the trees and fencerows. In the distance, a solitary thunderhead floated in the cerulean sky, trailing a narrow veil of rain beneath it.

There was still an hour before he had to lock the house for the last time. Then he would spend the night at Jack's house and leave in the morning without looking back. Until then, he gazed intently at the landscape he had known since birth. He wanted to imprint the vista of this perfect summer evening in his mind as an eidetic memory. His eyes took in the details of the familiar longing for amazement as if seeing them for the first time. Then it was time to leave. Much too soon, he thought. He drew a breath, put the key in the lock and heard the phone ring inside.

Jack Meade rocked gently in the hammock, as content as a baby in its mother's arms. He listened to the radio play-by-play as the Blue Jays clobbered his beloved Twins out of a pennant shot. He licked his lips and thought a beer would be nice. But not yet. He promised Boston he would wait for him to toast the end of summer. Folding thick, muscular arms across his chest, he closed his eyes and counted his blessings. But for the kindness of others, he wouldn't be the county sheriff or have a family. He felt blessed by the grace Father Carson often preached on.

He was born in Featherstone and baptized Jacques Baptiste Dubois, the only child of Clemente and Tanya Dubois. They moved to Minnesota from Baton Rouge to escape Jim Crow and made their living as a carpenter and a maid. Clemente's ancestors were French and Choctaw, while Tanya's were Spanish and African. They were the only "colored" family listed in the county's 1940 census. Jack was eight when his parents died in a car wreck. Boston was his closest pal, neither boy had a sibling and each wanted the other as a brother. Jack remembered his Papa saying the Meades were "sump'un." Even as a kid, he noticed how adults deferred to Boston's father like he was royalty. Boston begged his parents until they adopted Jack. However, adding Meade as his second surname didn't automatically confer their status on him. He soon realized people considered him a tawny orphan, a charity case who got lucky. He had to prove and prove and prove himself for acceptance. Now he was the county sheriff seeking a third term. But it wasn't easy.

He dropped a foot to the ground and pushed. As he swayed, he relived the pleasure of Boston's company for the summer. You and he went through all that stuff in the house. Lordy, it was like a hundred Christmases all at once. There were the Lionel trains, Gene Autry comic books, a battered Monopoly game, cap guns, baseball cards, ticket stubs and yearbooks. And our joint fortieth-birthday hangovers were worth the pain, too. This was our longest time together since college. Jeez, that's nearly twenty years. But we're family. Now the kids know their uncle is more than a name. "Christ, I wish he'd stay."

"Jack," Kris called from the back door. "It's Beverly Norgaard. She sounds hysterical."

"Now what," he grunted on the way to the kitchen. "Alright, calm down," he said into the phone. "Don't worry, Bev. I'll go look." He hung up, scowling in puzzlement. Then he turned to Kris. "Peder is six hours overdue from biking to St. Ansgar."

"Send a deputy. Boston's coming. We're going eat in an hour."

"Do you think he's going sit here and eat while Peder is missing?" He dialed again, explained the mission and said, "I'll pick you up in ten minutes." Back in uniform, Jack patted Kris on her ample rump as he went out the door. "I hope this won't take long."

With its flashing lights, Jack barreled the department's Suburban past the red-brick commercial buildings of downtown Featherstone. Passing St. Paul's Lutheran Church, he thought of Pastor Norgaard, whose congregation numbered several thousand. If anything happened to Peder, the whole town would feel the Norgaard's pain. It's up to you to see that it doesn't happen.

Though he wasn't one to fret, Peder's absence sat uneasily with him. The youth was a competitive cyclist. St. Ansgar was an easy hour-

and-a-quarter ride. Even if he rode farther, he was the kind of kid who would call his folks. He could fix a broken chain, flat tire or any other mechanical problem. But no one had phoned. That troubled him. As a father, he knew the kind of nightmare the Norgaards faced.

Jack passed the city limits, rushed along a mile of gravel road and then up San Juan Lane to the house. Boston stepped off the veranda, climbed into the Suburban and they turned down the ridge and onto the road to St. Ansgar.

"Beverly said he was going to the Breuer farm. You know anything more?"

"Nope." Boston breathed on his glasses and polished them. "He was going to shoot photos of the Shiner's Prairie country school. That and what's left of Breuer's farmhouse."

Jack radioed the dispatcher and told him in sheriff-speak which deputies he wanted on standby for tomorrow. As much as he ached for the Norgaards, he knew what Peder meant to Boston. "Don't worry. We'll find him," he said with a gentle fist bump to his shoulder.

"Yeah, right," Boston exhaled through his teeth.

Jack caught the undertone. It went with the rigid set of his brother's jaw that held his emotions in check. Despite Boston's stoicism—maybe because of it—there was no one Jack wanted more than him to ride shotgun. He's always had your back—you've always had his. How many brothers can say that?

Ginger O'Meara was washing lettuce when she glimpsed the sheriff's Suburban rush past her house. She couldn't see their faces but guessed it was Jack and Boston. If it were a police matter, one of them would call her tonight. Boston was more likely to call than Jack. Those two still seemed as tight-knit as in high school. Their bond had often shut her out when she was Boston's steady girl. That was long ago, she reminded herself. That's long over—*thank God.*

She blew a lock of chestnut hair out of her eyes and put the lettuce in a strainer. Then she gouged the eyes from two potatoes and put them in the oven. Today's visit with Mama left her feeling blue, and rubbing the chicken breast with sage offered some consolation. Mama was a hard-hearted woman married to a passive, alcoholic railroad man. Her childhood had front-row seats to the parents' nightly quarrels over drinking, money and status. They lived in a rented house that smelled of fried onions. Most of her wardrobe came second-hand. Mama made the children recite the rosary nightly and forced them to confession on Saturday. Her brothers eagerly joined the Marines. Her older sister joined a convent. Mama disowned Ginger after she eloped with a Protestant and then divorced him in less than a year.

After that, you began drinking heavily. There was no cutting back. That's when you ran away. That's when you drank and drank and... she put the chicken in a pan... and then you tried to make it up with Mama. She set the oven to 350 degrees. She still had all the letters to Mama that came back unopened. Her emotions welled up at the recollections. You've been sober for ten years. You can thank God and Meghan for that.

She had returned to Featherstone unannounced that winter. After two decades of exile, she hoped her sudden reappearance would shock Mama into talking, woman to woman. After that, reconciliation—maybe. She prayed daily for a miracle—something as pure and cleansing as a spring rain. Unfortunately, the spring rain hadn't fallen. At least it hadn't yet.

Nothing went as she had hoped. She found Mama living in a squalid apartment above a shop off an alley. Her heart pounded in her throat as she knocked on the door. It cracked open. A crone squinted at her and shrieked. Ginger got her foot in the door and forced her way in. Oh my God. What a mess, she remembered. After gaining power of attorney, she moved Mama into the Bethel Oaks care center. In the nine months since, Mama had yet to utter her name.

Today's visit, like her others, began with a centering breath and a silent repetition of *love is patient, love is kind, bears all things, believes all things, hopes all things*. Then she crossed herself and entered the nursing home. The stuffy air smelled of stale food and disinfectant; the halls carried the addled murmurs of minds drift. An attendant led her to Mama's sun-filled room with a crucifix above the bed.

"Agnes, you have a visitor," the attendant said in a singsong. Ginger entered, kissed the wrinkled forehead and looked for a flash of recognition.

"M-M-Meghan," Mama stuttered.

"No. I'm Ginger. Meghan's my older sister. Remember?"

"No-no-no. I want my nun."

Though this happened at every visit, Mama's non-recognition still hurt. Ginger hid it, however, and talked about things that used to interest Mama—new recipes, clothes, a childhood memory. Not a flicker. Today she felt more desperate than usual for a connection. She took the rosary from the dresser and wrapped the beads around Mama's fingers. As she did, the old woman looked into her eyes. Ginger saw a glimmer as if a small light had switched on. She leaned in close and whispered, "Hail Mary full of grace, the Lord is with Thee—"

"—Blessed art thou among women," Mama replied in full throat. "And blessed is the fruit of thy womb, Jesus. Holy Mary…" she continued, and her strident voice brought attendants to the door. Then Agnes plunged into the Gloria and the Our Father before starting the next Hail Mary. Ginger felt her heart race as they chanted. It seemed Agnes O'Meara was miraculously present. They recited the verses twice more, and for a few minutes, Ginger tried to believe they connected. Then the prayers ended, and Mama's presence dissipated like smoke.

The worst thing happened just as Ginger was leaving when the attendant asked if she had a sister who was a nun. She asked because Mama said her only daughter was a nun. *Only* daughter.

She left Bethel Oaks in tears. "Mama is still mean," she sobbed as she put the chicken to bake. "Her silence isn't dementia—it's spite. I'll never be the blessed fruit of her womb—never. It's not fair," she railed and buried her face in a dish towel.

"Alright, Jester, alright," she said a moment later. Putting down the towel, she stroked the border collie that pranced about nudging its bowl. Then she scooped out food and added a few scraps. "At least you give unconditional love."

While the potatoes and chicken baked, she sat on the screened back porch. Sipping from a mug of herbal tea, she listened to the crickets and let her thoughts drift to things that might have been. What if you had come back sooner? What if you had come back before Mama's dementia? What if—stop it, she scolded herself. Dwelling on what you can't change is the portal to darkness. "I have the *Statesman* and Mama to care for. That's enough," she told herself. But it didn't feel like enough.

Then there's Boston, she thought. Another person with whom you must reconcile, if that's even possible. The odds seem remote. Too much pain left over from going steady in high school. He gave you his class ring as a promise to marry after college. Then he dumped you after a year at Columbia. That old grudge still sat inside her like a chunk of granite. You were desperate for income to support Mama and applied for the editor's job at the last minute even though you expected rejection. Then he interviewed you on the spot—that was a surprise. The job offer hit you like a three-day drunk. He's friendly in a professional sort of way, but he's still as guarded as you remember. Maybe more so. So, exactly why did he hire you? Not out of sentiment. There isn't any in him. Most likely, it was because you're experienced and immediately available so he can return to Chicago. Now you're colleagues. Could you ever be friends?

The brothers drove south and west on the asphalt road through the Alton Moraine that flanked the south-flowing Tatanka River. This was familiar country where they used to hunt pheasants. The cagy birds often hid where they least expected them and Boston wondered if Peder was hidden where they least expected to find him. He left the question unasked and counted the "For Sale" signs tacked to the mailbox posts. The farmers were casualties of falling grain prices and rising interest rates. Many had mortgaged their farms to the hilt during good times to buy more land or machinery. Then their world collapsed in 1980 when the U.S. canceled grain sales to the Soviets because they invaded Afghanistan. Unsold grain added to the existing surplus and depressed grain prices more just as the interest rates rose on farm loans. It seemed an abstract economic problem at the national level but a personal catastrophe locally.

"I hate to see these auction signs," he said.

"*Uh-huh*," Jack grunted. "Daniels told me one farm in three is near bankruptcy. He oughta know… he holds the mortgages. I hate doing sheriff's sales, especially when it's a third- or fourth-generation farm. I did one by Waterford last week. The next day, the owner got drunk and ran into an abutment. Killed him. Suicide, I suspect."

"Anything you can do?"

"Not a goddamned thing. Folks are scared. Paranoid. They blame bankers, believe it's the corporations or Jews or the government. Two hundred farmers drove tractors to the state capitol and demanded relief. I heard some lost their farms. A few pack guns to the foreclosure sales."

"You're the right man for the times, Jack."

"Thanks. I just wish it wasn't an election year."

"You'll be fine," Boston said and felt his muscles tense as they approached the Tatanka River, a stream that flowed along a wider and deeper channel scoured long ago by a glacial river. The road ran atop the remains of an earthen dam to a one-lane bridge spanning the washed-out spillway. Heights made him queasy, especially the memorial cross, where, years ago, three teens in a car plunged to eternity.

A mile on, they found trampled grass and bike tracks at Shiner's Prairie School. They assumed Peder made them. Then they drove through St. Ansgar, a dying, unincorporated village of vacant houses in weedy lots. Plywood covered the windows of the brick Lutheran Church, and the Texaco station lacked pumps. The machine shop, grain elevator and general store had already closed for the day. It appeared the village had shut down for the night, if not forever.

"I haven't been here in a while," Jack said. "It looks worse than I remember."

"Why would you come here?"

"Because they elected me. It's my job to be present. Especially now. Farm folks feel forgotten by the government—any government. I owe 'em my attention."

They left the town on a gravel road, and Boston looked for bike tracks on the road's shoulder. He saw none. Then Jack turned down the grassy trail through a patch of woods and stopped at a fieldstone foundation. The tornado's debris of shredded cornstalks, tarpaper, insulation and paper still adorned the stubby tree limbs like the trashy decorations left from a frat house bacchanal.

Boston drew a long breath. "It's not like him to change plans without notice. It's odd we haven't seen any sign of him."

"Yeah, I know. Look, it's nearly sunset, so let's split up to look around."

As Jack went east, Boston turned west toward the creek. Peder found Kaplan's body there, and now he was missing. The congruence worried him. As he passed the fieldstone foundation, the pale, round cobbles reminded him of skulls he had seen in a catacomb. He shivered.

He struck a track along Clay Creek. The grass and weeds were newly trampled, and his hopes rose. It was probably Peder's trail. He spotted a fresh shoeprint in a patch of damp gray clay. His hopes sank. The print came from a hard-soled shoe several sizes smaller than Peder's sneakers. He followed the bank until it joined another track. Probably Jack's. He returned to the farmyard, where his brother leaned against the Suburban's fender. Jack shook his head.

"I ran into tracks, but they're not his."

"Probably some guys training their hunting dogs. It's that time of year." Jack rubbed his short, curly hair. "This isn't typical," he sighed. "It's usually a toddler or a senior who—"

"—I know, the first forty-eight hours are critical. After that, they don't turn up until a farmer picks corn or… I know how it goes."

"I know you do. Sorry."

"This doesn't make sense," Boston said, slamming his fist on the Suburban. "Peder has ridden all over the county—many times. His bike isn't built for off-roading. He'd stop at a farm if he got lost. Someone would call if he had an accident. I've got a feeling that—"

"Don't speculate. Too many unknowns. Stick to the facts."

"Facts? There aren't any," he barked. "Peder's missing. That's the only fact."

"Look, my department is trained in this stuff. Playing detective doesn't help."

Boston stuffed his flash of anger at Jack's superior air. Alright, asshole, have it your way, he thought, getting into the Suburban. He sat in a sullen silence while Jack radioed the dispatcher and ordered the Alton County Search and Rescue, the Civil Air Patrol and the saddle club posse to assemble by the St. Ansgar church at daybreak.

Jack dreaded the idea of mounting a search. Peder could be anywhere among the two hundred square miles of cornfields, groves and marshes in the county's west end. However, he had no other choice.

"Sorry," he said, fist-bumping Boston's shoulder. "It's all I can do." Then he was silent until the approach to the Tatanka River. "Watch for deer," he said. "They're invisible at dusk."

"I know that," Boston snapped and then lapsed into silence and thought about Peder and what he should do next. "I'll stay a couple more days," he said as they arrived at the house. "'Til we find Peder."

"Good. Grab your stuff. Kris has a room all ready for you."

"Thanks, but no thanks. It's late. I've a couple things to do here," he lied, still irritated at Jack's officious dismissal of his ideas.

"Well, okay then. I'll keep ya posted."

The house now felt tomb-like when Boston opened the door, and Rusty wasn't there to greet him. Until this morning, his father's Irish setter had been his constant companion. Rusty's presence created an impression that members of the family still lived there. He wasn't lonely with the dog lying at his feet, if not on them. He often talked to the dog, who listened without argument. But no more. He gave Rusty to Jack's kids, Ben and Lily, earlier that morning. Now the house felt cavernous. He opened a window and let in the sounds of crickets. Without Rusty, they would have to keep him company.

"Something happened to Peder before he got to Breuer's," he muttered while standing in the corner turret of the house. "We know he was at Shiner's Prairie. That's all we know." He dropped into a wing chair with a notebook. "Stick to the facts, he says. Ha!" then he began listing the facts:

Peder's tracks at Shiner's Prairie.

No signs after country school.

No bike tracks to or at Breuer farm.

No phone calls.

No witnesses or calls if something happened in St. Ansgar.

Farm search didn't include nearby woods or pasture.

He flipped a page.

Did Peder vanish between St. A and the farm?

How did he vanish?

Did someone take him? Why?

He put down the pencil, closed his eyes and listened to the crickets' pulsing stridulations. Worries flit about his mind like bats in a cave. Did someone take him, or did he run away? Then he shook his head. No, not likely. That left abduction. Perverts grabbed kids every day, usually for sex. But usually pre-teens. Peder was too old and too strong to be abducted. Ransom wasn't likely. Pastors weren't wealthy. Then why?

The cloud of worries followed him to the Adirondack chair on the darkened veranda, where the air felt cooler. Abduction. Why would anyone go after Peder? He was well-liked. A hero when he found Kaplan. But that ended when everyone knew he was a murdered cop. Then folks criticized the paper for the coverage. He wrote another question: What is it no one wants to know about Kaplan?

"You should've known better," he whispered. "You let him turn Kaplan's death into a crusade. That's what you would've done at seventeen—except Dad would've stopped you. That's when the threats started. You should've stopped…"

His stomach growled, a reminder he hadn't eaten since breakfast. The house had no groceries, and it was too late to eat in town. He took a suitcase from the car and, against better judgment, retrieved the bottle of whiskey. A double for his supper. Then he stripped to his underwear and lay on the sofa with the canvas dust cover as a blanket. Though he felt exhausted, he couldn't sleep because memories of Peder flickered in his mind like clips of silent film. He downed another shot. Even that didn't numb the bone-deep premonition that Peder was dead and his body, like Kaplan's, was stashed where it couldn't be found.

CHAPTER 2

Raucous cawing in the oaks woke Boston at dawn. "Shut the fuck up," he yelled at the window. Then he rose, muttering more curses at the murder of crows raging at an owl in the oaks around the house. A glance at the whiskey bottle told him why his head throbbed and his lips felt dry. Shuffling half-naked into the kitchen, he sleepily opened a cupboard. "Shit!" he yelled and slammed it. The kitchen had no coffee or aspirin or anything else. A long shower eased the headache. Then he dressed in yesterday's chinos and a polo shirt. Though still shaky, he drove the Jeep into town for breakfast.

The Streamliner Restaurant took its name from the stainless-steel dining car split like a banana and fused onto a brick building. He had hung out there in high school, and its chrome stools, lunch counter and booths hadn't changed. Even the jukebox kept the oldies. Besides the *Statesman*, this was the downtown place where he felt most at home, beginning with Chiara's joyous "*buon giorno*." She was a young war bride when he was in school and now as much an institution as the Streamliner itself.

"I know what I want," he told her before he settled into a booth. She brought him coffee. When she didn't ask about Peder, he assumed she hadn't heard. Just as well. He didn't feel like talking. It was better if Jack delivered the news when there was some.

He wished this wasn't Daphne Peterson's day off. Her company always gave him a lift ever since June, when he was the day's last customer, and she chatted with him while he ate. That was when he fell for the sassy, girl-next-door insouciance and corn-flower blue eyes. In his memory, she had remained a pesky, flat-chested six-grader with an embarrassing crush on him during his senior year. Now she was neither annoying nor flat-chested. The Daphne who bedded him owned the Streamliner and wanted an intimate but discrete companionship. It was an ideal affair in the wake of the divorce. Yesterday, she treated him to a farewell lunch at her house that included a special "dessert" between the satin sheets on her large bed. "One for the road," she called it. He sighed. It was all of that.

The poached eggs and toast settled his stomach, and he shoved aside the empty plate. Leaning on his elbows, he cradled the coffee cup in both hands and thought about Peder. Someone must have picked him up, he thought. And his bicycle, too. Not a pedophile, of that he felt certain. His gut said it was someone connected to Kaplan's death. Somehow, he had to get Jack to see beyond the convenient. That could take days, but he couldn't do it by phone from Chicago. Only one course lay open. He didn't like it, but he had to ask for another week of leave.

Betting on the outcome, he bought a week's worth of groceries at the IGA. Ginger lived in a house a half-mile from his. *Uh-oh*, he thought as he passed it. You should have called her last night. She'll be pissed if she heard it from someone else. He decided against stopping and went home. You're better off telling her over the phone rather than face-to-face. He dialed, her phone rang four times and clicked to a cheery greeting on the answering machine. He hung up and put a sticky note on the phone as a reminder to call again.

Seated on the veranda with a mug of coffee, he considered what could have happened to Peder between Shiner's Prairie and Breuer's farm. He couldn't get lost. Not on the grid of gravel roads that intersected every mile. Someone would have seen him if he were lying in the ditch. No tracks—no signs of Peder. What does that tell you? It tells you someone nabbed him and his bike. But why? Is someone afraid he knows too much about Kaplan's death? This wouldn't have happened on Dad's watch. And you should have known better than to let Peder have so much latitude. He was too much like the sorcerer's apprentice. It's on you if he's missing because of Kaplan. But his brief flash of honesty didn't erase the feeling of guilt.

He glanced at his watch and rose from the chair in frustration. Nearly mid-morning. If Peder weren't missing, you'd be halfway to Chicago by now, he thought. Instead, you better call Braydon and beg him to extend your leave. He won't like it. Not with his heart set on retiring as soon as you succeed him as editor-in-chief. You worked hard for that. You can't give it up now. Just a week's extension. Just until Peder turns up.

He picked up the phone, noticed the pounding beneath his ribs and hung up. The last encounter with Henry Vanderbilt Braydon was over coffee in his private office. After the pleasantries, his normally irascible boss said the magazine's directors had endorsed his nomination of Boston as the new editor. That included moving into the corner suite on the twenty-first floor with views of the Loop and Lake Michigan. He had walked out of the meeting giddier than when falling in love. Then Jack called an hour later with news of Dad's death. He remembered Braydon's don't-fuck-with-me glare when he asked for a three-month leave. After a sharp argument and a bit of bluff, the editor gave in. "All right, Meade. Labor Day. If you're not back then…" Braydon didn't finish. He didn't have to. He didn't shoot blanks. A few more days. That's all you need, he thought. Just a few days. Then he drew a breath and dialed.

After a few moments of pleasantries, he pitched the extension. Braydon greeted it with a barrage of obscenities that would be audible across the room. "Goddamn you, Meade. I said Labor Day and meant it. I'm going to retire and nominate—"

"Do what you have to, Henry. I've got to do the same," he wheezed against the tightness in his chest.

"Alright," Braydon growled. "Until next week." He hung up without a goodbye.

"Well, I guess hara-kiri isn't that hard."

Though it was only mid-morning, Jack moved as slowly as if he had already worked a long day digging trenches. Worrying over Peder had sabotaged his sleep. Instead of snuggling abed with Kris, like they planned, he drove to St. Ansgar in the dark and arrived as the sun cleared the horizon. The day broke still and overly warm.

Accountants, clerks, mechanics, teachers, farmers and the Lutheran choir joined the search. Jack stood beneath a graveyard elm, organized search teams, and assigned them to areas he had marked on the maps. Saddle club members rode along the ditches, creeks and fence lines. The search and rescue teams scoured the woodlots and weed patches. Two Civil Air Patrol planes circled the cornfields. A squad of deputies combed the Breuer farm while another pair interviewed nearby farmers.

A mounted searcher reported to Jack from the saddle. The sheriff nodded, pulled his lower lip and drew a red line across a search area marked on the map. The horseman took a new assignment, touched his cap and trotted off. In four hours, the number of searched areas equaled the unsearched ones. Jack chewed on his lower lip. Nothing yet.

His spirits lifted when he saw the black Jeep Wagoneer pull up to the church. Maybe Boston would have fresh ideas about where to look. And if not, at least you'll have his company. But any hope of brotherly inspiration quickly faded when he saw him kicking furiously at pebbles while he walked. That was never a good sign. He shook his head in answer to the question Boston was about to ask.

Boston's stoic "yeah" floated out on a long exhalation between clenched teeth. Then he turned and looked into the distance, removed his glasses and rubbed the scar. "Have you found anything?" he asked, still looking away.

"Not yet." Jack pointed to the crossed-out areas on the maps. "Nothing at Breuer's farm. We're pushing farther out. Talking to farmers. Any ideas?"

"I've got a feeling someone took him—"

"What gives you that—"

"Something to do with Kap—"

"Now, don't start that. He's been dead forty years," Jack said.

"Sorry."

Boston said little after that, peeved anew at his brother's stubbornness but wasn't in the mood to argue.

"I'm glad you're here," Jack said, fist-bumping his shoulder. "I know you've got my back." A searcher reported in a moment later. Jack gave him a new assignment and the searcher left. "Hey, remember when we punched out the Sabine brothers?"

"Third grade. Three days' suspension."

"Yup. Worth every minute. After that, Pinky quit calling me Sambo."

Why did he bring that up, Boston wondered.

Jack thought again about how this present moment began with a third-grade melee and suspension that had bonded them. They had backed each other ever since though they were an unlikely pair. He thought of their bond as something like epoxy and resin. Boston was the brains who played the piano, and he the brawn who played football. We're different, but it works, he told himself. Well, most of the time, anyway.

"I see you've got all the help you need," Boston said as he gazed at the organized bustle in the cemetery. "I guess I'll see you later."

"Hey, where ya going?"

"Home," he said over his shoulder. "I'm useless—like tits on a boar."

"Well… okay then. I'll call ya later," Jack said and turned to the maps. Don't take it personally, he told himself. It's just Boston being upset and hiding it, as usual. A moment later, he heard the sharp squeal of rubber on the asphalt as the Jeep shot away. He pursed his lips and shook his head. Not a good sign.

CHAPTER 3

Boston returned home pissed with himself for tearing out of St. Ansgar like a moody juvenile. Jack's doing all anyone can, and you, you act like he should've solved it by now. He heaved a sigh and sank into momentary self-pity. Maybe you ought to leave tomorrow and start life fresh on Tuesday.

Quitting never sat well with him. A fine line separated dedication from stubbornness, he thought, but damned if he knew where to draw it. Settling into the Adirondack chair, he reviewed his notes on Kaplan. Maybe there was an overlooked name or fact that could send the search in a new direction. Abduction still seemed likely, but every cop he knew hated second-guessing by reporters. Jack was no exception. Yet, more than once, he and other reporters had reached the truth before the cops.

Arne Heistad, Nelson Ferrall and other Chamber of Commerce leaders had complained the loudest about the Kaplan stories. Bad press, like a murder, might knock Featherstone out of the running for an insurance headquarters. What a crock. The anonymous messages and threats began when Peder interviewed people who had met Kaplan. He turned a fresh page and wrote a question, "Why does Kaplan's death upset them after thirty-five years?"

The day turned torrid at mid-afternoon, and he went inside for a beer—a sandwich in a can. Then he saw the yellow sticky note stuck to the phone. "Oh shit, you should've called hours ago," he muttered. "At least I can say I tried this morning." He dialed Ginger's number and braced for a sharp reaction.

"Well, hello there," she said, surprised. "You made good time. How's Chicago?"

"I'm here… at home."

"Oh. I thought you were leaving today."

"Uh… so did I." When he told her what happened, he heard a gasp followed by staticky silence. "Ginger…"

"Why didn't you call last night? *I'm* the editor—aren't I?"

He flinched as if he had touched a hot stove. "I screwed up. I'm sorry," he said, rubbing the scar. When it came to ire, she hadn't changed. "I tried earlier but missed you. I'll tell Jack to call you."

"Oh, don't bother. You know he won't as long as you're in town."

More staticky silence. Jesus, she still doesn't like him, he realized. Get over it.

"I'm… stunned," she whispered. "I'm sorry. I know how close you and Peder were… How do you…" She didn't finish the question, knowing how closely he guarded his feelings. That's where your troubles used to start, she remembered. Just as well that he rarely opens up.

"He meant a lot to me… like a son," he said and cleared his throat. "I've got a feeling it's tied to Kaplan. Jack won't—"

"Will you please draft something?" she asked. "You know more than anyone. Judd's on call. Dictate it. He'll get it in tomorrow's edition."

Long ago, he could read her mood from the tone of her voice. Now, he wished she would keep talking—about anything—just stay on the line and share the silence—even shared silence felt better than being alone. He listened to the static until it seemed weird and then promised to dictate a piece and call her when he knew more.

It took five minutes to draft and dictate a short piece for Judd. Then he poured whiskey over ice and took the drink to the veranda. As muggy as it felt outside, it was even more so inside the house. He wished for Rusty's company so he could scratch his head and to listen to him breathe. Propping his feet on the railing, he considered his options. Stay until Peder turned up or go to Chicago? The search might last a week. After that… if they didn't find him… what?

He longed for Jack to call with news, good news. And while he waited, he paced the veranda to work off the anxiety. It was nearly 6:00 p.m. and getting dark. No news struck him as bad news, and it seemed about to get worse. All afternoon he had watched the clouds build up until they sheathed the whole sky in layers of blue and gray. Lightning flickered, followed by thunder. With nothing to do, he watched the storm advance until wind-driven sheets of rain forced him indoors. He fixed a hurried supper and ate it as he stood at the kitchen counter near the wall phone. He willed it to ring, but it didn't.

The storm abated to showers, and he resumed his vigil on the veranda. Seeing headlights on the county road below the hill, he rose halfway out of the chair, hoping it was Jack. The car passed his lane and vanished in the gloom. Dejected, he sat at the piano and poured his anxiety into Beethoven's "Moonlight Sonata." Then Jack called.

"Here's what I know," he said in resignation. "He passed the St. Ansgar store about ten o'clock yesterday."

"Anything else?"

"That's it. We'll search again tomorrow. This damned rain doesn't help. Any ideas?"

"Check the abandoned farmhouses. And the woods along the Tatanka."

"Okay, thanks. What're your plans?"

"I don't know," he said. "I've got a week's extension. After that… uh… we'll see."

He called Ginger with the news. Then he settled into a living room chair with a drink. Turning the tumbler in his hand. Yesterday's pee-in-your-pants excitement over leaving now seemed ages ago. He felt like a passenger on a rudderless ship at the mercy of a gale. "Braydon is my patron," he said to the tumbler, "but Peder needs an advocate. Christ, I wish I knew what to do." He recalled his father used to say that to live is to choose. He tossed off the drink. "I'm not going to choose tonight," he mumbled on his way upstairs to bed.

CHAPTER 4

Boston woke on Labor Day with a dry mouth and a throbbing headache. He was dying to leave and angry that his conscience held him back until he knew something definite. Or until Jack opened up to ideas besides his own. He felt as stuck as a bug on flypaper. He phoned the realtor, who wasn't in and left her a message canceling any showings scheduled for the week. It wasn't much, but it restored his feeling of control. Then he garaged the BMW and mowed the lawn.

Jack phoned at midday. "I know you're worried," he said. "So, am I. The teams are still searching. I just got home. We're grilling burgers later. Drag your sorry ass over here, and let's worry together."

He arrived while his brother and Ben were throwing the football in a joyous competition. Jack had an heir, a successor, something he would never have. The scene reminded him again of his failure as a husband. Vicky got tired of waiting to start a family. You promised but postponed it until he had another promotion and then another. Selfish. You put ambition ahead of her desire. Well, you got the promotion you wanted but lost her on the way. Now she's remarried and pregnant. He didn't have to wonder who was happier now. He knew.

"Hey, c'mon and play," Jack called and fired the ball at him. He caught it and threw it back, faking a good time but half-wishing he hadn't come. Then Jack handed him a beer. The brothers lounged in lawn chairs and listened to the play-by-play of the Twins battling the White Sox. Between swigs, they bantered about which team played better ball, but Boston heard Jack's undercurrent of worry.

"I think someone grabbed Peder," Boston said. "That's why there's no sign of him. We got threats over his interviews."

"Oh, yeah. First you mentioned that. Who from?"

"Mostly anonymous—except George Filbert."

"Filbert—from the lumberyard? Oh, c'mon." Jack rolled his dark eyes. "I know George. He's a sour old man but—"

"He told Peder to leave Kaplan alone, or he'd end up the same way."

"That sounds like advice, not a threat."

They bickered a moment before Jack called the Cubs a second-rate ball team. Boston took the bait to defend them. Then Jack's pager buzzed. "Hey, maybe some news," he said on his way into the kitchen phone. He returned in uniform a few minutes later. "Peder's dead," he said, just above a whisper, "in a coulee near Rock Dell."

Jack's ample use of the lights and siren sent the Labor Day traffic scurrying onto the shoulders like frightened chicks before a hawk. A sidelong glance at Boston's face told him his brother was burrowed deep inside himself. He probably hoped it was a mistaken identity, some other kid and not Peder. If only that were true, he wished. They neared Rock Dell, and Jack left the highway for a narrow, sandy track that snaked down a wooded coulee between a limestone wall and a deep ravine. He parked behind a grader where its driver talked to an officer.

"What do we know?" Jack asked the balding deputy.

"Not much. Snappy here called it in." Deputy Townsend nodded at the skinny man who sucked on a cigarette as he shifted from foot to foot like an antsy kid who needed to pee. "He's down there," Townsend said, jerking a thumb over his shoulder. "It happened before the rain."

The tall, blond youth in a green T-shirt lay face down among some gooseberry bushes twenty feet below the road. A bike and helmet lay nearby. Jack wiped his eyes and swallowed. Much too easy to imagine Ben lying there. Thom and Beverly Norgaard weighed heavily on him. Never easy to give anyone the news that a loved one is dead. Especially a kid. Even harder when they're friends. He knew his words would break their hearts.

Meanwhile, an ambulance arrived, and the two medics talked with Jack as they unloaded a stretcher. Then the husky young men clambered over slabs of limestone to reach the body. Their voices drifted up to Jack, but he couldn't make out their words. Then they strapped Peder to the litter and side-stepped over the rocks and up to the road.

"It looks like he broke his neck," one medic said. "No sign of internal injuries. No broken arms or legs."

"Leave him here for a minute," Jack ordered and squatted to examine the body. He felt the shirt still damp from the rain. No signs of a struggle. Most likely, it's an accident. An autopsy will tell you more. Then he shuddered at the sight of tiny flies' eggs around Peder's eyes.

Boston watched Townsend climb out of the ravine. He laid the silver bicycle and a green helmet on the edge of the road. Something of Peder's was missing. It was always with him, but he couldn't think what it was. Only that it wasn't with him.

"What do you think, Chuck," Jack asked and scratched his head.

"An accident," Townsend said. "He could've lost control and went over the edge. More likely a hit and run, though," he added, pointing to the bike's bent front wheel. "Too bad Snappy graded the road. Otherwise, we could reconstruct it from the tracks."

"Where's his pack," Boston asked, recalling the missing item.

"Isn't one. Just his bike and helmet," Townsend said.

"His pack should be there, too. He always had it."

"Well, like I said—"

"*Uh*, it's a blind curve," Jack interrupted to head off an argument. He looked up and down the grade. "I wonder how fast—"

"Forty's a lethal speed," Townsend interjected. "It could've knocked him backward. Broke his neck in the fall."

Jack turned to Boston. "What about the pack?"

"Teal-colored with red piping. It was strapped to his seat. See the bungee cords? It would've had his camera, a water bottle and a notebook."

"That's right. He was taking pictures. Let's look again."

"Whoever hit him might've took it," Townsend offered as he scrambled after Jack.

"Might've took it," Boston muttered, pissed at the deputy's condescension. "He doesn't know Peder." He paced the distance from Peder to the blind curve. About sixty feet. Not enough space for a car to stop or swerve. Well, he thought, maybe know-it-all Townsend is right. Maybe Peder was standing by his bike. A glancing blow could have pitched him backward into the ravine headfirst, but so what? Why is he here?

Jack returned from the ravine rubbing his arm where he brushed the nettles. He talked to the EMTs. Then they put Peder's body in the ambulance. Townsend followed them. Snappy crushed out a cigarette, climbed onto the grader and stirred its engine to life as if nothing had happened.

"Look at this," Boston said, pointing to bits of dark paint on the silver bike. "If a car hit him, it might tell you the kind."

Jack grunted agreement. "This road isn't used much. We'll check the vehicles the locals own. Might turn up a match or someone who saw something." He loaded the bike and helmet into the Suburban. "You alright?" he asked, laying an arm across Boston's shoulder. "I know he meant a lot to you."

"He did. How did he get here if he was in St. Ansgar yesterday?"

"Maybe he extended his ride—training for the Iron Man race."

"No. Not without calling his folks. We're fifty miles from St. Ansgar. This road doesn't go anyplace he'd want to go. His bike isn't built for sand roads. And where's his pack. Saying someone stole it is bullshit. This doesn't make sense."

"*Uh-huh.*"

"I've got a feeling someone else is involved."

"Well, stop guessing. Stick to the facts."

"Here's a fact. He talked to Eliot Ferrall a couple weeks ago."

"*Hmm*. Well, he lives near Hennessey. That's close by. Let's see what he knows." Jack drove down the coulee and turned onto the valley road along Hennessey Creek, his favorite trout stream. His running recollection of the lunkers that lurked below the riffles did not lighten Boston's mood.

"What do you know about Ferrall," Boston asked.

"He's Calvin's older brother. World War Two Marine vet. Wrote a famous anti-war book. Can't say as I've met him. You know anything?"

"He lives alone. After Peter's article about Kaplan, Ferrall invited him to look at some historical materials he'd collected. Peder visited twice and said he didn't have anything interesting. Instead, he pumped Peder for everything he knew about Kaplan."

"*Hmm*," Jack rumbled without saying more.

Twenty minutes later, they stopped in front of a limestone farmhouse with green shutters. A limp American flag hung from a pole. Beds of asters and delphinium bloomed beside well-pruned shrubs verging the shady lawn. They sat in the Suburban for a moment and waited for Ferrall to come out of the house. When he didn't, they got out.

"Wait here," Jack said, putting on his uniform hat. He stepped onto the open porch and knocked. The front door swung ajar. "Hel-lo-oh," he called. "Anyone here? It's Sheriff Meade." Silence. He glanced at Boston, shrugged and entered the kitchen.

It was a simple but impressive farmhouse with high-end furniture and Amana appliances. Going from room to room, he noted the perfectly made bed, the clean floor and the tidy rolltop desk. Nothing seemed amiss or out of place. He returned to the porch, closed the door and made certain it latched.

"Ship-shape," he said as he walked to the Suburban. "Once a Marine, always a Marine. It could pass a white-glove inspection. Let's check the barn."

The barn was built into the hillside so hay wagons could drive into the loft. Instead of hay, it held a Ford tractor, rotary mower, small plow and garden equipment. Everything was clean, oiled and in its place. Nothing of interest there. They went below to the workshop that had been a milking parlor. Its floor and workbenches were as clean as the loft. The hand tools hung on a pegboard against their painted silhouettes. None were missing.

"Take a look at these," Jack said and squatted outside amid a web of tire tracks in the gravel. "Lots of this tread, so it's probably Ferrall's. Those buggy tracks must've come from his Amish neighbors. Then there are these." He pointed to a tread that crossed the others. "It came in and went out before Ferrall left." Jack wrote "call me" on the back of his business card and jammed it into the porch door. "You know, this place is too fucking tidy," he said, sliding into the Suburban. "Any reason Ferrall would go after Peder? Seems like the neat ones are the worst."

"No. Not unless he's tied to Kaplan's death."

"What about Filbert?"

"Evidently, Filbert didn't like Kaplan. He never said why."

"Anything else?" Jack drummed thick fingers on the steering wheel.

"Pinky, Arne Heistad and Nelson Ferrall complained a lot. Claimed the paper's interest in Kaplan had upset some important people."

"Who?"

"They won't say."

"That's just like them," Jack spat out the window. Just hearing their names made the muscles tighten between his shoulders. "Give me what you know. I want to solve this now." Then he started the engine.

"Hey, don't rush it. There are a lot of questions to sort out."

"*Hmm*, yeah," Jack said, now certain his brother wanted to be his partner in any investigation. He'll expect daily updates and second-guess every move. Not a good look while running for reelection. "Look, I know you and Peder were close," he said. "Of course, you want to help. I appreciate it. But I see you're torn between staying and going. There's nothing you can do here. So, go on back to Chicago. You've earned that promotion. Meanwhile, I'll keep you posted on things here."

CHAPTER 5

Ginger lounged in a lawn chair under an oak. Reading *The Witches of Eastwick* made her sleepy, and she thumbed over a page before dropping the novel in the grass. Then she closed her eyes and wondered if Boston would stick around until Peder turned up. That might take a week. Maybe more. He forgot to tell you about Peder, she thought, still irritated at the lapse. Not a good start. What else has he forgotten to tell you? If he stays, will he take over the *Statesman*? If only you had the witches' special powers—especially if he stays. Yeah, well, you've always been able to manage him.

The idea he might stay awakened her. The things he revealed at last week's luncheon might be useful. His invitation to a county club luncheon wasn't to catch up on their personal lives. Oh no, that would be too intimate, she thought sarcastically. No, he wanted to catch up on their post-college professional years as context for their long-distance collaboration. Context, ha! She remembered stifling a laugh when he said it.

He had fidgeted at first, like an insecure eighth-grade boy on his first date who asked innocuous questions. Just when you thought this was a pointless exercise, he asked how you started writing. You took it as a cue and said, "I'm an alcoholic." You said it straight, as a fact, and looked him in the eyes. "I started writing in recovery—it's how I explain myself to myself." After that, it seemed you talked a blue streak, words like water from a fire hose. You felt no shame flooding him with the sordid details of marriage and divorce, booze and weed, blackouts and recovery. While you talked, he wore that impassive "I'm listening" expression you've always hated. Then he rubbed the scar and pushed aside his half-finished beer. Yeah, well, you gave him context. Maybe he understands you now.

She looked up and watched Jester shag a squirrel across the lawn. "Sic 'em," she yelled, knowing he would never get close. When the squirrel zipped up the tree, the white dog with black ears bounded to her side and licked her hand. She picked up the book and sucked on a cube from the glass of iced tea. After another page, the phone's ring intruded on her reading. Dashing inside, she hoped it wasn't Bethel Oaks. She had had enough Mama-drama for one week.

It was Boston. She moaned at the news and braced herself against the kitchen wall. "Oh, I'm so sorry. Yes, of course, it's all right. Go ahead. Write it." She listened a moment more, wrinkling her brow. "Okay. Yes, I'll help you. Hold on. Give me ten minutes." Then, without wiping her tears, she grabbed the keys and rushed to her car in cut-offs and a tank top. "Oh, Mother of God, why Peder?"

Boston had composed the news story in his head on the drive back to Featherstone and wanted to get it ready for tomorrow. But that wasn't the only reason he turned down Jack's invitation to supper. Jack urged you to leave, but yesterday he begged you to stay.

He entered the *Statesman*'s newsroom, empty for the Labor Day afternoon. That was fine. Words came easier without others around. The IBM desk computer warmed up, and the cursor blinked patiently like a horse awaiting the *giddyap*. He wrote the lead and then stopped. Drafting a story wasn't his prerogative now. He had hired Ginger with a promise to keep his hands off. You better clear this with her, he thought. Besides, you're too emotional to write straight. Then he ended the call. Thank God she's coming to help you.

Hearing flip-flops in the corridor, he wiped his eyes and stood at the desk. She entered, wet-eyed, and leaned against him. Her breach of his personal space made him uneasy, but he closed his arms around her for a moment.

"Sorry," she said, stepping back and sniffling. "I needed a shoulder. Yours was handy." Then she pulled a Kleenex from the box on his desk. "Tell me what happened."

He laid out a narrative, but it was garbled with questions and suspicions. She stopped him, dragged a chair next to his and asked question after question to dig out the details. Each answer led to another question. After half an hour, they had a coherent story with the words he couldn't find by himself.

Her command at a moment of crisis amazed him. In barely two breaths, she switched from grieving to taking charge. How the hell does she do it, he wondered. Before he could ponder further, she interrupted his thoughts with questions about the text. As they discussed it, her job interview played in the back of his mind. She wasn't on the list of six finalists. She simply materialized out of the distant past. A twist of fate that—

"Let's present it this way," she said, breaking into his thoughts. "Are you paying attention?"

"Oh, yeah. Where were we…" He swallowed, startled.

"This phrase… *ah*, it's too emotional."

He struck it. "Jack has a press conference tomorrow," he said.

"Good. I'll send Robin and Ellen. *Uh*… you want a by-line?"

He shook his head. The press of a key sent the story to the printer. They read it again, made a few changes and then left a clean copy on the news editor's desk.

"Are you okay," she asked, peering into his face.

"Yeah. I'll be okay." He faked a smile and avoided eye contact.

"All right then, will I see you tomorrow?"

"Yeah. Tomorrow for sure. And thanks." He watched her walk past the reporters' desks and vanish down the stairs. You'd be up shit crick now if she hadn't applied, he reminded himself. What a godsend. You were in a real bind when the top candidates flunked their interviews. Christ, not one knew how to keep a newspaper profitable. You couldn't leave without a competent editor, but there wasn't time to launch a new search. Then Hazel put a folder on the desk and said another candidate was waiting downstairs. Another candidate, he thought. This had to be a drop-in. You didn't open the folder. Why bother. Resumes were mostly creative nonfiction.

You stood at the window with your back to the door, he remembered. It was raining, and you were feeling sorry for yourself. Then you heard, "Hi-ya, Boston," that gave you a chill. *Oh my God—Mary Virginia O'Meara!* And there she stood in your doorway. Her amber eyes, freckled nose, wide mouth and chestnut hair were as you remembered.

No wonder your greeting stumbled off the tongue like a drunk. But you both laughed together to cover up. You wondered if the suit and heels meant she was now a professional woman or was she still the spitfire you remembered? You decided to give her the courtesy of an interview and only half-listened to her professional recitation until she talked about turning a Colorado newspaper profitable. After that, she hit all your marks. That's when you realized that she *was* the editor you needed. Except she was Ginger. So, you slept on it to be certain and offered her the job in the morning. None of the old issues cropped up in the month of transition. We've both matured. It's a professional relationship. That's what you want, and that's how it has to be.

Ginger sat in her car and let tears stream down her cheeks. "Damn," she cried, unable to find Kleenex in her purse. She sobbed, resting her head on the steering wheel as her shoulders heaved up and down. When finished, she drew a breath, wiped her nose on the shirttail and drove home. She had known Peder for a month, but it felt like years instead. He was so sweet—he was the un-Boston you could've fallen for at seventeen. She longed to talk to someone who knew him. Even Boston. But he wasn't available. He was too withdrawn and stuffing his pain. Well, at least you have Jester.

She lived in the "Egg Lady's house," as it was called, and the only decent rental she could afford. Years ago, it belonged to a woman who raised chickens and sold eggs and pullets to housewives, including Mama. The story-and-a-half farmhouse a mile out of town had a kitchen, bath, parlor and two bedrooms. Perfect for her. She brewed a pot of tea, took it to the back porch and sat in a rattan chair with her legs tucked beneath her. Amid the cricket song, she emptied her sorrow in prayers for Peder and those whose lives he had touched. She believed everything was connected at a spiritual level and believed Peder's death would ripple through the cosmos until it touched everyone, including her.

The hour she just spent with Boston raised the question that had haunted her all month. How does he see you? If he has an opinion, it's vague because he's kept you at arm's length. Maybe you have been wrong about him. A lot has happened since college. And to both of you, too. People change. He gave you a chance, so it's only right that you give him one. She sipped some tea, but it was cold, and she set it aside. So, is it you, or is it him?

She giggled a moment later at another memory from their country club luncheon. After you confessed to drinking and recovery, you said, "I showed you mine, now show me yours." She used to say that when making out reached the point of undressing. Saying it then made him blush—and made him human, too. It took hemming and hawing before he told you about his father's obsession with him as the successor. He regretted saying, "Give up my career to live in your shadow. Not a chance. I know it hurt him," he admitted. That's quite an admission coming from him. It must have shamed him because he dropped his voice when he said it. Then he said the divorce was his fault, too. Maybe he's changed, but it's hard to tell. He seems sad and lonely.

She put away those thoughts and watched the day's last light briefly paint a band of clouds in hues of apricot, rose and lilac. Moments later, the darkness absorbed the colors into itself. On the cusp of night, she saw the first stars appear and the dark, angular silhouette of the house atop San Juan Hill. Seeing a light bloom in a window, she knew Boston had returned home. She remembered her long-ago dream of living in that house. Well, it wasn't to be. Seeing his house on the hill and hers in its shadow was a reminder of her place in his world. You really don't know him now, she told herself. It's probably best that you don't.

⁂

Boston's thoughts took a darker turn after Ginger left him at the *Statesman*. Peder's death was a fact. No suspense about it. Death was a fact he could face, but the pain was something else. That took time. But there wasn't time now to dwell on it. With so much to do, this wasn't the time to dissect the stew of anger, fear and grief simmering inside him. He had to act.

Locking the *Statesman*, he went for a walk to clear his head. The Green was Featherstone's epicenter. The block of grass, flowers and trees surrounded a Civil War memorial. Two and three-story brick commercial buildings lined the surrounding streets. Citizen's State Bank anchored one end, and the county courthouse faced it from the other. Mingled among commercial blocks were the Masonic Temple, a hotel and an opera house, now a movie theater. All of the stores had closed except Rexall Drug, and a pod of youths waited outside the Alhambra theater for tickets to *Indiana Jones and the Temple of Doom*.

Walking worked off some of his pain but not the anger at Jack's attempts to shut him out. It felt like a betrayal that burrowed inside him like a stubborn badger. When a lap around the quad didn't quiet him, he walked to Holy Name Church, where he used to serve at the altar. Dad often said confession was good for the soul. Maybe so. Over the summer, he had come to trust the bearded priest with whom he shared dinner, drinks and weekly chess games.

"Come in, come in," Frank Carson said. "I'm glad to see you. I just returned from visiting the Norgaards." He shook his head. "They're devastated. Have you seen them?"

"No. I'm not up to it today. Peder's death raises a problem for me."

"What's on your mind?" he asked, removing his Roman collar.

"It's about Jack. I want to talk confidentially… like the confessional."

"What about Jack?" Carson settled into an overstuffed armchair and unbuttoned his shirt. He was Jack's pastor and a sheriff's department chaplain. So was Thom Norgaard.

"He's avoiding tough questions about Peder's death. He's ready to call it accidental."

"I don't understand."

"We found Peder where he shouldn't have been," he said in a rush. "His pack and camera are missing... the injuries aren't those of an accident... I pointed out the inconsistencies... he doesn't want to hear them. Doesn't want to know people made threats over the Kaplan stories."

"What do you want from me?" Carson leaned back in the chair and scratched his beard.

"Just listen while I think out loud. Tell me if I'm full of shit." Then he elaborated on what he thought happened and why Jack didn't want to investigate.

"I don't know what's in Jack's head. Neither do you. He's trained in police work, you're not. Be patient... especially with yourself. Follow your conscience."

Conscience be damned, he thought after he left the rectory. Carson's advice added to his frustration. You and Jack have never differed like this. You've never felt shut out, separated by a wall of... It hurts. It hurts worse than the divorce.

Boston thought he heard an echo from the switch of the foyer light in the tomb-like darkness of the house. He didn't feel like eating anything. A drink would be better. He poured whiskey over ice and went to the veranda. From the chair, he watched the lights wink on across Featherstone and imagined each light as a phone call about Peder's death flashing from house to house. Almost everyone would know about it by the time they read tomorrow's paper. Company would be better than liquor right now, but it had to be someone unconditional, like Rusty or Kris, but not Jack. Not tonight. He saw lights at the Egg Lady's house. Ginger would understand. She knew Peder but your personal lives are out of bounds. He finished his drink and made another.

CHAPTER 6

PEDER NORGAARD KILLED led the *Stateman*'s issue for the day. The news made Pinky Sabine uneasy. "Everything's going to hell," he muttered under his breath. He fretted over the *Statesman*'s article as he dressed the store window manikin. The story said he died on Saturday. His body and bike were found on Monday near Rock Dell. The sheriff's department was investigating the cause of death. Now he worried his outspoken criticism of the Kaplan stories would draw attention to him. How much did Jack already know?

He looked up at the sound of women's voices passing the show window. It's the damned economy, he thought. The moms haven't checked out the special offers. The Back-to-School Sale doesn't meet projections, either. Nobody's buying suits. You can't afford steaks. Jorgenson has to repo pick-ups. Bet the pastors see less in their plates, too. He scowled. The women probably shop at the outlet mall up the four-lane. Those big boxes offer ten percent less than you can. "Sonofabitch," he sputtered and yanked the manikin as if it were a disobedient child.

Sabine's Emporium, like the other commercial buildings, was three stories of patterned bricks. After the great fire of 1883, the city rebuilt it in the Romanesque style that featured tall arched windows, cornices and turrets. It had an ideal location catty-corner to the Green. Pinky began managing the store in high school and found it was a bitch to run. He thought that's why his old man drank himself to death in the back room. It gives you a living but not the life you wanted. A sour thought. You wanted college, but it was out of reach. Then you thought the district's athletic scholarship was in the bag when your touchdown sealed the Falcons' second consecutive state football title. But Jack Meade got it because he was the team's captain. Another reason to back Jager for sheriff.

Pinky finished dressing the manikin and saw the man he envied most—Nelson Ferrall on his way to the Streamliner for coffee. That was what he did most mornings. And why not, Pinky thought? Nels has it made in the shade. His old man set him up as the president of Citizen's State Bank. Now he buys designer suits in Minneapolis. Pinky smoothed his thinning hair and stepped outside wearing today's special—a striped seer-sucker jacket with double-knit slacks.

"G'morning, Pinky, how'd the sale go?" Nelson smiled and fingered his soft mustache.

"Lousy, like everything else these days."

"This'll cheer you. Meade is leaving."

"Good. He's not one of us. Not like his old man."

"That'll be the end of—" They fell silent until several women passed. "That'll be the end of the Kaplan business and—"

"Meade put the kid up to it," Pinky interjected.

"Heard anything more about it—"

"No. You think we'll be questioned on account of—"

"Doubt it. Say, you were in the same grade as the new editor, right?"

"Yeah. She and Meade were an item then. I hear he's doing Daphne now."

"Well, I think we'd all like to." Nelson grinned, showing even, white teeth against his summer tan. "I've seen you eyeing her ass."

"And you, too."

"Well, I guess we've got something in common. Look, Pinky, I need your help getting what's-her-name, the editor, on our side. I'll call you later," he said over his shoulder as he sauntered toward the Streamliner.

"Shit," Boston snapped and hurled back the covers. It was Tuesday, the day he was supposed to receive kudos as the *Outlook's* new editor-in-chief. Instead, he was trapped in the boonies between conscience and duty. Worse, his head throbbed like an abscessed tooth. He couldn't recall if he had two doubles or three last night. Too many, anyway.

A hot shower and two aspirins got him moving. Then he made coffee and thought about Jack. He used to be thorough. Detail minded. Used to love working trig and calculus problems. Once he bragged about interviewing subjects until he pumped them dry. Now he doesn't want to ask the obvious questions about Peder's death. Probably afraid of who might be involved. It never stopped him before. No, more likely, it's the racial undercurrent from Jager's camp. Though he doubted Peder's death was accidental, he didn't like doubting Jack. At the same time, he didn't trust him to investigate on his own. Maybe you can use the *Statesman* to help him find the truth. You'll need Ginger's okay on that.

He dressed for the office and arrived as the *Statesman*'s staff stood about the newsroom in morose clusters. The trill of unanswered phones cut through the low susurrations of grief. News editor Robin Jensen wept openly. Cub reporter Ellen McGovern seemed stunned into silence. Business writer Dub Willard pulled on an elephantine earlobe. Hazel Watkins, the business manager, scurried about comforting the others like a hostess. But for the absence of whiskey, the gathering might have been a wake. Boston deflected their questions and said they might learn something from Jack's press conference at 11:00.

Ginger arrived a few minutes later as outwardly composed as if she hadn't heard the news. Then she called the editors into the regular daily meeting to plan the next issue. An update on Peder's death was but one of several stories. Afterward, she and two reporters went to the press conference.

Boston skipped the presser and sat at his desk doodling on a legal pad. *Goddamn, you Jack*, he seethed as if talking to his brother. You don't want my help, but you won't get far without it, he thought. We both know someone killed Peder. It's as obvious as my nose. But you won't admit it. Someone in town did it. That's what you're afraid of.

And you're afraid I'll ask the questions you want to dodge. And that's just what I'll do. He ripped the doodle from the tablet, crumpled it and hurled the ball toward the wastebasket. It missed.

Ginger returned from the courthouse, closed his office door and sat down. "How're you doing?" she asked and blew her nose.

"You can't tell?"

"Yeah, well, me too, but I can't grieve in front of them."

He nodded. "What did Jack say?"

"He's investigating an accident. Do you buy it?"

He shook his head. "For lots of reasons. Mainly because Jack's dodging tough questions. That's not like him." He stood, removed his glasses and walked to the window. "I hate to say it, but… everyone will buy an accident… even the Norgaards. That way, he doesn't have to implicate anyone before the election." He paused, weighing what he had just said. As harsh as it was, he felt it had the heft of truth.

"Yeah, well, he's your brother, so tell me how you want us to play it."

"Thanks for asking," he said with a pained smile and replaced the glasses. "Report it straight." Then he thought about how to ask her for something without begging or demanding. "I want to pick up Peder's research. It's why I think he's dead. And I want to work from here. That okay with you?"

She said nothing for what seemed like a long time. "What about your promotion?"

"I extended my leave. I'll go back once Jack's on track."

She drew a deep, loud breath. "Am I still in charge? If I'm not—"

"You're in charge, of course," he said. "I don't want to run the paper. That's why I hired you. But I need a home base. I need the *Statesman*'s leverage to get Jack—"

"It's your paper. Staying is okay. It's okay as long as we have ground rules," she said in a tone that ruled out a contradiction.

"Ground rules—what do you mean?"

"I want—no—I insist—I expect you to follow the same rules as the reporters. That includes keeping me in the loop the same way Peder informed you." Then she relaxed and cocked her head to one side as her lips curled in the impish smile he remembered. The one he used to like. “We didn’t budget a salary for you, so you’ll work for nothing—and report to me.”

“It’s a deal,” he laughed, and her tease took some weight off his chest.

Jack left the presser pleased that the reporters didn’t pursue many questions. Peder’s death was an odd case with incomplete evidence, but that didn’t mean it was a murder. Until the autopsy and forensic reports said otherwise, it was an accidental death. You can always reopen it if new evidence turns up, he thought, fetching coffee from the office urn. He took a large slurp and settled behind his desk and wished he had a Danish to go with it.

A deputy stuck his head in the door. “Sir, someone killed Eliot Ferrall. A neighbor called it in.”

“Alright, tell Mary I want to see her—right now.”

Detective Sergeant Mary Kasson bustled into his office like a plump sparrow to her nest. She listened closely as he told her what he knew. After she fluttered out, he called the *Statesman*. While he waited for Boston to join him, he made a note of what he knew about Ferrall. He was single, lived alone on a farm and was alienated from his brother Calvin. For some reason, he was interested in Peder’s research of Kaplan’s life.

“Call Ginger from now on,” Boston said as he got into the Suburban. “She’s the editor.”

“But you’re the boss.”

“I’m not the boss. Just the owner. It’s time you treat her with respect.”

He snorted. Ginger was just a grown-up version of the conniving bitch who wrapped Boston around her finger. He couldn’t say no. Vicky was the same. He’s got a blind spot about women. Never looks under the hood. Ginger has been on board a month. They haven’t blown up yet—but give them time. No way are you going to call her.

They took the highway east to Hennessey in the bluff country and then along the valley road to a forest track. Jack stopped in a clearing at the base of a wooded ridge. A half-dozen newly felled trees lay tangled like jackstraws. Cattle bawled from a pasture on the ridge above. Deputies moved about the scene near a dark pick-up, and Detective Kasson talked to an older man seated on a stump.

"What do we have, Mary," Jack asked.

"This is Jakob Strutt," she said, nodding to the bearded Amish man who said nothing and gazed at the leaves under his brogans. Mary told Jack he pastured cattle on the ridge and noticed the downed trees on Friday evening. He told Ferrall early Saturday morning. The pickup was there that afternoon. Then he didn't see Ferrall for a couple days. That was unusual. When he saw the pickup today, he sensed something wrong and hiked down to check. "Ferrall's in there," she said, nodding toward the pickup. "I looked through the windshield." She wrinkled her nose. "Bad."

"C'mon," Jack said, drawing on latex gloves. The pick-up's windows were shut. Peering through the windshield, he saw Ferrall seated behind the wheel with his head tipped back and his eyes open. His bearded face appeared swollen. Jack opened the passenger door but stepped aside as the cab's putrid air engulfed Boston, who had crowded in to look.

"Ripe, ain't it," Jack laughed as his brother gagged. When the cab cleared, he examined the powder burn behind Ferrall's right ear. Then he saw the small automatic pistol on the floor below his right hand. Jack opened the driver's door and examined the exit wound above the left temple. As expected, there was a slug in the cab above his head. He nodded. A straightforward case of suicide. He shut the door as reverently as if closing a casket.

"What do you think," Kasson asked as she tucked a lock of grayish hair behind her ear.

"Suicide." Jack scratched his head. "Thanks for your help, Mister Strutt. I'm sorry for the loss of your friend. Mary, stay on top of things here. I'll swing by Ferrall's house on my way back. When you get there, dust it for prints, look for a note or anything else."

"Ugh… I hate the smell of death," Jack said as they walked to the Suburban. He swigged water from a thermos and then spit. Two deaths in prominent families in one week. Nothing good can come out of that, he thought, especially in an election year. People expect answers. Fast. They drove to Ferrall's house. The business card with the "call me" note remained stuck in the doorjamb. Jack turned it in his thick fingers, tapped it against his palm and felt the tension return to the back of his neck.

"He was already dead when we stopped," he said sadly as he got behind the wheel. "Hard to know what leads to suicide—"

"If it was suicide."

"It seems pretty clear-cut. So, what's your idea?"

"I've got a couple," he said, ignoring Jack's defensive tone. "Maybe Ferrall was up to something when he invited Peder to look at documents. Then pumped him for what he'd learned about Kaplan."

"Maybe you're onto something," he said, pulling on his lip. "If he killed Kaplan, he'd worry about what Peder knew. So, he invites him to visit again and kills him."

"Logical, but it overlooks a couple a questions. Peder was in St. Ansgar at mid-morning."

"That's right. The preliminary is that he died around midday."

"That's a problem. He couldn't ride fifty miles from St. Ansgar to the ravine in three hours and die at midday. So, someone brought him."

"*Uh-huh*. Maybe so."

"I don't think it was Ferrall. He wouldn't know where to grab him. Even if he did, he didn't have time to kill him, stage the accident and then shoot himself."

"Maybe someone hit him on the road to Breuer's farm. Then they panicked, loaded him up, then dropped him at Rock Dell to protect themselves."

"That's a stretch. And there's the question of his pack."

"Crazy people do crazy things," Jack said as if that were obvious. "Look, I know you want to help, but there's nothing you can do. So, leave it to me."

Boston bit his tongue. Jack's running scared, he thought. Now he's afraid of any ideas but his own. His theories make no sense. And he wants you gone just when he needs your help. How can you help him when he doesn't want it?

CHAPTER 7

Boston returned to the *Statesman* that afternoon and discovered Ginger had left to visit her mother. Tomorrow's paper had already gone to make-up, but he roughed out a story. He called Ginger at home that evening with the news. She suggested they talk about it in the morning.

"Do you think Ferrall killed himself?" she asked over coffee.

"No. We don't know enough yet, but it appears he died about the time Peder did."

"Here's my idea," she said. "Ferrall was well-known as an anti-war author, a military hero and a champion of the Amish. That merits a sensitive but good-sized story right there. I'd like you to take that on. Meanwhile, we'll report whatever Jack releases."

"I like that," he said. "I'll have to rely on public information. It would be insensitive to interview Calvin just now. I also heard he and Eliot haven't spoken in decades. A well-researched story might force Jack to look deeper. His accident theory is full of holes, but he refuses to admit it. He wants to call Ferrall's death a suicide. Get this—he thinks Ferrall murdered Kaplan and then killed Peder to prevent disclosure. Then he cracked up and shot himself. It's a tidy theory and hard to disprove with Kaplan, Peder and Ferrall dead."

"What did you say?"

"I shot it full of holes. He doesn't want to consider murder. I've got to help him."

"Yeah, well, does he want your help?" She raised an eyebrow.

"No. But he needs it. Right now, he's grasping at straws. I'm worried. Now bear with me, please," he begged, palms up. "My gut says Peder's death is linked to Kaplan's."

"Is Jack afraid of finding out it's someone local just before the election?"

"That's it, exactly," he said, again glad he hired her. "Have you seen Jager's campaign signs? The orange and black dog whistle saying, 'Elect Dwayne Jager Sheriff—He's one of us!'"

"Yeah, I've seen them," she said. "It's insidious, but who's going to buy that?"

"Jack does. He believes he's losing. I want to investigate the deaths on the side, but I need him to feed me what he knows."

"How will we make that work?"

We? She wants in—as an equal. "I don't know. He wants information about threats over the Kaplan stories. Maybe I can get something in return. We need more info than we have."

"Alright," she nodded, getting to her feet. "I'll back you—just keep me posted."

She left, and he laughed. You're an unpaid reporter at your own newspaper. She didn't give you explicit orders, but you know what she wants, and you know better than to ignore her wishes. Ginger has virtues, but forgiveness isn't one you recall. He chewed on the end of a pencil and considered trading information. It worked with police contacts when he was an *Outlook* reporter. Would it work with Jack? He set down a chronology of the complaints and complainers:

June 11: Peder finds Kaplan's body.

June 12: Peder's article on tornado and body. He is a hero for two weeks.

June 26: Kaplan identified.

June 30: Autopsy. Kaplan murdered. No investigation.

July 2: Editorial demands investigation. Complaints begin.

Below that, he listed the names and dates of the complainers. Most sat on the Chamber of Commerce board and were anxious about the city's image. Arne Heistad, Doug Jorgenson, Nelson Ferrall, Pinky Sabine, Wendy Hillstrom, George Filbert and a few others feared it would poison the city's chances at landing a regional insurance office. Then he added more notes:

> July–August: Peder researched Kaplan in newspaper files. No complaints.
>
> August 3–14: Peder interviewed people who met Kaplan. Anonymous threats.
>
> August 15: Filbert makes personal threat in my office.

He reviewed what he had. Small potatoes, he thought. Even Filbert's direct threat was—what? He stomped into your office, pointed a finger and yelled, "Goddamn you… you and that kid… leave it alone or you'll end up…" And you were too pissed off to let him finish. Just grabbed him by the throat, shoved him into the corridor and yelled, "Get the hell out." Jack has all but rejected this already. He refilled his mug. Then he struck out descriptive phrases until the notes were strictly factual. Free of adjectives and adverbs, the facts look unimpressive—like shorn sheep.

"You need more trade goods than this," he muttered. "If Peder died because of an interest in Kaplan, the motive must be in his research." He hadn't seen the file for a couple of weeks. Not since the threats began. Someone stashed the three-ring binder at the bottom of a supply cabinet. Between its black vinyl covers were four inches of notes, newspaper clippings and photocopied articles about gangsters and wartime black markets.

He recalled the day Peder put it on his desk, pleased with his work. How had he compiled all that in scarcely two weeks? Then he remembered his own single-minded obsessions at that age. He read each page of the binder. The Minneapolis clippings rarely mentioned Kaplan. Of course not; he worked undercover. The *Statesman* ran a story about him in 1949 after the Minneapolis police came looking for him. Kaplan had told everyone he was an agent of the Federal Deposit Insurance Corporation. That made it easier to interview bankers and businessmen. Nothing in the files implicated anyone in Featherstone. So, what was it about Kaplan that made Filbert livid? Boston finished, disappointed the binder held nothing juicy to trade with Jack.

Then he noticed a bulge in the pocket of the binder's back cover. Something new. It wasn't there a few weeks ago. He fished out the lump—a small silver pin shaped like a halo. A virginity pin. He remembered them from high school. Some guys gave them to their steady girlfriends. They wore them on the left if they were virgins and on the right if they had "done it"—or claimed they had. It was wrapped inside notepaper advertising Jorgenson Motors. A hand-written note in purple ink dotted the "i"s with tiny hearts. "Peder. Give this to me after we do it. Soon! Love always, Patty."

"Well, I'll—be—damned," he said slowly as he turned the pin in his fingers. Then he laughed. "Peder, I had no idea. Doing it on the sly. Well, that's the fun part," he whispered, tickled that Peder was exploring sex. Then he frowned. Patty gave him the pin to give to her. So, was sex her idea? And whose pin is it now?

Ginger looked up from editing a page of copy when he entered her office and closed the door behind him. She shoved the reading glasses onto her forehead. "What is it?"

"This was in Peder's binder," he said, giving her the pin. Then the note. He couldn't help grinning.

She giggled. "Ooh, Peder had a secret. I'm so glad," she said, suddenly misty-eyed. "I guess Patty wanted him to pop her cherry. You remember that, don't you? A rite of passage. So, what are you going to do with it?"

"I'm wondering how to… uh… handle this," he said, squirming at a reference to popping her cherry. "The pin might be a clue or it might not. If this is what we think it is, I can't show it to the Norgaards. Do you think it's possible an angry dad killed Peder?"

"You mean Doug Jorgenson." She raised her eyebrows. "Be careful. He's a power in the county. You remember him—big-time jock, two grades ahead us. Does he have a daughter named Patty?"

"I don't know. I thought I'd ask. I'll keep the note secret."

"Yeah, well, it's your funeral," she said, putting on her glasses. "Please be careful."

He parked the Jeep among the full line of pick-ups, SUVs and sedans on the lot of Jorgenson GMC Motors. The show window had a "Jorgenson for County Commission" sign. If he has a daughter named Patty, what then, he wondered? Nothing, probably. He entered the showroom and asked for Jorgenson. Then he looked over a sporty El Camino while he waited. The burly dealer stepped out of his frosted glass office with a salesman's ready smile and a candidate's outstretched hand.

"Hey, I thought you'd left. What can I do for you? Looking to trade?"

"No, not today. Can we talk in private? A personal matter."

Jorgenson shrugged. "Sure, what's on your mind?" They entered his office.

Boston stood and Jorgenson sat behind his desk. Now that he was there, Boston realized he had made an impulsive move and didn't have a plan. Jorgenson was friendly on the surface, but he had criticized Peder's interviews. What might he do if he caught Peder and Patty together?

"Do you recognize this," he asked, holding out the pin.

"No. Any reason I should?" He turned it in his fingers and then guffawed. "Yeah, I remember giving one to… *ah*… what was her name? A cheerleader with big knockers. Year behind me in high school. Got preggers and…" he laughed.

"It was in Peder's things at the office. Do you have a daughter named Patty?"

"Yeah. Why?" Jorgenson's head jerked and his eyes narrowed.

"I thought she might want the keepsake."

"Why do you think it's for my Patty?"

"It was wrapped in your office note paper."

"I give notepads to a lot of folks—including the pastor. It's advertising. Here," he said, tossing one to him. "You've got the wrong Patty. Now, unless there's something else," he said, opening the door, "I think we're done here."

Boston was almost to the outer door when Jorgenson called after him. "Hey, I'm sorry. I didn't mean to be rude. It's just that… uh… dads can be overprotective, you know. I'll ask Patty if she was seeing him. If I learn anything, I'll call you."

Boston sat in the Jeep for a moment. What did you learn from that? The pin, or what it stood for, pissed off Jorgenson. Do you buy that overprotective father line? What would he do if he had caught them *in flagrante delicto*?

CHAPTER 8

Calvin Ferrall sat in his private office, uncapped a Mont Blanc fountain pen and signed his name to several documents for Boston. As a banker and a financial advisor, he was fascinated by the way people viewed money. Forty years in the wealth profession, as he thought of it, had given him a reputation for acumen. London Meade had followed his guidance for years and accumulated a trust for his sons. He recalled London as a friend, a man who put the city's interest ahead of his own. A good man to play golf with, too. But Boston wasn't cut from his father's cloth. His big city ego didn't sit well with many in town though that didn't bother him. He slid the forms into a manila envelope for the mail. Once processed, the funds Boston inherited would transfer to his account in Chicago.

Ferrall Financial Services occupied the second floor of Citizen's State Bank. His father bought it from the receivers in 1932. Calvin succeeded his father as its owner and president twenty years later. Then Nelson became its president in 1979. The plaques, awards and autographed photos of politicians on the reception room walls testified to Calvin's civic leadership. The Danish modern furniture in the waiting room signaled his success.

He leaned back in the chair and thought of Eliot and how he walked out of the family thirty-five years ago. Never spoke to us again. He became dead to us. But his death was not as upsetting as viewing the corpse to confirm his identity. Even cleaned up, he looked ghastly. Calvin remembered shuddering at the sight of him. Ever since, he endured nightly flashbacks to their shared bedroom above the St. Ansgar general store, going to the miserable shitter out back, bathing in a galvanized wash tub and walking to Shiner's Prairie school with sack lunches. You and he were born different men, he reflected. You worked in the store with your father and studied business. He read books, got a philosophy degree and then joined the Marines. "Why, Eliot?"

A glance at his Rolex reminded him it was time to dedicate a playground—his gift to the children of Featherstone. He slipped on his suit coat and closed the office. Standing at the foot of the stairs, he gazed transfixed by the light coming through the Tiffany windows. This has to be the best building Louis Sullivan ever designed, he thought. And thanks to Dora's dogged effort, this jewel box with its terra cotta décor is listed on the National Register.

A crowd of parents and elementary school children cheered him from the bleachers at the Little League field. Some called out his name. He answered them with a grin and a wave. Though he didn't drink, he appreciated the attention as if it were a fine wine because it produced a similar effect. He stood on the platform with the mayor.

"Good afternoon, mothers and fathers, boys and girls," the mayor began, adjusting the squawk on the microphone. "Even though I'm on the ballot, I won't make an election speech." The crowd roared with laughter and applause. "This playground is a welcome gift to the east side children. We're here to dedicate it and thank our benefactor, Calvin Ferrall." More applause.

Calvin adjusted the spectacles, glanced at some notes and began. "This playground fulfills a childhood dream." Then he described growing up in St. Ansgar, swinging in a tire hung from a tree and playing baseball in a vacant lot with hubcaps as bases. "A fully-equipped playground is as important to public well-being as a church," he continued, warming to the subject. "Here, the children play games. Games develop young bodies and minds. Sports teach them to play by the rules and work as a team. Those are the civic virtues we will need in the next generation of city leaders." He smiled. "I will be a grandfather in November. Someday, I will bring my grandchild here."

The crowd applauded. Then he joined the mayor in snipping the wide, yellow ribbon with ceremonial shears to let a mob of eager children scramble onto the jungle gym at Ferrall Park.

Frank Carson prepared the *ragout Bolognese* with the care of performing a sacramental rite. Sniffing the aroma, he knew it would taste even better than it smelled. Tonight was his turn to cook dinner for the weekly soiree with Boston. He and London started these gatherings years ago. After dinner and chess games, he and London sipped drinks and quoted passages from poetry, literature or Scripture and challenged the other to name its author. London drew from Sophocles, Chekov, Dickens, Sartre and others. Sometimes he stumped Carson with lines from the minor prophets. Boston had accepted his invitation to continue the tradition. Though not as learned as his father, Carson enjoyed Boston's company. He felt comfortable being his natural self around him. Maybe that was because he wasn't a practicing Catholic and didn't have idealized views of priestly life.

After devouring *ragout*, bread and wine, they matched wits with ivory and ebony pieces. Carson opened a gambit with a pawn, Boston countered with a knight, but Carson's bishop took it two moves. After a half hour and a snifter of brandy, Carson said, "check." Four moves more and "checkmate."

"Checkmate," Boston said, throwing up his hands. "The story of my week."

"What are you talking about?"

"I can't return to Chicago until Jack sees Peder's death wasn't an accident."

"I recall you said that." He frowned and stroked his salt-and-pepper beard.

"Someone killed Peder."

"Don't you think Jack will get to the bottom of it?"

"Not as long as he's afraid of losing the election. He's ignoring tough questions."

"And you're out to save Jack?"

"I have to. We've always backed each other. If I don't, he'll betray himself. Sooner or later, it'll destroy him."

"So, which is stronger? Staying or going?"

"Right now, they're equal," he said, releasing his breath in a *whoosh* of exasperation. "If I stay much longer, I'll lose my promotion. If I don't stay, Jack will screw up, and the Norgaards won't get justice. And worse, once Jack realizes it, it will eat him up."

"You've got a good heart." Carson leaned forward and patted his knee. "Take it from me, you can't save someone until they're ready. Until then, you must wait."

"Yeah," he exhaled through his teeth. "Wait. That's just what I don't have time to do."

While Boston slept, his mind cranked through probabilities that Filbert, Eliot or Jorgenson murdered Peder. The possible motives weren't congruent. Filbert hated Kaplan, possibly because he was Jewish. Maybe Eliot killed Kaplan and feared Peder's interest. Or maybe Jorgenson lashed out because he caught Peder fucking his daughter. He woke in the morning with more maybes than certainties.

He returned to the office and Peder's binder. One section contained the notes of the interviews with those who had met Kaplan. The accounts were random; some were bizarre or anecdotes without context. He read them again. Filbert claimed Kaplan had an affair with Emma Peterson. That's an odd thing to mention. What's his point? He remembered Emma. Daphne's mother owned the Streamliner when he was in high school. Back then, he thought she was a sexy older woman. Then he laughed. He was sixteen, and Emma was maybe forty—sexy but hardly old. Peder had interviewed Mabel Gunderson. He remembers his father privately referred to her as the town crier. She often aired the juiciest items before anyone else heard them. If there was an Emma-Kaplan affair, she would know. He called her and said he was following up on Peder's interview. She invited him to coffee. When he arrived at her house, the fleshy widow ushered him into a living room overstuffed with knick-knacks and a coffee table loaded with oatmeal cookies, a pitcher of coffee and China cups.

"I'm so glad you called," she began without waiting for a question. "I can't stop thinking about Peder. Such a sweet boy. And his poor parents. It's terrible," she said and passed him a cup of coffee. Mabel's preparations encouraged him. This was a big deal to her. A good chance she would tell others about it. If word of it reached the killer, it might flush him out. It was a chancy gambit but worth a shot.

"I'm continuing Peder's research. It's a tribute," he began. "What do you remember about Kaplan?"

Mabel's bosom heaved as she took a breath and said Kaplan was a gentle man with the kindest eyes she had ever seen. "Kind, deep and I think… sad. My husband introduced us. Some people said awful things about him. Maybe because he was Jewish—but so was Jesus. We invited him to dinner anyway." So far, Mabel repeated everything he already knew from Peder's binder.

He took another cookie. "Tell me about the rumor of Kaplan's affair with Emma."

"It's a lie," she snapped, and her face colored. "Emma had a lover. True. But I know it wasn't him. She told me that."

"How did the rumor start?"

"George Filbert. He did it to get even."

"Get even, with whom?"

"Emma." She perched on the edge of her seat and lowered her voice. "The Marines kicked him out, you know. Dishonorable. He tried courting Emma but… if you met him, you'd know he isn't a man to sweep a gal off her feet." She giggled. "Emma worked at Sabine's before her pregnancy. George kept asking until she told him, 'get lost.'" Mabel's face beamed with the smugness of a naughty schoolgirl. "We didn't know she had a man. The rumor began when her pregnancy showed. A scandal, you know. Questions about who did it. That sort of thing. It started right after Kaplan vanished. George did it to humiliate her."

Why continue the vendetta after Emma and Kaplan were dead, he wondered? Did Filbert kill him? He let the question pass. Mabel clearly didn't like Filbert. He guessed she would have said something if she suspected him.

He returned to the office overdosed on cookies with more questions than before. Was there bad blood between Eliot and Filbert? Filbert was a Marine corporal and Eliot a lieutenant colonel. Why didn't Emma marry her lover? Was her rejection of Filbert his motive to kill Kaplan? What does Daphne know?

CHAPTER 9

Mabel's interview added a few new facts. These, added to the others, shifted his perspective on Peder's death the way turning a kaleidoscope altered the visible design. No matter what he learned, the picture changed and changed again. Damn it. I'm trapped in a hall of mirrors, he thought, feeling farther from an answer than before. Is it time to throw in the towel and leave it to Jack?

He needed to think and walked from the office to the Green under a thin, gray overcast sky. A coal train wailed at a southside crossing. The damp wind carried the oily odor of soybeans from the track-side elevators. It mingled with diesel exhaust from a passing school bus. Then someone called his name. Turning, he watched Pinky scamper across the street in suede tassel loafers. The former wide receiver was never his friend in high school or now. Neither man offered the other a hand.

"Say, Boston, I just want to… you know, we all feel bad about Peder," he stuttered.

"We?"

"All of us at the Chamber, I mean. And… and myself personally, too, for sure. We criticized his work but… you know… it wasn't personal."

"Thanks, but don't tell me. Tell the Norgaards."

"Well, he worked for you. It just seems that… anyway, I'm really sorry." He was about to pivot but turned back. "Say, I thought you were going to Chicago."

"Eventually," he replied in an even tone to discourage further questions.

"Oh. Well… anyway…" he said, unsure of himself.

Boston knit his brow as Pinky scurried back to the Emporium. He's covering his ass in case the shit hits the fan, he guessed. Heistad, Nelson and the other Chamber leaders haven't said a word about the deaths. Normally, they made pronouncements for something like that. Is their silence significant, or are you reading too much into it? He took two rapid circuits around the Green and returned to the office with no more clarity than before.

A plain manila envelope lay on his desk. Inside it was a copy of Kaplan's autopsy. The medical examiner's sterile prose described him as forty-eight years old, about five feet seven inches tall, and would have weighed about 150 pounds. His remains showed no signs of poison, gunshots or stabbing. There was an unhealed fracture at the base of his skull but dehydration was Kaplan's primary cause of death. Dehydration?

Detective Kasson's cover memo commented on the unhealed fracture. She thought it likely Kaplan was struck from behind before his death. He was probably unconscious or appeared dead when he was stuffed into the chest. Without water, he would have died within three days. It seemed possible he regained consciousness. Faint scratches inside the chest by his left-hand resembled letters. Maybe he tried to leave a message.

Three days. Boston closed his eyes and imagined Kaplan, conscious and doubled up in a dark space, unable to move, not knowing where he was, how he got there or if he would be found. Then dying slowly without hope. Stuffing a corpse in a chest was one thing. But a living man… who would do that?

The scratches seemed vague in the attached photo, even under a magnifying glass. They might be initials or a word or nothing. Boston opened Peder's binder and reviewed the few articles that mentioned Kaplan. He was a lawyer and an accountant. During World War II, he investigated black market dealers in rationed gas, tires and war materials for the Office of Price Administration. Afterward, he joined the Minneapolis Police and focused on the city's underworld. Except for an article in the *Statesman*, the other articles didn't connect him to Featherstone.

The last page in Peder's binder held a long, typed paragraph about a Minneapolis gangster called Isadore "Kid Cann" Blumenfeld, who bought bootleg liquor from farmers and sold it to Al Capone. Boston recalled hearing about him long ago. Juries acquitted Blumenfeld several times on charges of bribery, prostitution, liquor and nightclub kickbacks. Nosy reporters were bribed or threatened. Though charged, he was acquitted of murdering several reporters. After a prison term for jury tampering, he moved to Miami, where he and Meyer Lansky laundered money through real estate. Peder had pasted their obituaries side-by-side. Blumenfeld died in 1981. Lansky died in 1983. He shuddered. *Jesus—is the mob involved?*

He turned Blumenfeld's name over in his mind. Peder was curious. Maybe too curious. Kaplan was investigating the underworld when Kid Cann was at his peak. Did the gangster put a contract on Kaplan? The timing seems right. If the mob is involved, this case poses some real risk. The possibility chilled him. Now you know something you wish you didn't.

As it happened, he had received a few anonymous threats stuck to his windshield. They had an amateurish appearance, and he ignored them. Daily, he parked the Jeep in the alley behind the building and entered or left through the loading dock door. As he left this evening, he saw another paper pinned beneath the windshield wiper. He pulled it loose and turned it over. The third message, like the others, was spelled with letters cut from a magazine: "YOUR NEXT."

Daphne Peterson went home mid-afternoon, ready to burst. She dashed into her bungalow with the urgency of someone who needed to pee. For days, she had overheard the morbid breakfast gossip and jokes about Ferrall's death: *Whaddya expect, guy lived alone, snapped... Nah, Gantz shot him... said he would. Made it look like suicide... Way I hear it, he killed the kid and then himself—that's suspicious right there.* She felt filthy and hypocritical, tolerating such trash while pouring coffee. Seating herself in a chair, she tightened her belly and screamed like a woman giving birth. Then screamed again. She buried her face in a dishtowel until she had no more anger, grief and disgust. Then, drying her eyes, she blew her nose and washed her face to restore herself.

Boston will be along in an hour, she thought. Maybe he'll be in the mood for sex after supper. You want to be fucked hard… fucked to oblivion. Just fuck out all this talk. The meatloaf mix was raw and sticky, and as she kneaded it, she fantasized about tonight until she worked herself into a frenzy. Then the phone rang. Wiping a sticky hand on the café dress, she answered. It was Dora Ferrall, leader of the county arts council. Daphne was fond of her because she had drawn her into a circle of Featherstone's influential women. She was calling to ask if Daphne needed an escort to the council's gala next month.

"Thanks, Dora, but I have one," she lied. "Please thank Nelson for the offer," she said, making a grotesque face. Her affection for Dora didn't extend to Nelson, however. She had known him since first grade and never liked him. Especially now that he came to the Streamliner every weekday to ogle her from behind a newspaper. That was creepy. Lately, Chiara told her she had seen him stroking his crotch under the table. She guessed Nelson rigged her election to the Chamber's board of directors in hopes of a return favor. Fat chance of that.

She resumed kneading the meatloaf to reawaken her carnal fire. The summer affair with Boston had its limits. Her mother taught her that a woman must set boundaries if she wanted to live on her own terms. Boston was what she wanted, an intimate companion without obligations or a commitment. She hoped their one-for-the-road dessert would keep the affair going or give him a reason to return more often. So far, it hadn't. A part of him went missing after Peder died.

You want all of him tonight, she told herself. You want his heart, his arms, his dick. To get them, she took care tidying the living room, putting wood in the fireplace, picking records for soft music, setting the table and choosing the wine. She put freshly washed sheets on the bed and turned back the coverlet as an invitation. The doorbell rang as she was about to take a shower.

"Oh crap," she muttered, wiping her hands. "I hope he's not early." She opened the door.

"Are you okay," he asked, staring at her.

"I'm a mess but…" A glance at him told her he was emotionally drained. She pulled him into the house. "No, I'm not okay. Peder's dead. Mister Ferrall's dead, but I have to be cheerful to blowhards and their morbid talk." Tears and mascara dribbled down her cheeks. "Do you want a drink? I'm going to shower."

"No thanks. I don't feel like… I'm down, too."

"Supper will be ready shortly," she said. "It's meatloaf, peas and mashed potatoes—but it's from scratch. Give me a minute to get out of this… this… ugh!" She threw up her hands and ran to the bathroom.

Seeing Daphne depressed was something new. Maybe it was the gossip and rumors. Before the deaths, she had been upbeat, even on bad days. Somehow, she usually set aside her worries and irritations to have fun. Maybe it was all the talk about Peder. She was sweet to him. But she was naturally soft and compassionate, anyway.

Daphne returned to him wrapped in an aura of clean scents. She poured the wine, and they sat down to supper. Her usual routine was to eat with gusto while telling him the off-color stories she overheard at the counter. It was part of the foreplay, and she reveled in it. As usual, she dressed for the part with enough visible cleavage to jack him up. That didn't ignite his ardor tonight—or hers. A weak smile and furtive glances were all she could muster in the face of talk about his search for Peder's killer.

He suspected she was hot for a good romp in the sack. As much pleasure as she had given him, the prospect didn't excite him tonight. What's wrong with you? You've had a limp dick ever since Peder died. Something bothers her, too. Lately, she's not giving you a head's up on items that might become news. It's not that there aren't any. She just doesn't want to talk. She's dressed for sex, but I don't think her heart is in it. He watched as she picked at the peas.

"What do you hear about the deaths?"

"Trash talk mostly," she replied without meeting his eyes.

"What about Ferrall?"

"Nothing. Nobody knows him. Well, Calvin does, I guess."

"But everyone's got a theory?"

"Yeah. Someone said they heard..." and she drew a ragged breath. "I don't like talking about..." The sentence ended with a shake of the head.

Afterward, she lit the fire and turned on the stereo. As they sat close together on the sofa, he put an arm around her and she slid her hand onto his crotch.

"I want you," she said fiercely. "I want you to fuck my brains out, just fuck me, please." She squeezed his member to excite him. "If you help me out of this dress..." she purred, "maybe we can..."

Forget Peder, he thought as his hand caressed her breast and then undid a button. Their lovemaking often started by undoing one button and then another and another for a slow reveal. Forget Jack, he thought, exposing her nipples. Forget Ferrall. Forget everything, he told himself as she unzipped his pants. And then he heard a voice from somewhere in the recesses of his mind. Not tonight, bozo. She's hiding something. And you'll never find it in her pussy.

He paused and then rebuttoned her top, then stood and zipped his pants. "I'm sorry, I can't tonight." Then, seeing the distress in her eyes, said it wasn't because of her. "I don't want to unless I'm with you in the moment. And I'm not. I'm upset over Peder. That's where I am right now. I'm sorry." He kissed her neck and left.

Back in his house, he let his fingers glide over the piano keys as he considered what the little voice said to him. Daphne has always been straight with you, he thought. She told you how it felt growing up with the gossip about her unwed mother. Growing up without a father. You've trusted her candor. But is she? There are holes in her story where there shouldn't be any. She skipped over how her mother got the restaurant. Is she being candid or is it a sleight of hand, a magician's trick of distraction? If it is a trick, what is she hiding? Why play games with you? Unable to answer that, he felt a wiggle from the worm of doubt.

CHAPTER 10

Jack loved the law and believed he was as faithful to it as he was to Kris. The law could be as difficult as any marriage, but he didn't love it any less. Every morning, as he trotted up the courthouse steps, he paused and patted the column the same way he patted Kris on the rump. For love and luck. He checked with the desk officer on the way to his corner office at the east end of the building. The desk faced one window with a large print of mallards in a marsh on the wall behind it. Several chairs and a small worktable under the other window created a comfortable space for meetings with deputies and the public.

He carried a sidearm in his briefcase but seldom wore it. The belt and holster were uncomfortable sitting at the desk. Besides, the courthouse had enough armed officers for any uprising. As he saw it, his job was to see that citizens acted in legal and socially acceptable ways and take action when they didn't. He found that most troublemakers weren't inherently evil. They were usually acting out of their old traumas, fears or deeper impulses. Many times, he had managed a surrender by coaxing someone into a dialogue. Force was the last resort. He had never shot at anyone—thank God.

Captain Dwayne Jager often disagreed with this approach to policing. He argued that force or the threat of it was more effective than talk. In the last year, he had racked up a large number of arrests that turned out to be unnecessary. Now he had a reputation as a no-nonsense, law-and-order deputy challenging Jack for the office of sheriff. The deputy believed a sharply dressed officer induced immediate respect, if not subservience. Jack glanced out his window and snorted. His image-conscious deputy stood in front of the glass panel in the outer door and checked his appearance. He tugged the tailored shirt tight around his torso, adjusted the pistol belt and hung the aviator's sunglasses from a breast pocket. Jack thought he looked like a B-movie cop, but his challenge worried him.

Jack pulled on his lower lip. What are you feeling, he asked himself. "Name it, claim it and tame it," he whispered, repeating a phrase learned as a psychology student. Ever since Dad died, he had the feeling that people saw him in a different light. It was subtle, but he felt it. The "one of us phrase" is catching on, he thought. It's like they realize I'm not one of them but a stranger pretending to be a native—a colored kid who got lucky. How do you beat an Aryan poster boy?

Boston finished the call and put down the phone. Jack was on his way to pick his brain. That meant his brother wanted another point of view. As much as he hoped Jack wanted to talk about the deaths, he doubted that was the reason. Before Peder's death, he could predict what his brother would do or say. Sometimes, they could finish each other's sentences. What he knew about Jack's mode of thinking now seemed like an out-of-date map.

He wanted to run some ideas past Jack, but his brother was so touchy about his prerogatives as the sheriff that it seemed unwise. As a precaution, he stashed Peter's binder in a lower desk drawer. If Jack showed interest in Kaplan—which seemed unlikely—then he would bring it out. His brother entered a minute later, closed the door and sat at the table. Boston saw fear in his dark eyes instead of their usual openness and warmth.

"I'm going lose this election," he gasped. "My old supporters are too busy to campaign for me. They say they don't have money to give because business is bad. I know it's not true." Then he babbled on, spilling his guts in huge gusts of words punctuated by waving hands. "Jager's got a lot more lawn signs than I do, especially in well-off neighborhoods. I counted 'em. Those people vote. Some folks say I'm a you-know-what in the wood pile, a smoked Norwegian, definitely not one of us."

Boston put up a hand to slow him. "Folks don't buy that crap. You've won two elections. People know you—they don't know Jager."

"Easy for you to say… you're whi—" he slapped a hand over his mouth to stifle the word. "Sorry. There's a lot of that talk. My folks left Louisiana to escape it. As far as I can see, they didn't escape anything. It's worse when it's indirect. I'd rather have it out in the open." Jack's broad shoulders slumped, and he exhaled heavily.

"I know. You faced this in school, at the U and here. What's different this time?"

"They're picking on the kids."

"What… Why?"

"Some bigger kids picked on Lily. Said her daddy's a darkie who doesn't belong here. Ben flattened the biggest kid. The rest ran. I'm damned proud of him."

"Whose kids?"

"Guess? I don't know who's a friend anymore. I haven't felt this alone since my folks died," he said and sucked a ragged breath.

"You won two elections. What's changed?"

"It's because I wouldn't stop the Mexicans from organizing a union at Consolidated Canning. Arne Heistad and the Chamber demanded I lock up the leader. I didn't. No legal grounds." Jack rubbed his tired face. "It might have ended there, but Jager said immigrants bring in criminals. If he were sheriff, he would run a background check before they could work."

"That's bullshit."

"I know. But voters are buying it." Jack spit as he talked. "They claim I did nothing because the coloreds stick together."

"C'mon, people are smarter than—"

"You ought to live here more. People are scared, and Jager is stoking their fear. Between foreclosures, farm agitators, immigrants and the Posse Comitatus—"

"I thought the posse dissolved."

"No. The members rebranded themselves."

"Well, back to Jager."

"He's looking for the next big arrest. Just itching to catch Gantz in a parole violation."

"Who's Gantz?"

"Former posse member. He did time for stealing Ferrall's timber. Threatened to get even. He's on parole. Maybe he did get even."

"Why'd you hire Jager?"

"I screwed up. He left the Minneapolis police because of an internal investigation into excessive use of force. Blue wall. No charges. I found out a year after I hired him."

"*Hmm*. Maybe—"

"No, I *know* what you're thinking." Jack thumped the table. "No! I won't—"

"Why not? Voters deserve to know." Boston felt his temper rising.

"It's innuendo." Jack pointed a thick finger. "Don't… even… think… of it. I mean it."

The brothers locked eyes until Boston nodded. Then Jack slid a manila envelope across the table. The interoffice memo temporarily rotated the captains and lieutenants to other duties for two months. "It's cross-training. We do it every other year," he said. "I reassigned Jager to supervise traffic and water safety. He's going to shit bricks—he'll claim it's a demotion."

"Well, isn't it?"

"Thanks for listening," Jack said, less agitated than before. "I better get back now."

"Aw shit," Boston whispered after he left. His brother was in a corner with two suspicious deaths and a bigot gunning for his job. He threw down his pencil. Chicago seemed farther off than ever. Every campaign needs a Mac the Knife, he thought as he flipped through the Rolodex. He found the name of a friend and picked up the phone. Jack doesn't need to know.

Jack walked to the courthouse, wondering if people were avoiding him or was it his imagination. Most of them were on the other side of the street. Nobody looked his way or waved. The walk back to the office seemed longer than two blocks.

The preliminary medical reports on Peder Norgaard and Eliot Ferrall lay on the desk. He quickly read each one, looking for justification to close the cases. It wasn't there. In fact, the medical examiner's reports raised new questions. He rubbed his left eyelid to stop the twitching that began this morning. It stopped for a moment and then started again.

You need a Hail Mary pass with the evidence you've got, he thought, recalling his last state football tournament. We were down nineteen to fourteen on our thirty-yard line with less than a minute left. You called the play, received the ball, faked the rushers and threw a long bomb to Pinky for the winning touchdown. You need a break like that now. If Boston weren't hanging around, you could call Ferrall's death a suicide without raising questions.

He called deputies Thomas and Kasson to his office. While he waited, he shuffled through the pack of football cards, a memento from the time when his gods were Jim Brown, Bart Starr and Deacon Jones. Then he heard Thomas limping down the corridor and shoved the deck into a drawer.

Tall and taciturn by nature, Leonard Thomas followed departmental procedures to the letter, and Jack trusted him completely. He was now the temporary chief deputy in Jager's place. Thomas ran a hand across his grizzled crew cut and took a chair. Detective Kasson arrived in seeming disarray while shoving papers into her shoulder bag. She sat across from Thomas while Jack stood.

"Mary, what's your take on the evidence of Ferrall's death?"

She shrugged. "I'm struck by the evidence we didn't find." She listed no blood in the cab. No fingerprints on the gun or cartridge. The bullet through the head didn't align with the slug in the cab. "I can go on," she added.

"Maybe Ferrall jerked from the shot," Thomas suggested.

"Even so, there should be some blood in the cab."

"And what's your conclusion," Jack asked.

"It's obvious he was shot outside the truck."

"*Uh-huh*," he nodded, seeing facts torpedo any hope of closing the case quickly. "Anything else?"

"It's not a suicide. Ferrall's friends said he didn't own a gun. Didn't like them, in fact. The gun didn't have serial numbers—acid. We have no suspects but Gantz, so…" she shrugged again and raised her hands. "It's murder."

"For now, let's stick to possible suicide until we know more," Jack said, looking from one officer to the other. "Same with Peder. It's still an accident, either self-inflicted or hit-and-run. Keep looking for cars, drivers or anyone who might have seen him near Rock Dell. I've got an appointment with Calvin. Maybe he can tell me something useful."

Calvin greeted Jack in his private office. They shook hands, and Calvin gestured toward an upholstered chair. "Please have a seat, Jack."

"Thanks. I'll only be a minute," he said and remained standing. "I'm sorry about your brother's death."

"Thank you for those sentiments," he said and took his place behind the desk. "This is so tragic." He removed his spectacles and wiped his eyes. "He was my only living relative." Then he replaced the glasses and laced his fingers until the index pair formed a steeple. "What can I tell you?"

"He may have shot himself, but we're not certain. He didn't leave a note."

"Poor Eliot," he sighed, wagging his head. He continued shaking it as Jack asked about his brother's associates, his friends and his state of mind. Calvin said he knew almost nothing about his brother's personal life or the state of his mind.

"Well, can you tell me anything?"

"To be honest, very little," he said, looking up at Jack. "He returned from the war a different man. He changed inside. Changed so much I did not know what to make of him. He would not talk about the war, so I suspect he must have suffered horribly. He was badly wounded, you know. And he saw so many men killed. When he returned, he worked with us for three or four years. Then he cut us off. Never explained why. He has not spoken to me since. Not even at mother's funeral."

"Any sign of mental illness?"

"That is possible. I mean, it is possible he snapped like those Viet Nam veterans. I regret I did not do more. Reach out to him."

"Did he have enemies who might have killed him?"

"*Enemies?*" Calvin glanced at Jack. "I thought you said suicide."

"We have to consider all possibilities. Did he have enemies?"

"No one. Except Gantz. Beyond him, no one I know of."

After Jack left, Calvin remained behind the desk, mortified. Not from anything Jack said but embarrassed he couldn't tell him much about Eliot. What will people think if they know that, he wondered? Most might say they are sorry for your loss and let it go. But they expect you to show grief. How are you going to do that after so many years?

He closed the office and went to his Town Car. Then he yawned, still drained after last night's go-round with Dora over her drinking. One of many clashes in recent years. He thought she drank more now than in the past. He didn't drink and had never understood why she did. Maybe she learned it from her parents. You loved her precociousness at nineteen. She shook up your life as a young banker. When you needed to marry six months after meeting, she turned it into a romantic adventure. Nelson was the result. She changed when Nelson was in college, and you were busy earning some real money. You thought building her a big house on Sioux Point would rekindle the magic. But her drinking picked up after that. That was after six years on the Minneapolis Orchestra's advisory board. If there is a connection, it is not obvious. He shook his head. What is the allure of liquor?

He drove to the Holy Name rectory to discuss Eliot's memorial service. The Ferrall's weren't Catholics or anything else, but Eliot had led the campaign to restore St. Brigid's Church in Hennessey. The parishioners wanted to honor him. Carson had already agreed to conduct the memorial and wanted to know the family's preferences. Calvin and Dora would attend, of course. It was expected.

CHAPTER 11

The sonorous pealing from St. Paul's Lutheran Church announced Peder Norgaard's funeral. Ginger closed the *Statesman* to let the staff attend. Many downtown shops and offices closed as well. She waited for Boston in the church vestibule and studied the long shafts of sunlight pouring through the clerestory windows. A single stream fell on the Norgaards and the casket. It reminded her of the sun's rays in Baroque religious paintings. God had surely touched Peder.

Boston arrived late, accepted the proffered program without a word and sat with her along a wall. The mourners stood to sing "Lord of all Hopefulness," and Ginger sang through her tears. In a sidelong glance, she saw Boston stand as stiff as a pillar. He stared ahead, his jaw as rigid as a steel railing. This is tearing him apart, she guessed. Of course, it is. Except for Jack, he has rarely gotten close to anyone. But Peder was different. She started to grasp his hand but drew back. He'll resent it. You're not his keeper. Not unless he asks. And he's not one to ask.

Boston heard the remembrances of Peder but felt them as indictments of his negligence. The words went past him as he blamed himself for letting Peder's curiosity over Kaplan run amok. Two people are dead as a result as surely as if you pulled the trigger. How can you live with that? Before he knew it, the associate pastor raised his hand and pronounced the benediction. A classmate picked up the urn of Peder's ashes and recessed in the company of three others. The Norgaards followed them, and then the ushers released the mourners, row by row. Amid the throng, Boston saw Pinky and his wife, Heistad, all the Ferralls and Robin Jensen with most of the *Statesman*'s crew. Then he saw Jack and Kris. Behind them, he saw Jorgenson with his wife and his buxom daughter. It was obvious why Peder or any hormonal youth would be drawn to her. Equally obvious was why her father might be over-protective. Boston tensed up amid the crowd of Norgaard friends and family, fearful that someone would turn on him in front of the others.

The people ignored him and spiraled down the stairs to the reception in the Fellowship Room. Ginger paused at the top step. Boston motioned her to go on. He couldn't face the Norgaards today. Or tomorrow. What he wanted to say to them would have to wait for a better time. A time when he knew the truth of Peder's death. He turned away, and Ginger descended the stairs.

"I fucked up," he muttered as he entered the house. "I fucked up big-time." He dreaded being alone again though the idea of company repelled him. It would be nice to have Rusty because he would be there, ready to give him solace without asking how he felt. Rusty would know without asking. Without Rusty, he turned to the hair of the dog for consolation. It was expensive, but it tasted flat.

Then he heard his father's voice in the back of his head. The uninvited messages come more often these days. Don't rush a story, the old man said. Let it ripen. A rushed story is usually a wrong story. Mistakes have consequences. He thought of his editorial demanding an investigation into Kaplan's death. You did it to please Peder. The difference is Dad would've consulted Jack before writing it.

"I had no right to ask Peder to do what Jack won't," he said as he fixed another drink. It had even less flavor than the first. He stood, holding onto a chair for balance. After a moment, he called Jack at home.

"I missed you at the reception," he said. "Didn't you go?"

"No. I can't… can't face the Norgaards right now. I wish I hadn't asked Peder to—"

"Leave it alone. It's not your fault."

"I can't. Can you tell me more… off the record?"

Jack sighed. "Go see Father Frank. Absolution isn't my job." Then he relented and promised to send the coroner's reports as soon as they were out. He said Peder's death raised questions, but he didn't have enough to launch a murder investigation.

"What about Filbert?"

"I need more than a crabby comment. You got anything more?"

"I'll get you something tomorrow," he promised. Then he tossed off his drink and stumbled on the way upstairs to bed.

A large breakfast and two aspirins buffered what was now Boston's daily headache. Even hung over, he knew trading information with Jack would work only if he had something fresh. "Let's get off your ass and work like a reporter," he muttered, slipping into a blazer and knotting his tie. Then he stopped at the office.

"Oooh, look-in' good," Ginger cooed from his office doorway. "All dolled up. I like it."

"I'm going to Ferrall's memorial service."

"Oh—and hide behind tombstones to spot the killer."

"Ha ha," he said, irked at the sarcasm. "It's just a hunch something will turn up."

"Yeah, well, it's your funeral," she quipped, laughing on her way down the hall.

Boston left Featherstone and took the state highway east toward Hennessey. He thought Hennessey would be an ideal place to live if he could travel back in time. The village struck him as an innocent place, like the hamlets in Currier and Ives lithographs. Daly's Tavern and St. Brigid's Church, the houses of sin and redemption, faced each other across the town's only intersection. Scattered around them were several bed and breakfast inns, a motel, gas station, machine shop, feed, hardware, antique and general stores. The outfitter in the old grist mill rented bikes and fishing tackle. Despite this image, he knew life there was more complicated.

Amish buggies, cars and pick-ups lined both sides of the shady street. He entered the church and nodded to Strutt and an Amish man on a back bench. The pews were already full, but he squeezed into a spot by the fifth station of the cross. He liked the simple, clean design of the church with the Virgin's statue on the altar's right. On the wall beside him was an icon of Simon of Cyrene bearing Jesus's cross. Then the Ferrall family entered and sat in the reserved pew by the casket. Calvin appeared grim, Dora held a handkerchief to her veiled face and Nelson gazed at the Virgin.

Carson stood at the narthex in a cassock, surplice and stole. "The Lord be with you," he intoned. "And with your spirit," the members replied. After a prayer, a friend of Eliot's read verses from Ecclesiasticus beginning with, "let us now praise famous men." Another read from the Gospel of John about Jesus washing his disciples' feet. One by one, friends recounted his military service, underwriting the school's music program and defending the Amish ways against prejudice. Boston glanced at Saint Simon's icon. Eliot was like the saint, he thought. He bore the burdens of others. Once a Marine, always a Marine. He was clearly integral to this community and cared about others, but he left his family. Boston held that thought and let it marinate.

After a final prayer and the blessing, the mourners followed the casket to the cemetery, where the veteran's honor guard fired volleys. Then the bugler held the last note of taps as long as his breath allowed. Carson read the words of committal. Then he nodded toward the Ferralls. Calvin tossed the first clod onto the casket. It struck with a dull thud. In turn, Dora, Nelson and Eliot's friends tossed handfuls of earth as they left in silence. Boston studied each face. If one of them was his killer, he didn't see him.

"Why are you here," Carson asked as Boston approached. The priest removed the stole, kissed it and laid it on the back seat of his VW. Then he peeled off the surplice.

"I thought I might learn something. Now, I'm not sure. What do you make of it?" he asked as he leaned against the Beetle.

"I don't know. Eliot was their patron saint. Not a candidate for suicide." Carson peeled off the cassock and folded it.

"That's my conclusion."

“Between us, the Ferralls puzzle me,” he said, loosening his collar. “Calvin showed no emotion, but Dora cried. Calvin gave me the impression that she and Nelson didn’t know him.”

“Sometimes, death revives old family issues,” Boston said.

“Or settles them.”

Carson’s comment rattled about in Boston’s mind as he returned to Featherstone. Calvin and Eliot were pillars of their respective communities. Each had a distinctive career. But somewhere in the past, something alienated Eliot from his family. Or was it the other way around? Where is the fault line? When he parked in the alley behind the office, he wasn’t certain he had learned anything.

Ginger tapped on his doorway. “Well, did the killer show up?”

“If he did, I didn’t see him,” he said. “Eliot was a saint. Father Frank and I don’t think it was suicide.” He noticed her smile seemed at odds with the pain he saw in her eyes, but he didn’t ask why. She could tell him if she felt a need to.

“Oh. So, nothing new.”

“It confirms my belief he didn’t kill himself. I also learned a lot from the eulogies that I can work into the article about him.”

“These came in early this morning,” Robin Jensen said. She laid a batch of faxes on Boston’s desk. “I kept them ’til now. Couldn’t help but peek.”

“Thanks,” he said with a smile, certain he knew the contents. “Do me another favor. Forget you ever saw them. Okay?”

“Saw what?” she asked, eyes wide in feigned innocence. Then she sashayed out of his office with her single braid swinging across her back. He admired her. Though Robin still dressed like it was 1969 on campus, she was a professional’s professional—an astute news editor and a graceful writer. When he approached her about the editor’s job, she refused because it was too much for a single mother with three kids. But if anything happened to Ginger, Robin was his backup.

He closed his door and opened the folder. Zeke Costas at the *Minneapolis StarTribune* had faxed copies of reporting on Jager and included off-the-record interviews and internal memos about the internal investigation. What he read confirmed his sense of Jager. He used excessive force on and off duty. Investigators noted that many he had arrested suffered needless cuts and bruises. One suspect had a dislocated shoulder. Jager beat a man unconscious while working as the off-duty security at a biker bar. His girlfriend filed assault charges but withdrew them when he left Minneapolis. Public knowledge would sink his candidacy. However, Jack said no. For now, he locked the file in his drawer.

Meanwhile, he still owed Jack a summary of those who complained or threatened him over the Kaplan stories. He leaned back in his father's high swivel chair—the one a district judge gave him. He dubbed it the "uneasy chair" because custodians of truth shouldn't sit easy in their chairs. Dad was a scrupulous custodian of truth. How would he deal with Jack in this situation? With patience, I guess. And Jack would listen to him. He swiveled back and forth in the chair, ambivalent over the promise to give Jack information on the threats he received. Though he barely knew the men on his list, putting their names on paper made him uneasy. How will Jack treat the information, he wondered, as genuine threats or tattling? You're violating your own ethics by sharing information with a cop—even if he is your brother. You're a reporter, not a cop, but if it's for a greater good… he chewed on his lower lip. Then he started the list with the date Jack determined Kaplan was murdered and quoted his editorial:

> To Kaplan's family, his death is always today's news. After so many years, they deserve to know what happened. Justice delayed is still justice denied. His death requires bringing his killer to account, if only posthumously.

At the time, it felt like one of the best lines he had ever written. As good as Dad's words, except the old man wouldn't have written it. His father had a subtle way of winning people to his opinion without offending them. A rare talent that he didn't inherit.

He threw down the pencil. You shouldn't have promised, he thought in disgust. Then he picked it up and drove it across the legal tablet. Line after line of sharply slanted script recorded every scintilla of complaint, negative opinion and veiled threat. Then he got up and walked around the Green to clear his head. Returning to the office, he picked up the pencil and crossed out every word of supposition and bias until only facts remained. Then he typed up the report and printed two copies. He locked one in his desk and sealed the other in an envelope marked: "Sheriff Jack Meade, Personal and Confidential." He left it at the courthouse, happy to be rid of what he considered garbage.

"I don't remember when we've been so far apart," he muttered while taking stock of bread and cheese in the kitchen pantry. "We've always patched it up before day's end." He laid out two slices of wheat bread and slathered them with mayo. "All that is gone," he said, adding slices of cheese and ham. He bought groceries yesterday with the intention of cooking a full meal, but the ambition had left him. Instead, he ate the sandwich with chips and washed it down with whiskey. "Don't take it personally," he said, but he felt abandoned and took it personally. "Why should I care if he doesn't want help? I ought to let him struggle. It's what he wants. It's what he deserves." He sighed. "I can't do that." Feeling blue, he mixed a second drink.

CHAPTER 12

Jack returned to his office after presiding over a sheriff's sale and hurled his jacket at a chair. He had just presided over the legal process of dispossessing a family. Nothing went right. He had hoped the neighbors would buy Otto's mortgage for pennies and sell it back to him. After a few low bids, a well-heeled Texan got it for cash. The crowd jeered. It turned ugly when deputies restrained agitators from the New Farms group. He gulped water, but it didn't wash away the sour taste in his mouth.

Boston's envelope lay on his desk, and the sight raised his hopes. Maybe it contained a who or a why that could move at least one case to closure. He grunted as he read the first sentence: "The trouble began with an editorial demanding an investigation into Kaplan's death." Kaplan, just as you thought, he groused and continued reading: "I assigned Peder to research Kaplan's past. The research in newspaper archives raised no complaints. He interviewed seven people who met Kaplan, and only George Filbert complained. Eliot Ferrall's interest isn't clear." Then his eyes ran down the list of those who seemed most concerned:

> George Filbert. Peder interviewed him at the lumberyard. He seemed angry and made Peder uneasy. Never said Kaplan's name but referred to him as "that Jew." He claimed his investigation was a cover for an affair with Emma Peterson. He told Peder: "Nobody cares about Jews. Leave it alone or you will end up

> the same way." We received anonymous mail threats after that. The voicemail threats sound like Filbert. He threatened me in my office.

Jack nodded. Sounds like Filbert, he thought. Wish he'd do us all a favor and die. He made a check by the name and wrote: "Bears watching."

> Mabel Gunderson: County library board. Friend of Emma Peterson. Her husband was a cashier at Commerce Bank. She met Kaplan. Said he faced prejudice. People treated Emma badly because she was unmarried and pregnant. The rumor about his affair began after Emma refused Filbert's marriage proposals.

He chewed on Filbert's interest in Emma. Did he kill Kaplan out of jealousy? And then kill Peder to prevent exposure? Unlikely but…

> Warren Schmidt: He is elderly. Used to own Post House Bar and Lounge. Kaplan talked to him several times. Asked about his contacts in the Minneapolis liquor business.

> Calvin Ferrall: Told Peder he never met Kaplan, but his father did. Didn't know what he was investigating. Calvin invited me to a catered dinner at his home and expressed a "hope" there wouldn't be any more stories about Kaplan when there were so many positive ones to tell.

Calvin's name surprised him. He looked out for the city more than anyone. What was sinister about entertaining as a way to get things done?

> Eliot Ferrall: Peder interviewed him. He never met Kaplan but asked Peder about what he knew.

"Now we're getting somewhere," Jack muttered under his breath. Eliot lived alone, offered to show Peder documents at his house. For sex? No proof—sex cases often end up as murder-suicide. But there's no sign of sex in the autopsy. It's still an accident and a suicide, he decided.

> John Vreeland: Elderly farm worker. Kaplan was supposed to talk to him but never showed up. Vreeland saw Breuer make liquor during Prohibition.

Vreeland seemed irrelevant. Breuer died in 1942.

> Arne Heistad. Peder didn't interview him, but he demanded we drop the Kaplan stories because they hurt the city's chances of landing the Primus Insurance headquarters. He said, "Some important subscribers object to an investigation. Take my advice. Leave it alone." I asked who said so, but he refused to say.

Heistad. *Hmm.* Jack's eyes flicked across the paragraph again. Arne is pushy when he wants something, he thought. He's built like a boiler with arms thicker than thighs. Probably strong enough to snap someone's neck. Then, *nah*, the evidence is too thin.

> Nelson Ferrall. Seems to be the intermediary for whoever is unhappy. He hasn't threatened but helps those who do. I asked why the people refused to call me. He said it was because Featherstone is small, and everyone knows everyone. No one likes conflict. Nelson hasn't uttered an opinion of his own.

Not like his old man, Jack reacted as he sucked on a lozenge. No guts. No opinion. A playboy messenger. The last name startled him.

> Emery Daniels. President of Commerce Bank. Met Kaplan several times and gave Peder an interview. Said he talked to many businesses. Daniels thought he was investigating someone. In a private conversation, he told me there was "a lot of consternation" within the Chamber over the paper's coverage of

> Kaplan. From Filbert and Heistad in particular. They claimed Peder had Kaplan's case notes. (Not true.) Daniels said some intended to hurt me financially. He dismissed the talk about Primus Mutual as wishful thinking. I think he knows more than he told me.

Jack finished reading and blew out his breath. You know them all, he thought. None have so much as a parking ticket. Each is a wheel in the community. They won't like being questioned. Good chance they'll remember it on election day. Filbert's threat looks like the only one with meat. The rest are hot air. Then he called in Thomas and handed him the memo.

"Pretty thin," he said after reading it. "Hardly worth following."

"I made the mistake of asking for it. He'll be on my ass if I don't follow up. No one's a suspect. I want to know where each was over Labor Day weekend. Be discrete. Oh, and don't interview Daniels just yet."

CHAPTER 13

Chronic fatigue was new to Boston, and muscle aches added to his daily headaches. He rose in the morning feeling as if he had aged a decade overnight. This wasn't the exhaustion he knew as a reporter embedded with the Marines in Viet Nam. It was different. A soul fatigue, if that was possible. Maybe it was that infamous "mid-life crisis" he didn't believe in. Maybe he was just getting old. Whatever it was, it was happening to him. He didn't like it.

The dresser had no clean shirts. He pulled one from the laundry bag, wrinkled but clean enough. He stumbled on his way down the back stairs. The refrigerator had no eggs or milk. He meant to buy groceries yesterday but forgot. He brewed coffee and took it into the great room. Current issues of *Time*, *Atlantic*, *The Economist*, *The New York Times* and other weeklies and monthlies lay in drifts around the wing chair with an empty bottle and two tumblers. What a mess, he thought. You're falling apart, but what the hell? Why stop? He drew a breath. Alright. No groceries, so I'll eat breakfast in town.

The light rain splattering the windshield added to his melancholy. He slipped into the Streamliner, didn't see Daphne and gave Chiara his order. The scrambled eggs and toast calmed his queasy stomach. Propped on his elbows, he cradled a coffee cup and shuffled through his next steps. Jack's investigation hasn't moved in two weeks. Braydon is pissed you haven't returned. If you don't return, you can kiss the promotion bye-bye. So, you have a simple choice—Peder or the promotion. You can't have both.

He left, still undecided and drove to the Ever-Clean Laundry. Ernie Ketcham greeted him with his usual testiness. Boston dropped a bag of dirty clothes on the counter. They would be ready at day's end Ketcham said around the cigarette in the corner of his mouth. Then Boston picked up the groceries he had forgotten to buy yesterday. Discount Liquors was the last stop on the way home. Luxuriating in the shower, he weighed whether to stay or return to Chicago. When he couldn't decide, he cooked enough spaghetti for lunch and two dinners. Still undecided, he went to the *Statesman*.

"What is it," Ginger asked as he entered and closed the door.

"I've decided to stay until Jack's on track," he said rapidly. "I don't know for how long. That still okay with you?"

"I thought we settled that. You don't need permission. You own the place. But if you get in my way, you'll know it." Then she smiled, and he noticed the small creases, like parentheses, around the corners of her mouth. It was a friendly smile, but he also knew she wasn't kidding. Then she motioned him to sit.

"Yesterday, you offered to help me with Mama. Well, you can. I want you to listen. That's all." She stood in front of the desk, clasping and unclasping her hands. "You're the only one in the office who knew Mama when she was… Mama. I don't want sympathy or advice. Just understanding from someone with a moral compass."

He nodded and broke eye contact, so she had emotional space to talk. She was silent at first, perhaps to gather her thoughts. During the pause, he noticed the details of her office. Though equal to his in size, it had a smaller desk, a table, and a credenza. Her personal items included a photo of Jester, a dish of smooth pebbles from a mountain stream, the serenity prayer in needlepoint and a diploma from the University of California-Davis. A framed portrait of Agnes O'Meara stood on the credenza.

"Mama may never say my name," she said, drawing a deep breath. "They tell me her dementia has progressed beyond even partial recovery. We'll never have a conversation."

"I'm sorry. I had no idea—"

"Mama's gone, an empty shell. I hate caring for a stranger who doesn't know me," she wailed.

He fidgeted and leaned forward, tempted to rise and stand by her. But she didn't want sympathy or pity, only his ear. Christ, this is hard.

She wiped her eyes and blew her nose. Her misery revived the agony he felt as his mother died of cancer. He was fifteen. She was his soulmate more than his father. After she died, it was Jack and Ginger, not Dad, who pulled him through the grief.

"I wanted to reconcile—now I can't," she sobbed. "We connect saying the rosary—but it's just a reflex. It's not real."

Her story aroused his remembered grief, the kind that's stored and emerges later in moments of compassion. He felt it but knew she didn't want it. At least, not now.

"That's my reality," she said, blowing her nose. "Here's what I want to know," she said, switching moods, now sharp and intense. "Every day, I ask God to end Mama's suffering. It means ending her life. Is that immoral?"

Her question shook him. *Jesus! Who are you to have an opinion?* This is something for Carson. She's desperate and trusts you. Knowing that gave him a chill. He shifted in the chair, uncertain he had an answer. "No," he said, looking into her eyes. "No. I don't think it's immoral. Just the opposite. You visit Mama though it hurts. She's not present to you, but you're present to her. You want what's best for her. Didn't catechism teach us it's Christ-like to suffer with others? That's what you're doing. Honoring her with your suffering. But indifference… that's immoral." After he said it, they looked at each other without speaking for a long moment.

"Thank you," she sniffled. "I needed to hear that."

"I'm honored you asked me. You're doing right by her."

"I had to get that out… so you'll understand… so that when I'm difficult… I mean, when I'm more difficult than usual," she added with a giggle and wiped her cheek.

He laughed with her, remembering how difficult she could be. But she trusted him, and he trusted her. It seemed that between Mama's decline and Peder's death, they were somehow bound together, if only temporarily. He felt at ease. Then she smiled, and it was like the sun appearing from behind a cloud. In her moment of despair, he saw beauty in her at forty he had never seen at twenty. The image stayed with him for the rest of the day.

Minnesota's weather turned abruptly rambunctious at the September equinox as it usually did. The cold rain and fog felt like an excuse to stay abed. Dora woke a little woozy from last night's brandy and an argument with Calvin. "What I drink is none of his business," she muttered and wrapped herself in a robe. She peered through the bedroom window overlooking Lake Iosco. Below her, two fishermen in an aluminum boat plowed a dark furrow across the lake's foggy surface. You might have to give this up, she thought, but you'd hate that.

Calvin bought all of Sioux Point on Lake Iosco and built the huge, ultramodern house she had designed. The large windows and views up and down the lake made it ideal for holding galas and parties that supported the arts. They used to have lots of fun, but his light-hearted mien had faded. After he retired from the bank, instead of relaxing, he opened a financial service business that absorbed all his attention. She soon felt neglected, as if he had taken a mistress. Today was Saturday, and another empty weekend loomed before her.

The idea of starting life over began as whimsy. Slowly, her "what if" game of fantasy had acquired a life of its own. She thought of little else lately save starting over with another man. Is it possible to get out of this loveless marriage in one piece? He'll fight you all the way. Calvin, you're nothing like Claudio. He played violin in the Minneapolis Orchestra. You went to the orchestra's advisory board meetings monthly. Never missed one in six years. You spent a night or two with Claudio in Minneapolis while he celebrated your beauty as you lay naked in his bed. His fingers used to make you shiver as they glided lightly over your skin. He was a maestro of romance. Then he left Minnesota for the symphonic orchestra in Madrid. Then you went from him to martinis.

She turned this way and that before the full-length mirror. Despite thirty-six years of marriage, neither her face nor figure sagged. She still attracted looks from younger men. It didn't work when Boston came to dinner so Calvin could press him for positive stories. You planned it, to sit across from him, but the black, off-the-shoulder dress didn't do the trick. His eyes betrayed little, he ignored your signals, and you haven't seen him since. An open affair in Featherstone is impossible, of course, but it is fun to keep in practice.

She dressed and entered the kitchen. Calvin looked up from the *Statesman* and then continued reading without a greeting.

"Anything interesting," she asked, adding a jigger of vodka to her orange juice.

"Nothing much. Did you send a card to the Norgaards?"

"Yes, of course. Are you going to the office? I thought you were staying here today."

"Something came up. I will be gone for a couple hours."

Dora tossed off her breakfast drink and looked at the glass. Is this an orange juice or a screwdriver, she wondered. Then she weighed whether to make another. These days, you get more company from vodka and brandy than Calvin. At least he doesn't play around like Nelson. Maybe you should be grateful for that.

After two cups of coffee and cinnamon toast, she tackled the agenda for her baby, the Arts Council. It was a good cause in itself. Even better were the friendships with women around the state. She organized the council twenty years ago and discovered the county had dozens of unknown but good painters, sculptors, weavers, musicians and potters. They worked other jobs and professions but came together now and then to perform or display their work. As much as she loved the council, she wanted to pass the torch and thought of Daphne as her successor.

CHAPTER 14

The gentle patter of autumn rain reminded Jack of his childhood when he made model airplanes in his room. He would like to sleep in today, but Kris was already up and dressed in nursing scrubs. She kissed him on her way to the hospital. He made Ben and Lily breakfast and then drove them to school on the way to the office. The final autopsies and forensic reports on Norgaard and Ferrall lay on his desk. He read them with a silent prayer he would see something to support a firm explanation of their deaths.

Eliot Ferrall died on September first between 2:00 and 4:00 p.m. from a single gunshot behind the right ear. He was sixty-six years old and in excellent health; he stood five-feet-ten inches tall and weighed 182 pounds. His body held no traces of drugs or alcohol. He didn't leave a suicide note. The weapon was a Colt .32 automatic with three rounds in the clip. Ferrall's friends said he didn't own a gun. Acid had removed the serial number. Delmar Gantz said he was working in the state forest that day, and a ranger would vouch for him. So far, the deputies hadn't found the ranger. Jack fluttered his lips in frustration. It looked like a suicide, but it wasn't. It was a homicide. And that could be complicated.

Peder Norgaard died September first between 11:00 a.m. and 1:00 p.m. He was seventeen years old, in excellent health, stood six-feet-two inches tall, weighed 156 pounds. His body had no traces of drugs or alcohol. He died instantly from a severed spinal cord. His wrists had faint bruises. The fractures in his sternum, ribs, and the cuts on his legs and chest occurred after he died. His knees and elbows had grass stains. Dark paint on the bike matched a color used on General Motors vehicles. His parents said he took his pack and camera with him. "Oh, shit," Jack blurted, convinced his re-election depended on this case. He started a list of questions:

Did Peder vanish between St. Ansgar and Rock Dell?

Grass stains—crawling?

Where is the pack?

Type of GM vehicle hit the bike?

Cause of broken neck and other fractures?

Why did Eliot Ferrall leave family?

Did Ferrall-Norgaard share interest in Kaplan?

Reasons for suicide?

Can Gantz confirm alibi?

He finished the list and called in Kasson and Thomas. He trusted Kasson's intuition and Thomas's innate skepticism. Between them, they might see something he overlooked. Anything to advance the cases toward conclusions. He asked Kasson for her take on Peder's death.

"Ambiguous at best," she said. "The body and bike at the outside of the curve look like an accident. However, the medical examiner says a fall couldn't sever the spinal cord. Falling would have caused a concussion or cracked his cranium. No sign of that. He wasn't wearing his helmet. So, if he fell head-down, there'd be dirt and lacerations on his scalp. There weren't any. And some injuries occurred after his death. So, we're looking at a murder, not an accident."

"Anything else, Mary?"

"Talk to Boston some more," she said, tucking back a lock of hair. "He seems to think Peder's research worried people. Maybe Kaplan's killer or an associate is still around."

"Still around—after forty years?" Jack stood at the window and watched the rain splatter the puddles. "Think Ferrall was that someone? He was a Marine. Left Featherstone about the time Kaplan vanished. He pumped Peder about his research. Any other suspects?"

"Filbert and Heistad don't have alibis for that weekend," Thomas said in his dry, matter-of-fact voice. "Filbert made the only threat, if that's what it was."

Jack grunted. "Heistad was a soldier. Think he's strong enough to twist Peder's neck?"

"Maybe, but why," Thomas asked. "Here's the deal, Jack. Peder was in St. Ansgar at ten. He died between eleven and one. There's not enough time to ride from there to the coulee. I think we're looking for a third party."

"Hold that thought," Jack said, feeling boxed in. "Well, what if Ferrall called Peder? What if he arranged to pick him up? You know, to show him documents like before. Then killed him. A couple hours later, he cracked up and then shot himself."

"There's a problem with that…" Thomas said, rubbing his crew cut. "The problem is this, Ferrall owned a Dodge truck, not a GMC. So, his paint won't match the stuff on the bike. Like I said, we're looking for a third party."

"If Ferrall killed Kaplan, Peder's research might worry him," Kasson added. Then she furrowed her brow. "But… like Len said, Ferrall would have to intercept Peder, kill him and then fake a hit-and-run a couple hours before shooting himself. That's impossible. It makes no sense," she said vehemently, shaking her head. "None at all."

"Suicides are often inexplicable, you know," Jack countered. "Moving on. Any evidence Filbert sent the phone and mail threats?"

"It seems likely," she said. "The cut-out letters came from a construction catalog. The voicemail is fuzzy. We can't identify him with certainty."

"What else do we know?"

"Filbert owns a dark Chevy," Thomas said. "The lumberyard pick-ups are GMCs."

"Then there's motive," Jack continued. "If Filbert killed Kaplan, he might kill Peder."

"Why would he kill Kaplan," Kasson asked.

"Maybe because he was Jewish. Or maybe because he believed he and Emma Peterson had an affair." Then he shrugged. "I want you to finish checking out their alibis. I don't want you to investigate Filbert yet. Not until we have some probable cause. Mary, what are the chances Ferrall shot himself for personal reasons and someone else killed Peder?"

"Two independent deaths make a lot more sense than anything else."

"And what about Gantz?"

"He had a motive," Thomas said. "But I doubt he was involved."

"Why?" Jack snapped, sensing he was about to hit another dead end. "Maybe he cut the trees to lure him into the woods. Then killed him and staged the suicide."

"I think somebody else cut the trees," Thomas said in a flat voice as if he knew for certain. "Gantz is a pro, a creature of habit. In his other thefts, he took walnut and oak, not boxelder and elm. He cut the trees flush with the ground to hide his theft. And he stole one tree at a time. Usually at night. Gantz doesn't have the brains to set a trap or stage a suicide. Besides, he knows he'd be our first suspect."

Kasson nodded in agreement. "Maybe the trees aren't connected to Ferrall's death."

"Maybe," Jack said absently. "But why would anyone cut the trees? That's enough for now," he said. "I want to think about it. You do the same." In the back of his mind, he wondered what the voters thought now that he and Jager were tops in the September primary. Only six weeks until the November election. In Jack's ideal world, he thought he would solve both cases in four weeks and then campaign on his success. But was a month enough time to put the cases to bed?

He stood at the window and watched raindrops dimple the puddles. If only evidence fell like rain. For now, the safest course seemed to lie with the evidence at hand. The simplest theory was usually the right one. He broke out a pack of notecards and wrote one fact on each. After that, he penned the names of people mentioned or involved on the other cards. Then he tried to match the names to the facts like a game of solitaire. It was a crude method but effective, he thought, unlike Jager's non-existent databases.

The cards raised more questions than they answered. Peder and Ferrall died the same day, less than four hours and ten miles apart. A coincidence? Death by broken neck, death by gunshot—different MOs. Separate killers—unrelated deaths? What was Ferrall's interest in Kaplan? What was Filbert's? Filbert had a GM vehicle and no alibi for the day. Filbert served in the Marines under Ferrall. He was booted dishonorably after machine-gunning Japanese prisoners. Why wait forty years for revenge? Jack put down the cards and opened his office window. He breathed in the damp air and listened to the soothing patter of the rain. He wished he was at home where he could curl up for a nap and sleep until after the election. He checked his watch, shrugged into his jacket and went home.

A night's sleep snuggled next to Kris didn't relieve the tension in his shoulders. It was only 7:30 a.m., but he had to be on his toes to brief Glenda Mercer. The county attorney had the office next to his. At this hour, she was all business. His knock on the door produced a commanding, "Come in."

Mercer stood at the window with her back to him as he entered. Her office décor radiated a chill from its somber oak wainscoting, massive desk and an absence of personal touches. The stolid, broad-shouldered woman of indeterminant middle age habitually stalked into rooms with an air of command. Her gruff voice, short gray hair and dark pinstripes impressed, if not intimidated, the judges, defense attorneys and cops. Especially the cops.

"Alright, Jack, what have you got?"

"Two suspicious deaths. No obvious motives or suspects." He saw her features congeal into a withering scowl. Not what she wanted to hear, he guessed. In turn, he felt anxious, like a wayward child in front of the school principal. He hastened to tell her the autopsies and skimpy evidence raised a lot of questions. Telling her there wasn't enough evidence for a murder investigation only deepened her scowl. Facing her was like standing in a cold-storage locker.

"You mean both deaths are probably homicides, but you don't want to say so?" she barked and threw her hands in the air.

He gave an "I don't know" shrug. "Gantz made a threat before prison, but nothing connects him to it—yet. Filbert made threats, but there's no motive or evidence on him either."

"So, where does that leave us?" Mercer sat behind the mammoth desk while Jack stood before her. "I mean, call the shot here—*sheriff*. I've got to impanel a grand jury."

"We're not ruling out anything," he said in his softest voice. "Not until we have clear evidence of homicide."

"You're certain the deaths are unconnected?" Mercer straightened the knot in her scarf. "Anything to their shared interest in Kaplan?"

"We looked at it, but there's nothing except Filbert's interest. We're being... *uh*... discrete about it. Peder interviewed him. The others he interviewed didn't object. All complaints were anonymous." Crap, he thought. Now she's aware of the Kaplan idea. Sooner or later, she'll come back to it. *Damn*.

"Did Ferrall kill the boy and shoot himself?"

"It's possible, but we haven't found sufficient evidence to call it."

Placing her palms on the desk, she heaved herself erect and leaned toward him. "Alright, you have an unknown murderer with two victims by different MOs. Or you have two unknown murderers with a victim each. Which is it?"

"I think we have one killer and one suicide. The deaths occurred on the same day," he added quickly. Her expression told him she didn't buy that theory, either.

"Alright, sheriff, keep me posted," she said, waving a hand in dismissal. "Oh, by the way," she added with an icy smile, "Congratulations on your primary win."

Jack walked the few yards to his office, his face warm and flushed with embarrassment from Mercer's verbal spanking. Thomas and Kasson waited for him. Until they turned up more evidence or suspects, he told them, the deaths were under investigation as an accident and a suicide. "Keep the cases under wraps. I don't want Jager mucking for headlines."

Thomas guffawed. "You know damned well he'll say something, facts or not."

"Yeah. If I'm lucky, it'll bite him in the ass."

CHAPTER 15

After years at the *Outlook*, the telex's chatter triggered a Pavlovian reflect in Boston's brain. Hearing its clatter meant a batch of fresh information he could sort, analyze, dissect, parse, synthesize and compress into a coherent story with a lead followed by several paragraphs. If only it was news of Peder, but he knew it wasn't so. Jack didn't use a telex. Then, when his brother called a moment later, Boston hoped for a breakthrough. That wish died when Jack said, "We need to talk." That meant he wanted a sympathetic ear while he thought out loud. Boston took a pair of Sprites from the newsroom refrigerator and waited for him.

Jack's appearance alarmed Boston. Even when under stress, his brother usually appeared as outwardly placid as a millpond. The furrows in his forehead added years to his looks. He gestured in spasms as he talked. "I've never had cases like—this is off-the-record, you understand," he stuttered. "I don't know what to do," he said as his satin baritone approached a scratchy falsetto.

"Well, where do things stand now?"

"Peder's death looks like an accident. Ferrall's looks like suicide," he said as his fingers made air quotes around "looks like." "Everyone on your list was in the clear Labor Day weekend except Filbert and Heistad. Neither had an alibi. We're certain Filbert sent the mail threats. Maybe the voicemails, too. But I can't figure out his obsession with Emma Peterson after all these years. If he didn't kill

Kaplan, it's unlikely he killed Peder." He paused, sipped the Sprite and drew a breath. "Glenda is impaneling a grand jury. If I don't get a break in these cases, folks are gonna think I don't know my job."

"So, you think they are murders?"

"I'd say so if I had a suspect or a motive or evidence."

"How about the autopsies?"

"I brought copies. You'll see what I mean." Then Jack stood up to leave.

"Sit down. There's something else," Boston said and handed him the virginity pin. "It was wrapped in this note."

Jack studied it, scratched his head and then laughed. "I remember these. You gave one to Ginger. What's your point?"

"It was in Peder's stuff. Apparently, he just discovered sex." Then he passed him the note. "I showed the pin to Jorgenson but not the note. He got his back up. Then he apologized for being an over-protective father."

"Are you suggesting he killed Peder for screwing Patty?"

"What if it was Lily in the same circumstances?"

"*Hmm*. I see what you mean. Maybe—"

"Jorgenson drives GMC vehicles. Protecting his daughter is a motive."

"Sure. But I don't see a tie-in with Eliot and Kaplan. Do you?" He heaved a sigh. "I've gotta go now. Thanks for listening. See you at supper, five-thirty sharp."

The campaign must be eating him up, Boston thought. He's running scared because of Jager's line that he isn't one of us. You can do a lot to help Jack, but you're deaf, dumb and blind when it comes to prejudice. You've got no experience with the subtle slights he endures. You're white and can't walk in his shoes. All you can do is listen to his footsteps.

Jack clomped into the house, gave Kris a quick kiss and said Boston would be along shortly.

"You better perk up, then," she retorted, arms akimbo.

"Yes, dear," he mumbled, unbuttoning his shirt on the way to the bedroom.

"You know, it's time to use your psychology degree on yourself," she called after him. "Think about what you'd tell others in the same boat. Then take your own advice."

"I guess so," he mumbled, sliding out of his trousers. She's right, he thought. You had that feeling about her when you met in psych class. That's what attracted you. Consider yourself blessed. Even that wasn't easy. He had met the Kaminskis only a few times and worried his ancestry would be a problem when they announced the engagement. They were gathered in the farmhouse living room after Sunday dinner. He and Kris sat on the sofa facing her parents in seated matching chairs under a photo of the pope. Ma Kaminski gasped when Jack asked for their blessing. Then Pa cleared his throat. "You're a good man, Jack. I like you but… *uh…* It's best if people marry their own kind." Then Kris beat him to a quick response. She lit into her father, saying she would marry with or without their blessing. Several months later, she glided up the aisle of St. Stanislaw's Church on Pa's arm. She's right, he thought, as he pulled the Twins jersey over his head. Shrink yourself.

"Did you know Ben and Lily are both on the honor roll," Jack asked, turning to Boston at supper. "Ben's going out for basketball this winter. Lily joined Brownie Scouts." He kept up a nonstop patter on their activities. That way Boston didn't have an opening to ask about the campaign or expound theories of the cases. Then Ben and Lily cleared the table, and Jack nodded toward the door to the basement rec room. "Game's on now." He had looked forward all afternoon to watching the ballgame with his brother and dissing his Chicago team.

"Too bad the Twins blew their pennant shot," Boston gloated.

"Yeah, but they still play better ball than the Cubs."

"The Cubs have a shot. Don't forget, the Sox just beat the Twins three out of four."

They bantered until Jack buried him with statistics. Then, sensing Boston's flagging interest, he braced for comments on the coroner's report—the last thing he wanted to talk about.

"I might believe Peder's death was accidental if it happened near St. Ansgar… if it wasn't a severed spinal cord… and he had his pack."

"Uh-huh. I know," Jack muttered and turned up the volume on the television.

"There're more questions than answers."

"Tell me about it," he grumped, sinking deeper into the chair, peeved and sorry he invited him to supper. *Jesus—can't he get off it just for tonight?*

"Let's talk—off the record. Let me help you," Boston said softly. "What's easier to prove—something that did happen or something that didn't?"

"I don't know. These are unconnected cases."

"What about Kaplan?"

"That's your supposition."

"Isn't it possible Kaplan's killer—?"

"Well, shit, anything's possible."

"You don't believe that—"

"Do you know how hard it is to get facts?"

"Yeah. I do it every day. It's called reporting."

"Look, I invited you to supper so we can watch the game, not to talk about my work. Stick a sock in it, for Christ's sake."

"Sorry, but I… uh—"

"I think the Minneapolis mob killed him and left him in Breuer's house. Now I'm done talking," Jack snapped, turning away. "Stay the hell out of it."

They sat for a moment in sullen silence. Jack stared fixedly at the game. The stiffened contours of his face were sharper in the flickering light of the television. Boston stood, thanked him for supper and said it was time to go home.

Jack followed him upstairs. A sidelong glance at Kris, and he knew she overheard their quarrel. And he also knew she was annoyed with him, and he would hear about it just as soon as Boston left. His brother was her pet, too.

"I wish he'd mind his own beeswax," he muttered. "Nothing but trouble."

"Stop it. He's trying to help you."
"Well, his help doesn't help."
"You're pushing him away just when you need him the most."
"He's meddling. I wish he'd go to Chicago."

CHAPTER 16

The fraternal squabble felt nastier than any Boston could remember from adolescence. It wasn't what Jack said so much as the rage he felt radiating from him. Their boyhood dustups had never lasted long. Dad made certain they reconciled quickly. "Don't let the sun set on your anger," he often admonished. But this one felt different. He went off to bed angry but certain he was right. No reason to make up with him, he thought. He doesn't want the evidence you have. He wants the evidence that doesn't exist. What a chickenshit way to side-step the issue. He's afraid it's someone he knows.

Boston rose in the same foul mood that he took to bed. He projected his disgust with Jack onto the coffee beans and took pleasure in grinding them. Strong, freshly brewed coffee soothed his irritation. It was warm enough to sit on the veranda in a sunny spot. So, where are you? he wondered. Jack has pared down the evidence to support a safe, simple but wrong conclusion. He's thinking too small. The devil isn't hiding in the details; he's roaming about a bigger picture. He finished his coffee and flicked the dregs onto the lawn.

Fully awake at last, he hiked down the hill and along the gravel road. He enjoyed walking for the exercise but also as a kind of kinetic meditation when he felt fully present. Body awareness shook loose ideas and insights trapped in his subconscious. Striding along, he listened to the cadence of his breathing and the crush of gravel underfoot. As he moved, he thought about Kid Cann. The mobster bought bootleg whiskey from farmers. Breuer made whiskey. Country stores traded in whiskey. Did Breuer trade it to a store that sold it to Kid Cann? Prohibition ended in 1933. Breuer died in 1942. Vreeland knew Breuer and Kaplan wanted to talk to him but about what?

He returned to the house toying with a tantalizing idea. Kaplan was looking for local associates of Kid Cann. *Nah*, that's impractical. Featherstone isn't big enough to hide a criminal enterprise. Not for long. A Cann-Kaplan-Peder connection—tenuous at best—too far-fetched. But someone local is the key. You've got to get Jack to look beyond his fears. But you need to be patient—patience requires time—time you don't have. At least not without another extension. He dialed the Chicago office, knowing he had chosen between Peder and promotion.

"I'm involved in a murder investigation," he told Braydon. "My newspaper is doing what the sheriff won't. A lot rides on what we can dig up. I'm sorry to put you in a jam, Henry. I can't say when I'll return. So, if you name someone else to replace you, I'll understand. You do what you must."

"Alright," Braydon growled. "You've pushed my buttons and found a soft spot. I started in newspapers. I'll hold off until you collect your scalp."

One down, one to go, Boston thought on the drive to the office. Now to bring Ginger up to speed. Her opinion of the autopsies and reports matters. She was tied up in meetings when he arrived, and he knew better than to interrupt her. When she finished, he entered her office as she reached for the phone. He saw her irritation when he put the reports on her desk.

"I can't read them until I return these calls," she said sharply, waving at the pink slips impaled on a spindle. "Come back in…" she glanced at her watch, "… come back in an hour." I wish he wouldn't barge in like he owns the place, she thought. Well, he does own it. At least he didn't pull rank. Even so, she savored the power to tell him "Not now" and make it stick.

She returned the calls and was reading the reports when he returned. Without looking up from the page, she raised a finger to show she needed another minute. He took a chair. While she read, she had a feeling he was looking at her, admiring her—as a woman. It raised goosebumps on her arms, and she prolonged the reading to enjoy the feeling. Then she shoved the glasses atop her head and looked at him.

"What do you make of it," he asked.

"You can't say an accident and a suicide. Not with a straight face." She shook her head vigorously. "No way. Too many awkward questions."

"That's how I see it."

"It's your call. Do we let it pass or raise the questions?"

"No, we don't let it pass. Report it straight. Jack wants our election endorsement. It's leverage."

That's a first, she thought, shocked at seeing daylight come between them. He's always sided with Jack over anyone else, including you. Now he's choosing Peder over Jack. Maybe he has changed.

They spent an hour devising scenarios with the facts at hand. Nothing made a strong case for an accident or a suicide. Every scenario led back to Peder's interest in Kaplan. Why was he in Featherstone? Who killed him? And why were city leaders eager to see the case go away?

"Thanks," he said as he stood to leave. "We're on track. And I'm not crazy."

"No, you aren't. What about the killers?"

"I think it's one killer or set of killers."

"Yeah, well, they must've thought Peder knew too much. So, maybe Kaplan's killer is still alive. What does Jack think about that?"

"He won't consider Kaplan until his killer buys an ad admitting it. I think he's afraid it's someone here." Boston shook his head. "He wants easy answers."

"So, are you saying he's afraid to investigate because of reelection?"

"Yeah. Jager's got him rattled with that 'one of us' bullshit. I'm worried. We had a blow-up last night. He cut me off from any more information."

"What, what can we do?"

We! The plural again. "We'll use the paper to investigate. I think we can..." then he paused. "Sorry. I'm not in charge now. I didn't mean... you tell me."

"Let's keep digging… for Peder's sake."

"Good. We'll investigate below the radar." He returned to his office buoyed by her words. Without Jack, she was the only one who could watch his back. God help the bastard who crosses her, he thought and rubbed the scar.

The medical examiner's sparse, technical prose said that Peder's spinal cord was severed by a sudden twist to his neck. Boston thought that fact could sink the accidental death theory. To be sure, he wanted more information about spinal injuries. Carnegie Library had a reference section. Maybe he could find something there. He recalled reading their copies of the *Chicago Tribune, The New York Times* and several other metropolitan dailies. He had read them in high school to burnish a fantasy he was a sophisticated man of the world. Walking the half-mile to the library burned off the buzz from the whiskey he kept in his desk drawer. He asked the reference librarian for medical encyclopedias.

The terminology was as thick as the tome itself; however, he understood enough to know an accident would have paralyzed Peder but not killed him. Not instantly, anyway. Severing a spinal cord at the neck by twisting it required an immobilized body. That would take at least two men, he thought. It might account for the bruises on Peder's wrists. You and Jack might agree on that. Whoever they were, they caught Peder after he left St. Ansgar. But where? Why drop him at Rock Dell and arrange an accident? Why not toss him in the Tatanka River, bury him or hide him in an abandoned building? Boston returned the books to the reference desk certain of two things. At least two men killed Peder. And two men would have to have a shared reason to kill. Money?

Filbert stood at the lumberyard office door in a seething rage as Deputy Thomas limped down the stairs. The first interview was bad enough about what he did over the Labor Day weekend. That's none of his goddamned business, he told himself. Now he's asking about anonymous threats against Meade. How long before he returns with a search warrant? "Son-of-a-bitch," he hissed to the empty office. "People will think I did it?" The gangly manager felt as if the walls were closing in. He shuddered and returned to the metal desk in his unadorned office. They're after me. With trembling fingers, he arranged and rearranged paper clips in five precise rows of six. Only a matter of time before Thomas returns. What do I do then?

A commotion in the yard brought him to the window. Below him, a crew was picking up a pallet of shingles that had tumbled off a forklift. "You stupid shit, pick that up," he yelled. "I oughta fire all of ya." Then Ducky Benson arrived to work his shift—late again. "You're fired," Filbert screamed. "Get your pay." It felt good to do it, but before Ducky could collect his money, Filbert rehired him because no one else wanted to work for him.

"All this is because of Meade," he snarled after Ducky left. "I warned him… I warned him… him and the kid… he's gonna pay for it." Still shaking, he shoved aside the hardware catalog and dialed the phone. "Arne, it's George. Thomas was here again and—"

"I know. He stopped to see me, too," the Chamber exec said.

"But Arne, I don't have an alibi. What do I do?"

"Calm down, for starters." Heistad said Thomas asked him a bunch of questions about Labor Day. "I was fishing up north. That isn't a crime. Neither is spending the weekend alone."

"I know, but it looks bad," Filbert whined. "He asked about me and Emma Peterson. About anonymous threats. And what I said to the Norgaard kid. I just know they suspect me." Holding the phone in one hand, he lined up his pencils with the other. "I'm worried, Arne. Meade's got the town worked up… I mean, how do we stop him?"

"George, sit tight," Heistad said. "Getting worked up makes it look like you're hiding something. I've heard from the others. Thomas is talking to everyone who complained about the Kaplan stories. When he doesn't find anything, he'll cross us off the list. It'll blow over. Jack's not going to pin anything on you or me. He's too worried about reelection. And come January, we'll have a new sheriff. Then this business will be over."

"Well, I hope you're right, Arne."

CHAPTER 17

Daphne went home at mid-afternoon in disgust because she didn't stop the lurid rumors at the breakfast counter. She shed bits of clothing on her way to the bathroom. A long soak in the tub didn't remove the dirty feeling inside. Wrapped in a flannel robe, she lay on the couch. Boston would come at six, and she hoped he would be horny. They hadn't screwed since Peder died. You'll feel better after a good fucking, she told herself.

He arrived, but she didn't detect a return of his hoped-for ardor. When he kissed her, his smooch felt chaste and dutiful, like kissing a relative. "Let's sit on the couch," she said, loosening the robe enough to expose ample cleavage. That usually lit his fire. Instead of snuggling as usual, he sat at an angle to look into her eyes. Then she realized tonight wasn't a visit; it was an interview.

He looked at her, liking everything he saw. Especially her candor. She used to tell him everything. Now, when he asked about the rumors she overheard, she shrugged or evaded his questions. He couldn't let it go at that.

"Did your mother tell you anything about Filbert or Kaplan?"

She licked her lips and coughed to free the reluctant reply stuck in her throat. "Mom knew him a little. He used to eat there. Said he was a sensitive man." She cried inside. Oh, why does he have to bring that up? "Mom was pregnant when he disappeared. That's when Filbert claimed Kaplan was the father… my father. Mom hated Filbert… she warned me about him. Thank God, he's never come into the Streamliner."

He nodded. "Have you heard any new rumors about Peder and Ferrall?

"Not much," she said, shaking her head. It loosened the French braid, and her dark hair tumbled around her shoulders. She bit her lip and considered what to tell him. If you name names, he'll tell Jack. People will guess you talked. Then you'll be in deep shit.

"Anything new?"

She drew a breath wishing he would say, "let's have dessert," but he didn't. "There's an ugly rumor going around," she began. Maybe giving him some of the truth might put him in the mood for… "No one is talking openly," she continued. "I overheard someone tell someone else…" (He doesn't need to know it was Nelson.) "… someone said Mister Ferrall was using Peder for sex. He killed him and then shot himself."

"*What!* What? Anything else?"

"I don't believe it," she said, remembering how the rumor had hit her like a gut punch. "Peder looked at me often enough… you know… the way you do," she said, cupping her breasts. "He definitely liked girls, boobs and ass. And we all adored him." She exhaled and fell silent for a moment. "It's too disgusting. I don't want to talk about it. Nobody knows Mister Ferrall. Let me fix the filet. Afterward, maybe we could…" and she winked an invitation at him.

"Thanks, but I'm not very hungry."

She snuggled against him and laid her head on his shoulder in resignation. The deaths have come between us, she thought, remembering how they used to eat, tell dirty jokes and hop in the sack for orgiastic romps. Not now. The memory saddened her. Everything has changed. You don't want to be in his investigation. You have to live here. He doesn't. You want to be his bitch and not his snitch.

CHAPTER 18

Boston sat at his desk and rubbed his eyes. Last night was a doozy. He was trapped in a nether world of angry voices, orders, accusations and condemnations saying, "Give it up… none of your business… you don't care… it's your ego… you're selfish… afraid to face… go to Chicago…" He woke with a woozy head and felt as if he had been sucked dry.

Falling asleep unaided was nearly impossible now. Two drinks used to do it; now it was three or four. Every morning he had a goddamned headache that two aspirin at breakfast aspirin couldn't kill. He finished a mug of office coffee, opened his lower desk drawer and added whiskey to the cup. A sip helped. Then he forced out his breath as if to expel the heaviness beneath his ribs.

Ginger stopped at his door. "Good morning. Are you alright?"

"*Uh-huh*. Bad night," he mumbled, running a hand over his bristly chin.

"Well, you've got a nice start on a beard," she added. "I'll talk to you later."

It's time you come clean with her, he thought. You've got to tell someone or bust. He got up, rushed to her office and closed the door. "Uh… there's something I've got to say," he said, doubling and releasing his fists. "I don't know how to say it."

"Just say it," she snapped, leaning her elbows on the desk.

"*Uh*, it's like this," he began, and his voice rose to the higher pitch of an over-wrought adolescent. He rambled about Jack's pseudo investigation, the evidence that proved nothing, the facts they needed but didn't have. Then he began repeating what he had already said. "What I mean is... why doesn't Jack look at..." and without waiting for a reply, he caromed onto a tangent about Gantz, who might have killed Ferrall.

"*Stop it*. You're not making sense. And I don't have all day."

He felt a flush crawl up his neck and into his cheeks. "I sent Peder to do Jack's job... put him at risk... ignored the threats," he moaned as he paced in front of her desk. "He's dead because of me... it's my fault... I killed him." His foot caught a chair leg, and he stumbled. "Goddamn it," he hissed and kicked the chair into the credenza. The crash toppled the portrait of Agnes O'Meara. He froze, mouth agape and breathing heavily. His gaze shifted from Ginger to the portrait to the chair and then back to her as if piecing together the sequence of events. "I'm sorry... sorry," he stuttered, a fool ashamed of losing self-control.

"Are you alright," Ginger asked, jumping up from the desk. In his gray eyes, she saw the confusion of someone who had opened a door and didn't know where he was. He's been drinking, she thought. Whatever he's sipping is probably in his desk. She weighed her next words. "You're not alright, are you?"

"I don't know," he moaned, then his expression hardened. It was as if an inner switch had flipped. His words issued through tightly clenched teeth. "I got Peder killed. Now I'm going to kill the sons-a-bitches who... I don't care how long it takes."

"Sit," she ordered, pointing to the chair. You know what he's going through, she told herself. And you know why. You've been there. Done that. He needs your help out of that dark hole—just like you did. Oh God, I need him sober. Let him listen to me, please. She leaned forward and looked into his face.

"What," he asked as he settled into the chair.

"Listen carefully," she said in a low voice. "Your personal life is none of my business—until it affects the paper. All of us have watched you unravel a little each day. You arrive late, forget to shave, your eyes are puffy, your clothes are a mess. You're falling apart. Peder's death is eating you up. And you're alone at night, drinking—a lot. Don't ask me how I know. I know. I just smelled it in your office. It's on your breath. Drinking won't bring back Peder. It won't ease your pain, either. I tried that. It doesn't work. And drinking won't solve his murder. You won't feel better until you feel pain. Trust me. I know how it works. I won't tell you not to drink, but I'm asking you to consider it—for your sake."

He listened with eyes downcast like a beaten man. His neck sank into his shoulders, and his hands lay limp as rags in his lap. Then he licked his lips and looked up at her.

In his eyes, she saw a child's helplessness. "I understand what you feel," she continued. "But you didn't kill Peder. Don't blame yourself for things you didn't do. I tried that, too. It doesn't work. Don't do this to yourself," she said, squeezing his arm. "Please."

"I should be dead, not him. It's not right." He rubbed his arm where she squeezed it.

"One more thing," she added, keeping eye contact. "This is your paper. I'm your employee. You working out of here is still okay by me on one condition."

"Condition—what condition?"

"You feel guilty. Alright, you're honest about it. But I saw something dangerous in you. I saw it when you threw Filbert out. And now, when you kicked the chair."

"What are—"

"You're out of control. Unstable. Your rage is a threat to you, your paper, your employees and any hope of catching Peder's killer. His death isn't about *you*." she said, raising her voice. "My condition is this—I have the last word on anything we do or publish about Kaplan, Peder and Ferrall. If not, I'll resign. Then you can take over." She waited with arms akimbo. The wait seemed like hours.

"Okay," he nodded, knowing she never bluffed. He met her gaze and nodded. "You have the last word."

"Good," she said, and her lips stretched wide in a smile. "Now, in a day or two, when you're completely sober, I'm sure you'll return to the man I truly know you to be. You're angry for the right reasons.

The anger is your heart talking. All that anger, frustration, pain—that's energy. Let's harness it."

He sat still for a moment. "Thanks… friend. May I have a Kleenex?"

CHAPTER 19

Nelson waited in his car for Jager to leave the courthouse. "The race is a dead heat," he said when the candidate got onto the Mercedes. "We've never had one this close."

"Got any polls?"

He shook his head. Instead of polls, the campaign team counted Jager's lawn signs in key neighborhoods. His outnumbered the Meade signs where voter turnout was usually highest.

"Thanks for your help, Nels. You've really put me in play."

"Aw, you're a quick study." He glanced in admiration at the man about his own age. "Where'd you learn to campaign?"

"Nowhere. I just say what I feel—what I think people want to hear. There's no real study to it. I just put it out there. It's like sales. You're good at that, Nels. You know how it's done. Give people a little information to show you're serious. But don't bury them with facts. They don't want facts. Campaigning is emotional, not logical."

"That's true." Nelson smoothed his mustache. "Once you're the sheriff, we'll be rid of union troublemakers."

"Consider it already done," the candidate said with a grin. "And the other greasers, too."

Nelson knew he had a winner in the deputy. As the Chamber's chairman, he wanted a business-friendly sheriff who would prevent problems like union organizing. When he saw Jager's potential, he offered to manage the campaign if he would challenge Jack. Thanks to his civic and commercial contacts, it was easy to get Jager in front of key groups. Tonight, it was the Kiwanis Club in Waterford, a charming valley town of professionals who worked in Rochester at the Mayo Clinic and IBM. Their support would add momentum and money. Eighty people awaited them in the banquet hall of the Lighthouse Supper Club. Standing at the podium, Nelson thought Jager looked and sounded like an ideal sheriff—lean, good-looking, plain-speaking and a man of action. With him as your right hand, he thought, you can be the county's next power broker.

"We can never hire enough deputies," Jager said. Then he held up a computer disk. "This thin wafer can hold volumes of information about criminals. Using these will put us out front. With computers and databases, we can spot potential criminals before they strike. This is where we'll see results when I'm your sheriff." The audience applauded. Afterward, he opened up for questions. "Yes, you in the back of the room," he pointed to a bald man with his hand in the air.

"When will we hear what happened to the Norgaard boy and the other fella?"

"Thanks for asking. That's a good question," he said. Then he said the sheriff reassigned the officers and put a less experienced one in charge of the investigation. "Let's face it, these are simple cases that he should've solved weeks ago. I guess the sheriff can't make up his mind. Law enforcement, like medicine and business, requires special talents, but not everyone has them. I think you'll agree it shows."

Jack loathed campaigning. The process struck him as a disgusting burlesque of the democratic process. Ideally, it should be an opportunity to educate the voters. However, that required a public with an attention span longer than five minutes. Too much of the election turned on trivia and personalities. He felt like a phony when selling himself. Switching from his uniform to civvies, he stood while Kris knotted his tie. Then she kissed him for luck. Tonight, he was speaking to the Commercial Club of Dayton Lake, a farming town twenty miles west of Featherstone. Four years ago, one or more supporters drove him to these events. They begged off this year. Too busy, they said. He suspected they were backing Jager.

The campaign already seemed like an exercise in futility, but he felt obliged to show up. On the drive, he considered his off-the-cuff message. It ought to be short, simple and touch the things that people knew or cared about. It won't be a big crowd. They scheduled his speech just when most of the residents were eating supper and watching the news.

He and the town cop finger waved as they passed each other at the intersection. Jack parked at the American Legion Hall, a Quonset hut next to the city's power plant. As he entered the nearly empty hall, he saw the Fire Marshal's certificate on the door. The room's capacity was limited to one hundred. The audience numbered perhaps twenty-five or so, and the host delayed the introduction a few minutes in case of stragglers.

"Alton is a large county with unique challenges and opportunities," Jack began, speaking to a middle-aged audience whose expressions were as impassive as cinderblock walls. He suspected few were familiar with computers. In fact, they might be leery of technology they didn't use. Maybe you should double down on what they understand, he thought. Talk about what they see and hear and know. Yeah, that might be your best counter to Jager's claims.

"You'll hear promises that databases can prevent crime," he said. "Sounds good, but it's a fantasy. Crime is a human activity. It's driven by impulses most of you recognize and understand." Warming to this, he said they possessed the highest technology. "You know more about your neighbors than a database. And you know who to call when someone is out of line. Our office is successful because you are its partners. No technology can replace your eyes, your ears and your common sense. No computer can replace what you know."

He continued in that vein, praising and complimenting them. In the end, he received their applause. Then someone asked about Peder Norgaard and Eliot Ferrall. How many times do you have to answer that, he wondered. Then he said the cases weren't as clear-cut as some people claimed. The families deserved to know the truth but finding it took time. A lame excuse, he realized. The questioner gave a non-committal nod. Then the hall emptied.

Jack didn't feel like Alton County's native son as he drove home in the dark. Being born in Featherstone isn't enough, he thought. Being born to Louisiana migrants makes you an outsider. Being adopted by the Meades wasn't enough, either. You grew up thinking, talking and acting like a Meade, but something is missing. Who would you be if Papa and Mama had lived? Maybe you'd know your true self as a man proud of his French, Spanish and African ancestry. Instead, you're a darker-skinned white man. The Black guys at the U excluded you. You didn't speak their lingo or share their attitude. You were too white to fit in with them, and you're too dark to fit in here. Black or white—you're nowhere. Not one of us.

"What's wrong," Kris asked when he walked in the door.

"Damned campaign. Jager and his 'he's one of us' crap. I'd like to quit."

"You stop that," she said, shaking her finger in his face. "You listen to me Jacques Baptiste DuBois Meade. You've beaten better men. Just do your job, you'll win."

"Not this time. The Chamber Board is backing Jager. If I lose the election, I'll be finished here. We'll have to move."

"Oh, for Pete's sake," she cried, throwing her arms in the air. "The Chamber Board has exactly fifteen members. The county has over seventy thousand citizens. The Chamber is afraid of a union organizer. The rest of us have other concerns." Planting her fists on her hips, a gesture he usually loved, she bored into him with blue eyes as hard and clear as January ice. "I'm sick and tired of hearing 'poor me, poor me.' You're going to win. Now get that into your big heart if not your thick head."

Ginger gathered the *Statesman*'s editorial team and two reporters into a conference on the campaigns for various offices. She wanted a recap of interviews with Jager and Jack in the hottest local contest. Clint Collier was a semi-retired old hand who enjoyed following new candidates like Jager. Ellen McGovern was assigned to Jack.

Clint hitched up his chair. He said Jager was stoking a fear of crime and promised to use computer technology to prevent it. In an interview, the deputy told him that a growing city like Featherstone would inevitably attract some criminals. If he were the sheriff, he would do background checks on new arrivals to pre-empt any potential criminals.

"That sounds like pie-in-the-sky," Ginger said. "Or maybe police-state tactics."

"Maybe both," Clint said. "The idea is catching on with those who have computers. And a big hit with the IBM folks in Waterford." He said Jager mentioned the Reagan Administration's plan to amnesty millions of undocumented immigrants. Since no one knew who they were, Jager said he would check on every Mexican who came to town. "Jager is doing well because his speeches are simple, define a problem and propose a solution," Clint said. "He looks like a man with a plan."

Ellen, the rookie reporter with a degree in political science, glanced at her notes on Jack's campaign. "There's no juice in anything he says, even when I interviewed him. His speeches fall flat because most of them are recitations of statistics about the county's low crime rate, the closed cases and the citations for efficiency. When I talked to him, it almost felt like he wasn't there. Just going through the motions to be polite. The bottom line is this, he's letting Jager set the agenda and then tries to counter-punch. He's losing because he hasn't laid out a vision."

"Alright, team," Ginger said. "We will endorse one of them eventually. Now, let's turn your interviews into stories about why each is running for sheriff and what each intends to do. Anything else," she asked.

"Yeah, there's an ugly racial side to this," Robin interjected. "I joined Curt at one of Jager's speeches. He came right out and said, 'I'm an experienced lawman, not some dark horse running for re-election.'"

"Dark horse," Ginger muttered. "That's below the belt. We won't print that."

"It's not the worst I've heard," she said. "Some are saying we'll be safer if the sheriff looks like the rest of us. In other words—"

"Keep tabs on that," Ginger said. "We won't cover it, at least not at the moment."

CHAPTER 20

Boston sat on a wrought-iron bench in front of the Civil War memorial feeling liberated from the morning headaches. That was because he did the unthinkable. Last night, he emptied a bottle of expensive Irish whiskey into the sink. This morning, when he put the bottle in the trash, the count of empties averaged a fifth every three days. Thank God she stopped you. Now there's no liquor in the house. Not even beer. You quit for Peder, for Ginger and for yourself most of all. Ginger deserves a monument, he thought, gazing at the memorial to martial valor. It took guts to confront you, guts to say what she did. It had to be compassion because of what happened to her. And she's right. It's not about you. Maybe that's why you slept well.

He started back to the office after two circuits around the Green. Then Jager stepped outside the building and stood in the center of the sidewalk with his feet apart. As Boston approached, the deputy put on the sunglasses and casually rested one hand on his holster.

"Hold on," Jager ordered, blocking his way. "I want to talk to you."

"Oh, what's on your mind?"

"Tell me about the murder cases. The investigation is stuck. It's time we pull together."

"Sorry, Mister Jager. Everything I know is the paper."

"It's *Captain* Jager. Now, what about the forensic reports."

Boston shook his head. "I'm not their custodian. Sharing reports is the sheriff's prerogative."

"Damn-it. The press is supposed to be neutral. Tell me about Peder's interviews."

"Nope. Reporter's notes are confidential. The sheriff hasn't seen them, either."

"Yeah, but you tell him everything you know."

"Here's the difference, *mister*," he said, staring at the deputy hiding behind the reflective lenses. "The sheriff is an elected official. You're a mere civil servant who reports to him. I go through channels for information. You should, too." Then he thought of Costa's fax. Is there a way to let him know what you've got? No, not without exposing Jack. "Now, excuse me mister, I have work to do," he said and moved on thinking, damn, but that felt good.

He reviewed the documents Costa sent. The internal investigation found ample evidence for excessive use of force if not depraved indifference. However, the police union scuttled any charges, and Jager left Minneapolis on his own. Still, even a hint might sink his candidacy. He shelved the file until he saw an opportunity for an "October surprise."

But Jager was right about a bogged-down investigation. It's time you swallow your pride and make peace with Jack, he thought. When he called his brother, the sulky voice said, "Oh, it's you," followed by, "There's nothing new. When there is, I'll call a press conference."

"Oh, c'mon, Jack. I called to apologize. Let's work together on this."

"Forget it. Go to Chicago. I'm done with you."

"You won't win this election by covering your ass and going through the motions," he said, furious and losing his grip. "Like it or not, I'm staying. If you won't do your job, I *will*," he blurted without forethought. He heard Jack bellow, "Go to hell," and then a click.

You know better than that, he cursed, feeling sick to his stomach. Ginger's right. You're out of control. Jack didn't deserve that. You hurt him more than Jager could. And you enjoyed it. Grow up, dipshit. Call and apologize. But he resisted the urge. Not now. Not until he could do it without groveling. It weighed on him for the rest of the day. He rubbed his face and thought about a drink to soften the edge. The choice was his, of course. But if he did, he would have to face himself if not Ginger. He went home, disgusted.

Over supper, he rehearsed an apology with words carefully chosen to balance contrition without conceding his opinion. It had to be done and soon. He glanced at the phone from time to time while he washed the dishes but put it off. Then it rang.

"What's gotten into you," Kris asked without saying hello. "Jack's hurt. He thinks you betrayed him. Now he doesn't want to talk to you. Wishes you'd go away. What's with you two?" He heard a voice he felt compelled to obey. It was a mother's tone, one that fused righteous rebuke with loving anger. He felt small. She's right, of course. You can accept Jack's anger because he'll eventually sweep it under the rug. But not Kris. Her anger is a higher order of magnitude. She won't forget it. Not for a moment. Not ever. She protects Jack like a fierce bantam hen with chicks.

"It's my fault. I'm frustrated. I questioned his integrity."

"I know," she said, closing off any wiggle room. "I need you—he needs you to back him up. So, patch it up—now."

"I will tomorrow. In person. I promise."

The gray, damp morning with the threat of a slow rain seemed made for an apology. Boston hoped the rain would wash away yesterday's rancor, a rain to give them a fresh start. He and Jack had squabbled in high school, but their anger never lasted. Dad expected them to apologize before the day ended. "Don't let the sun go down upon your wrath," he had often said, quoting from *Ephesians*.

He didn't call Jack immediately as he had promised Kris. Instead, he scoured the files on Kaplan, Peder and Ferrall for new evidence as a peace offering. Something to tie the deaths to one killer, one motive. And then, like magic, it popped off a page in the forensic report, or so he thought. He would go with it if Ginger's confirmed his hunch.

She was busy moving among the editors and reporters, stopping here and there to talk. He knew better than to interrupt her. While he waited, he admired her figure, now rounder in the derriere and bust than in high school but not as voluptuous as Daphne's. And then, aware of his gawking, he returned to his desk until she finished her rounds. When she was free, he asked her to see him. She sat in a chair at his table.

"I saw something that might link the deaths to one killer."

"Okay. What is it," she asked, clearly impatient.

"Clay." He held up the forensic report.

"Explain that," she ordered and crossed her arms.

"Peder's bike tires held clay. The coulee road was sand. So, he didn't ride that road. I noticed it when we found him, but I forgot it."

"So?" She waved her hands impatiently.

"So, there's no clay at Rock Dell. There is at St. Ansgar and Breuer's farm. I found a shoe print in it on the night we looked for him. Peder must have been there. Maybe they killed him there. The same party could have killed Eliot."

"Are you sure," she asked, her arms still folded.

"There was a little clay on Ferrall's porch. Neither he nor Peder had it on their shoes. So, there must be a third party."

"That makes sense," she said, releasing her arms. "Can you prove it?"

"No. Not until we locate the county's clay deposits. Will you check that?"

"Why? What's stopping you from checking?"

"I've got to apologize to Jack," he said, picking up the phone. "I lost my temper last night. It's time I eat crow in person. I promised his wife."

CHAPTER 21

Jack downed two aspirin. Besides the headache, he felt bruised after yesterday's quarrel with Boston. A falling out with him hurt. Losing his only relative was the last loss he wanted next to Kris and the kids. As a distraction, he leafed through the latest bulletin from the state's sheriff's association. This month's feature focused on how to hire good chief deputies. He dropped it in disgust and picked up the file on Ferrall. The man was dead. Calling it murder or suicide made no difference to the deceased. Later, if more information came in, he could reopen the case. The front desk officer told him he had a call on hold.

"Oh, it's you," he grumped when he recognized Boston's voice. "Yeah, you can come over if you want." Not that you give a shit, he thought. No wonder your head aches. He's worse than Jager.

Jack wore an impassive face as the brothers sat behind the closed door. He watched Boston squirm in the chair. His apologies never came readily. Kris must have called him, he guessed. She has a mother's way of taking him down a peg or two without hard feelings.

"I said something shitty yesterday," Boston began, looking into his dark eyes. "I hurt you. But I love you too much to let it fester. Walking over, I felt like I was wearing a sign that said, 'I'm an asshole.' I'm sorry. Forgive me?"

"Well, you *are* an asshole. But… you're still my brother. So, yeah, I forgive you."

"Thanks. It's just… I feel responsible for Peder's death and—"

"And you'd be in a cell if you were responsible. No one blames you. Stop blaming yourself. You couldn't see it coming. Nobody did."

"I should've seen it."

"Well, people do what they do for reasons we can't foresee."

He nodded, remembering it wasn't about him.

"Now, I need you," Jack said, putting his hands together as if in prayer. "I need a break before the election. Unless contrary evidence turns up, I'll call Ferrall's death a suicide." Saying it made him tired. He rubbed his face. "There's more to their deaths than I can prove. You got any ideas that don't involve Kaplan?"

Boston laid out what he learned in the medical encyclopedia. It would take two people to break Peder's neck. And the coroner said his ribs and sternum cracked after he died, probably when he was thrown into the ravine. In short, he wasn't killed in an accident because he was already dead.

"I know. We've had only six murders in eight years. In each case, the killer and victim knew each other."

"That's my point," he said. "Two unusual deaths and no local suspects. Look at it this way. Both cases are missing bits of evidence, like the pack. It's not likely two different killers hit the same day, within hours and miles of each other but for different reasons. Not likely, is it?"

"No, but it's possible."

"Possible? It's damn near impossible."

"Oh, and *you've* got a better idea?" Jack leaned back and folded his arms.

"Yeah. Killers who create ordinary accidents that aren't investigated."

"And your evidence of that? I need facts, confirmation, credible suspects and a motive. None of that exists." Jack wished he would quit playing detective. Well, fuck him, he thought. It's your job—not his. "Anything else?"

Boston mentioned the clay. It was in the bike tires, on Eliot's porch but not on his shoes or Peder's. Then he mentioned the shoe prints at the Breuer farm. "Maybe they killed Peder at or near the farm and dumped his body. Maybe they thought the search would end around St. Ansgar. Hardly anyone used the coulee road. The body might have rotted before you found it. And then you'd call it a hit-and-run."

"*Uh-huh*, I get your point," Jack said, nodding. "I'm surprised the search didn't turn up anything at the farm. I can't call it a homicide. Not until there's more evidence. Not until after the election. What about Ferrall?"

"That's more complicated."

"Gantz had a motive to kill—"

"Or someone else did. Kaplan is the key. I think his killer is still alive."

"Well, shit," Jack slumped in his chair. "Where do I start? It's a thirty-forty-year-old cold case. No evidence, no suspects. I still think the Minneapolis mob whacked him and left his body to throw off any investigation."

"You mean, throw it off the same way someone left Peder in the ravine?"

Jack glowered and growled in his throat. "No, that's not what I mean."

"If Peder and Ferrall didn't have clay on their shoes, how did it get on Ferrall's porch? If I can make that connection, so can you."

Jack felt his temples throb. He wished Boston would leave. "I don't know. And neither do you. Like Calvin said, the war unhinged him. Maybe he did kill Kaplan. He needed to find out what Peder knew. So, he lured him to his place, killed him, and then committed suicide."

"Bullshit. Even you don't believe it. And I'm damned sure your detective doesn't."

"We're running down rumors of something sexual. Murder-suicides happen all the time."

"Jack… you know better. You don't believe it. And even if you did, you'd never—never—say that to the Norgaards. Quit ignoring inconvenient facts."

"Like what?"

"There's no blood in the cab. He was shot behind the right ear. Did you know he was left-handed?"

Jack blinked. His eyelid twitched. "No… I didn't. Well, so what? This isn't your job."

"The hell it's not. Detectives and reporters are two of a kind. It is my job. I'm doing it for Peder. Doing it for you. Doing it because the election is skewing your judgment."

"Goddamn you," Jack sputtered and shot out of the chair and towered over Boston with doubled fists. "Get out—now."

"Are you angry at me or yourself?" he asked, looking up at him.

Jack's shoulders slumped. "Oh, maybe you're right. Maybe there's a link. Jesus Christ, it better be a good one. If I keep it simple, I can close one case before the election."

"It's what Jager would do. Don't become the thing you hate."

"I can't help it. I can't let him win."

Boston walked back to the *Statesman* battered by grit, leaves and loose papers blown by the wind. "Alright, asshole," he muttered in disgust. "We're brothers. We have to stick together. You want hard evidence. I'll get it—and shove it up your ass." Then he checked his anger and recalled Carson's counsel to be patient and wait until Jack asked for help. Alright, you'll wait, he promised himself and slept well that night.

Jack was happy to see him in the morning. The intrusion was welcome on several fronts, including a diversion from the chore of budget review. A necessary but tedious task. He gave Boston a sheepish smile and fetched a mug of coffee. Each made light of yesterday's testiness, and Jack said he had thought about the points his brother raised.

"Deputies questioned everyone who knew Peder and Ferrall—including Calvin, Peder's friends, the Amish guy and most of the folks in Hennessey."

"What'd they tell you?" Boston glanced at the duck picture behind Jack's desk. It brought up memories of happy days hunting from their blind at Sioux Point.

"Nothing," he said with a hang-dog face. Then he ran through every dead-end. Nothing points to a killer or a motive. "That's all I've got," he said, standing at the window with his back to Boston. "I've got what I've got. Not enough for a warrant. That's what I've got."

"What about Jorgenson? Has anyone talked to him?"

"Not yet. I don't want to question him while he's campaigning. We're not on great terms. It might look like I'm trying to throw his election. We don't even know if it was Jorgenson's daughter."

"Forget about the election. Let's focus on your investigation."

"Election has nothing to do with it. Look, I don't tell you how to run the paper, so don't tell me how to run the department."

Here we go again, Boston thought. "Risk goes with the job. We've always had each other's backs. Don't push me away. I put my career on hold to help you. For your sake, I want you to get the real killer."

"Yeah. Well, fuck you. I'll do this my way."

"Alright, have it your way," Boston said and left.

"Damn, you," Jack cussed but checked the impulse to follow and apologize. He waited a few minutes and phoned Boston's office. The call went to voicemail. He left a message. A rotten way to start the day, he thought. Oh, what the hell. Even if the Kaplan connection is far-fetched, there's no harm in looking. Maybe you can prove there's nothing. If something turns up, well fine.

He started with the Chamber of Commerce directory and took down the names of those who joined before 1948. That included most of the city's elder statesmen, such as Emery Daniels, Bill Kincaid, Jeff Anderson, George Filbert, Morgan Williams, Jack Hedstrom, Mitchell Palmer, Calvin Ferrall and a dozen others. You know them all, he thought. If Boston's right, one of them had a hand in killing Kaplan, Peder and Eliot. That seems unlikely but… He asked Thomas and Kasson to quietly check each name in the department's records. Then he left his office to speak to a group in Peddlers Grove.

CHAPTER 22

Dora Ferrall left the country club and got into her Audi coupe, still buzzed from the luncheon martinis. The Alton Arts Council met there because she picked up the tab. That way, she made sure the luncheon menu included martinis—happiness in a glass. What fun. Jimmy Krause waited on their table and blushed beautifully when she flirted with him. It was worth a big tip. The meeting ended several hours ago, but she lingered to go over the agenda and details.

Once on the road, she barreled down the center of the highway in the dusk toward her next martini at the end of the driveway on Sioux Point. An on-coming car flicked its headlights, but she blew past it without swerving to the right. A moment later, she saw it approaching in her rearview. Its flashing red-blue lights and siren startled her as she turned onto Sioux Point Road. The Audi fish-tailed on the gravel and slid sideways into the ditch in a cloud of dust that drifted past her. Dora sat immobile and confused. Then someone tapped on her window. She lowered it and looked into the young face of Deputy Nathan Larson.

"Are you alright, Missus Ferrall?"

"Yes, of course, I'm alright," she snapped and then clambered gracelessly out of the car. "It's your fault," she said, laying into him. "Your siren startled me—made me miss the corner." She stood unsteadily on the road, annoyed and embarrassed.

"Ma'am, have you been drinking?"

My God. He knows, she thought, alarmed. "No. I had a cocktail at lunch. Hours ago."

"Wait here," he said and walked to his cruiser. She shivered with fear, certain that he went for the breathalyzer equipment. To her relief, he returned with a citation book. He wrote a ticket for speeding and reckless driving. "You can contest this in court if you want."

"Thank you," she said, snatching the ticket from his hand. The fine was more than $150, but it was nothing. Just money. "May I go now," she asked with the hauteur of having just been subjected to the greatest indignity.

"I'm going to follow you home, ma'am. If you go over the limit, I'll arrest you."

She got into the car and giggled at his way of saying "ma'am" and "arrest." He's so cute when he tries to act stern. You're twice his age, she thought, but what fun if you could fool around with him. Maybe play games with his handcuffs. But her fantasy quickly gave way to gratitude. You were lucky he didn't give you a sobriety test. You know what the result would have been. A citation for driving under the influence, if not a trip to jail. No telling what Calvin would do if that happened. He might let you sit in jail overnight and hold it over you forever. She drove home with both hands on the wheel.

Why *do* you drink? This wasn't the first time she had asked herself that question. You have everything. Calvin earns more than enough to buy the things you want—the house on the lake, Caribbean vacations in winter, good cars and social status. Thanks to the spa sessions, you still look fortyish instead of fiftyish. The arts council gives you fulfillment and betters county life. You should be happy. And you would if you hadn't lost Calvin along the way. He has no joy.

She thought of Nelson, a darling child who was now as distant as Calvin. When he wasn't working, he was playing golf. God knows what else he was doing. Or with whom. He and Karen will be parents next month. A baby probably won't focus him on family life. Not for long. He has Karen where he wants her. While she tends to the baby, he can play around. Dora shook her head to clear it. A grandchild won't fix our troubles. Our problem is love. There isn't any.

Love. When was the last time you felt real love, she wondered. At least ten years ago with Claudio. He was everything you wanted in a lover. You were forty-one, he was thirty-three when you started the affair. Just a little flirtation at the gala in your house for the orchestra's supporters. It went quickly after that to a couple of nights a month during the orchestra advisory board meetings. With him, you felt fulfilled as a woman. Why didn't you follow him to Madrid? You haven't been happy since. Martinis are a poor substitute. Even Deputy Larson knows you're a lush. Turning into the long driveway, she vowed to take better care of herself from now on.

CHAPTER 23

Jack is just being Jack—intelligent, stubborn and insecure—Boston thought. I need his intelligence, not his stubbornness. He's stuck on thinking the deputies got everything useful about Ferrall from Hennessey's residents. After reading a summary of the deputies' interviews, he realized the deputies asked narrow questions aimed at determining whether Ferrall killed himself or Gantz did it. Narrow questions lead to narrow answers. A good reporter would cast a wider net. Well, it's not too late to ask those questions.

He stopped briefly in the office and then drove to Hennessey. One or two new facts, like a couple of key letters in a crossword, might fill in many blanks. Finding something useful might restore Jack's drive and self-confidence. His mood brightened on the drive. He savored the dry scent of autumn leaves. The first fall color flared in the trees. Huge combines gobbled wide swathes of soybean stalks, and migrating blackbirds whirled up in a dark cloud that passed over him. The level upland of corn and soybean fields gave way to swales and coulees. Smaller fields wrapped around the hillsides in contoured strips of alfalfa and corn, woods and pastures that added texture. Herds of black and white cows added life. He drove, suspecting that beneath the bucolic surface lived as many crime-prone residents as on any block in Chicago. Human motives were the same everywhere.

He got out of the Jeep in Hennessey, leaned against it and wiped his glasses. An Amish buggy clip-clopped past on the empty street. The bearded driver tapped the brim of his straw hat. Boston nodded in return. He watched a stout older woman in a scarf rake leaves onto her flowerbed. Her neighbor stacked storm windows. Then a pair of women lugging gravid grocery bags passed him, chattering like sparrows. Daily life in Hennessey seemed as transparent as glass. How could Ferrall live here while harboring a secret?

If there was an answer, he hoped to find it across the street at Daly's Tavern. He paused in the doorway until his eyes adjusted to the dim interior. Then he took a stool at the bar that ran the length of the tavern's left side with the beer taps midway. Shelves and racks of bottles covered the wall behind the bar. He glanced at a pair of old men at the end who shook dice over who would pay their tab. Empty booths lined the wall behind him. There was a jukebox and a small dance floor at the back. Chicagoans would pay through the nose to drink in a place like this. It had to be Hennessey's social hub where people visited, celebrated, remembered and forgot.

"What'll it be," the burly bartender asked as he polished a glass.

"A bump and a beer." He hoped the owner knew Ferrall.

"You're new here. I'm Cletus Daly," he said. He had quick blue eyes and a thick, black mustache. When Boston gave his name, the tavern keeper complimented the paper. Then he set down a shot of Jameson and drew a Harp lager from the tap.

"You've got the kind of place that keeps folks coming back." He tasted the whiskey and then the beer.

"They have to," Daly laughed. "It's the only place in town. Now… what can I do for you?"

"I'm working a story," he said, impressed at how quickly Daly caught on. "Hope you can give me some background."

"Background?" His gaze drifted warily toward the old men.

"Did Eliot Ferrall come in here?"

"I hope you're looking into his death. The sheriff ain't doing much."

He ignored the remark. "Did you know him well?"

"Know him? Sure, I knew him. We all did." Daly leaned closer. "Not much of a drinker. Maybe a beer on a hot day. A shot to celebrate something. Otherwise, an honest, sober man. You could trust him."

"Go on. So, he had friends?"

"Friends? Jesus, Mary and Joseph—hundreds of 'em." Daly waved his arms to encompass the room. Then he listed the things Ferrall did that Boston had heard at the funeral. Daly said he co-signed an unsecured note to remodel the tavern.

"Do you think he killed himself?"

"No. Never. Full of joy, he was. Hated guns."

"What about enemies?"

Daly shook his head. "No one had a beef. Well… those Gantz boys. They're wacko. Believe there's a Jewish plot to take over the world. Put white patriots in concentration camps. Crazy talk. Turner Diaries stuff. The trouble started when Ferrall refused his woods for their militia training. Then he caught 'em stealing timber. Del did two years. He threatened to get even. He just got out."

"And Eliot?"

"He lived quiet. Sociable, but no women that I know of. He often came in, ordered mineral water and talked about books or philosophy in a way anyone could understand. He respected what people thought. When you finish that, how 'bout another bump and a beer—on the house?"

He nodded but went easy on the whiskey. The codgers settled their tab and left the bar wheezing over an old joke. So far, Daly hadn't told him anything he didn't know.

"Notice any strangers about the time of Eliot's death? Say, out-of-towners?"

Daly hung up the bar towel, drew a breath and his gaze rolled up to the pressed tin ceiling. "Yeah… yeah," he nodded. "A couple guys. Maybe two days before Eliot's death. One had broad shoulders, high cheekbones, good hair. Friendlier of the two. Walked like a soldier. Had kind of a southern drawl. The other was shorter, wiry. Talked through his nose, had zits like a teenager. They ordered burgers and Cokes. Hardly said a word. They weren't weekenders or fishermen."

"Did you see their car?"

"*Uh*, yeah. Lemme see. Yeah, a dark Chevy Blazer. Looked new. Minnesota plates. Haven't seen it since."

At last, you're on the cusp of something, he thought. A few customers drifted in. He ordered a burger, fries and a cup of coffee. After a little more conversation, he left Daly's buoyed by evidence the deputies didn't have. He had a description of two strangers and the make and color of their car. The timing fit the deaths. The car might match the paint on Peder's bike.

Daly's directions to the Gantz farm took him down a gravel road past several dairy farms to a rutted driveway marked with the yellow Gadsden flag of the Alton County Militia. Next to it was nailed a hand-lettered warning: "Keep Out. Private Property Insured by Smith & Wesson."

The farmstead wasn't visible from the road, but he drove in anyway. As he parked next to a pair of GMC pick-ups, he felt as if he had entered a Viet Nam era firebase. A wall of shoulder-high logs topped with barbed wire ringed the weather-beaten house in need of paint, shingles and an attic window. He sat in the Jeep and waited for someone to appear. He had a queasy feeling Gantz was watching him. His fingers trembled slightly as he clipped a mini microphone inside his jacket sleeve and fed the cord to a cassette recorder. Then, seeing a face behind a dirty window, he turned on the recorder, zipped the cassette inside the jacket and got out of the Jeep.

"Stop right there," someone bellowed from behind the partially opened door. "Who are ya? Whaddya want?"

Boston stopped in the wall's sally-port. "I'm Boston Meade from the *Statesman*. I want to talk to Delmar Gantz."

The porch door opened wider. A bearded man in stained coveralls stepped outside pointing an automatic pistol. "This here's private prope'ty. Git your hands where I can see 'em."

"I'd like your opinion on Ferrall's death," he said, putting his hands forward, so the mini mic pointed at Gantz. "It'll only take a minute."

"I already tolt it to dem depudies," Gantz growled. "Don't know nothin' about his death 'cause me and LeRoy was loggin' that day. A ranger seen us. Good enough?"

"Why do you think he shot himself?" He doubted the deputies asked that.

The logger scratched his crotch as his gaze roamed the sky. "Shit, how do I know?" Gantz spit a gob. "I din't like the mudderfucker but he din't strike me for the kind to do that. He was a Marine—so was I. Know what I mean? Besides, he din't like guns."

Boston nodded, hoping to get Gantz off the defensive. "Anything else?"

"Me an' him—we din't see things the same. I ain't cryin' cuz the sumbitch is dead, but I think someone did him. Dunno know who." He shifted his weight from one foot to the other.

"Think back. See any strangers out here, then?" He studied the man's pouchy eyes and matted hair. He seemed older than his years.

"Oh, oh, wait, wait a sec," he said, and his eyes lit up. He scratched his beard. "Yeah, yeah. Them guys in the Blazer. Day or two before Ferrall got it."

"What guys?"

Gantz shoved the pistol into his pocket. "They were lookin' for Ferrall's place an' got lost. They come in here an' I give 'em directions."

"To his woods or his house?"

"His woods."

"They say why?"

"Come t' think, that's a strange 'un, too."

"*Oh*," he asked, hoping that Gantz knew something.

"Said they was buyin' some trees offa Ferrall. Wanted to inspect 'em first." He scratched his beard. "That ain't how ya buy timber. I know. Me 'n LeRoy buy timber all the time. Ferrall never sold timber. Lets them Ay-mish cut dead stuff for firewood and such. But that's it. These guys was fake loggers. Not like me. They had on new jeans and shirts. Looked like dudes. Had only a chainsaw. Bran' new. Din't have no axes, chains or loggin' tools."

Boston kept the hidden mic pointed toward Gantz and hoped he would keep talking.

"Me and LeRoy went an' looked after we heard about them trees." He spit. "Shitty work. High stumps. Limbs layin' atop of each other. Them branches all tangled. Amateurs. A pro woulda cut 'em to fall clear. An' woulda cut oaks an' walnuts, not worthless shit like them piss elms an' boxelders." He spit again, and his small eyes shifted side to side. "Me and Leroy, we didn't cut those trees. No sir."

"Why did they cut the trees?"

"T' throw blame at me. 'Cause I got a record." Then he railed about the people who were out to get him.

"Did you tell this to the deputies?"

"No. They din't ask an' I din't think of it 'til now."

"Thanks for your time, Mister Gantz. You've been a big help."

Gantz nodded. "Sure. Any time," he said, scratching his beard.

Boston left the compound, pulled onto the shoulder and pounded the steering wheel with glee. "Now I've got something." Two strangers seen by two witnesses at the time of Ferrall's death, and they're connected to the trees. Maybe connected to Peder.

It was nearly sundown when he followed the trail of horse droppings past Ferrall's house to the farm with an Amish buggy. A pair of horses stood nose to tail by the barn, the windmill clanked and the farmhouse window emitted the glow of an oil lamp. For an instant, Boston thought he had entered another century. He got out of the Jeep as a clean-shaven young man in glasses left the barn.

"Hey, does Jakob Strutt live here?"

"*Jah.*" The youth reentered the barn, and Boston heard them gabbling in German. Then the elder Strutt joined him in the twilight. He had a pink face but seemed worn down.

Boston began with condolences on Ferrall's death. Someone had told him the Amish weren't inclined to accuse anyone. Respecting that, he asked circumspect questions. He said Peder was like a son to him, and he wanted to understand why he and Ferrall died. Strutt's face betrayed nothing, and Boston sensed his reluctance. It was something he often met as a reporter. The reluctant ones often had the best information. Had he seen Peder at Ferrall's house?

Strutt looked down as he shuffled his feet. "*Jah.* I seen t'at boy two times. Once he come in a car and other on bicycle."

"Did you see the boy on the day Eliot died?"

"*Nein.*" The farmer kept his eyes on the ground. "He come a couple weeks before."

Then he asked if Strutt had seen anyone at Ferrall's house about the time he died. The older man's eyes flickered and looked down. When it seemed he wouldn't say more, Strutt said two men in a black car turned in at Ferrall's house as he went by. That was the afternoon after he told Ferrall about the trees. "*Es war der Tag als er starb*," It was on the day he died. Strutt wiped his eyes, then his nose. Sensing he had no more to say, Boston repeated his condolences and left.

He drove to Featherstone as the full moon rose behind him. Maybe you've turned a corner in the case, he mused. Three witnesses described the same two strangers in a dark Blazer before and on the day of Ferrall's death. It was the right car for the paint on the bike. It was the car at Ferrall's on the day he died. And Peder wasn't there that day. The strangers must have left the clay on Ferrall's porch. The two men weren't local. So, someone hired them. Knowing that, he felt contented with his work for the first time.

He entered the house happy. Standing at a turret window, he watched the moonlight wash the countryside with its peculiar highlights and shadows. It seemed a fitting end to the day's discoveries. He thought of telling Detective Kasson what he learned. Why not? She wasn't running for office. No—terrible idea. Jack would resent it. Take it as a betrayal. He decided to wait for confirmation before sharing it.

CHAPTER 24

Yesterday's hunch paid off. The chance foray into Hennessey has changed the game, Boston thought. Now there's a wind at your back. In his excitement last evening, he forgot to buy groceries and ate breakfast at the Streamliner. Pushing aside his plate, he reread yesterday's notes. Everything he learned wiped out Jack's accident-suicide theory. Still unknown were the men who cut Ferrall's trees, their relationship to Ferrall and whether they left gray mud on Ferrall's porch. Now, at least, he had a trail to follow. Then a shadow fell across his notebook.

Daphne stood by the booth with a coffee pot and a peeved expression. "I waited for you last night," she whispered. "You didn't even call."

"I'm sorry," he said. "I took a road trip and got back late. Forgive me?"

"Yes—this time." She refilled his cup and then left, still annoyed.

Chiara brought his check, and he was happy to be alone with his thoughts. Based on what Gantz told him, the strangers were equipped to cut trees. If they intended to frame Gantz, then someone local gave them the idea. He cradled the coffee cup in both hands. Last night's euphoria was wearing off. He didn't feel as close to finding the killer as he had. These new facts raised more questions. Two steps forward, one step back. He sipped the coffee, but it was cold. Besides, four cups were enough caffeine for one morning.

As he walked around the corner to the *Statesman*'s office, he wondered if Emery Daniels could tell him anything. The old banker had nudged him along all summer with a few indirect suggestions. So far, every one of his hints opened up a new lead or proved to be true. Maybe he had another. The old man was considered something of a sage.

"I always feel honored by a visit from the fourth estate," Daniels rumbled with good cheer when Boston entered the dimly lit office with its furniture of yesteryear. The banker's gray wool suit matched his hair and fiercely pointed eyebrows. The rheumy eyes behind the large glasses lent him the visage of a wise but predatory owl. "Please, sit down," Daniels said. "Tell me, what may I do for you today?"

Boston sat in a wooden chair, a piece of the austere office that seemed like something from a Dickens novel. Maybe the old banker's agile mind could unearth a fact, an insight, a lead that shed light on Kaplan. He recapped what Peder recorded in his interview. Then he mentioned Daniels's belief that Kaplan was investigating something related to the Minneapolis mob. "That's all Peder put in his notes. I wonder if there's more to it. Maybe he missed some details."

"That's perceptive of you," he said with a note of admiration. Then he cleared his throat. "I've thought of several things since the interview. And more since his death. They are complicated things. Possibly defamatory. What I didn't tell him is speculative. I held it back because I didn't think he was mature enough to handle it. I'm sure you understand."

"I appreciate your discretion. Can you tell me? What was Kaplan after? And why here?"

"Excellent questions," Daniels said, shifting in the large leather chair. "His credentials as an FDIC auditor made it easier for him to see the banks' records. As far as I know, no one refused him. However, I suspected he was a detective."

"Any idea what he was looking for?"

"As I said, he was sharp," Daniels tapped his forehead. "He read a balance sheet and found inconsistencies faster than most accountants. That's why I wondered what he might look for down here. Maybe it was—"

"Tax evasion? That's a—"

"That might be an element but not the whole of it."

"What else?"

"As I was about to say—money laundering—running illicit money through a legitimate business and altering the books to cover it." Daniels coughed raggedly, sipped from a glass of water and then blew his nose.

"Maybe something tied to the black market from his days at the OPA?"

"Maybe. I've been a banker fifty years," he said, clasping his hands. "A lot of businesses have risen and fallen with the times. Our leaders like to think we don't have crime here. I'm certain Kaplan was on to something. Maybe something connected to Kid Cann and the Minneapolis mob."

"Peder had some clippings about him."

"Yes. A dangerous man." Cann was running illegal slot machines, prostitution and liquor at the time. "All are high cash operations that need money laundering. Now, I'm speculating, you understand, but cash run through small-town businesses might be harder to trace than at a Minneapolis business. Of course, it's just a guess."

Money laundering. The phrase lit up Boston's mind like a flood light. "Anything else?"

"No. As to why or how his body ended up down here, well, who knows? One more thing," Daniels added as Boston rose to leave. "This is confidential. Kaplan spent a lot of time with Edmund Ferrall when he ran Citizen's State Bank. Talk to Calvin. He might know something. Just don't mention my name." Then the old man rose from his desk, extended his hand and rumbled goodbye and good luck.

He still knows more than he told you, Boston guessed on the walk back to the office. But he is wise and too shrewd to say anything open to libel. No matter; his leads have paid off so far. Is there trouble between him and the Ferralls?

CHAPTER 25

Autumn's shorter days and earlier twilights awakened Ginger's old demons. She heard them rustling in the back of her mind, pattering on tiny feet like mice in the attic. Back in the day, she used to calm them with a little liquid sunshine. It usually worked for a while, but they always returned for more. You know better than to give in, she told herself. You're not going to drink. Picking up the kitchen phone, she punched in the number for her AA sponsor. The Jeep's headlights swept into her yard before the call went through. She hung up. Boston's unexpected appearance banished the inner twilight. She threw open the front door, momentarily self-conscious in her baggy jeans and sweatshirt. Jester stood by her, barking.

"Hi. I just stopped to give you an update," he said.

"Well, come in. You're my first visitor." She gave him a Coke and ushered him into the living room. "It's warmer in there."

He followed her through the kitchen and heard Patsy Cline singing "… and I'm crazy for trying and crazy for—" just before Ginger turned off the stereo.

"I see you're still her fan."

"Yeah, well, why not? She sang honest songs." Then she waved him to the couch and settled into the armchair facing him. She thought he seemed happy. If so, it's the first time since Peder's death. Maybe his Jack troubles have blown over. Then, to her surprise, Jester jumped up beside him and nuzzled his hand. As he stroked the dog's ears, she hoped he was as comfortable around her as he was with Jester.

"So, how's it going with Jack," she asked, not because she liked him but because he was Boston's only family and she respected that. At least he has a brother. You haven't seen Sean or Clem in at least ten years. They enlisted to escape Mama's nagging them to become priests.

"Jack's still digging his foxhole," Boston said. "He thinks the simplest theory is the right one. That's true if he ignores half the evidence. I pointed that out. We still aren't talking." He said it as a matter of fact. "Nailing the killer depends on bringing him around. That's my job."

"You know, I've missed you the last two days… I mean…" She hoped he didn't take it the wrong way.

"I went to Hennessey yesterday on a hunch. I didn't see you today. Anything new?"

"A lot," she said, raising her eyebrows. "I looked at the deeds on recently foreclosed farms to check out a story. While I was at it, I checked the title to the Breuer farm. Intriguing chain of ownership. It was foreclosed and then rented back to its prior owner."

"Who owns it now?"

"I'll get to that," she said. Breuer bought the farm in 1893. Citizen's State Bank foreclosed on it in 1931 and leased it to Breuer a year later until he died in 1942.

"*Hmm,* that's unusual," he hummed as he stroked Jester's ears. The dog lay still with its eyes closed, breathing softly, seeming content.

"This is where it gets interesting," she continued, enjoying the back and forth. "Citizen's sold Breuer's farm to Dominion Properties in 1949." She smiled and held up her hand. "Wait for it—there's more." She paused again, playing with him the way she did in high school. "Guess who was a Dominion stockholder?"

He wagged his head. "No idea. Who?"

"Oh, c'mon. Guess."

"Alright," he laughed. "Edmund Ferrall."

"Who else?"

"Santa Claus."

Eliot Ferrall." She threw her hands in the air.

"And…?" He coaxed with his fingers.

"He was a director when Kaplan vanished. Maybe there's a connection."

He held up his hand. "Careful, concurrence and causation are different. Don't jump to conclusions."

"Dominion transferred title to Westar in 1976. Westar leases it to a neighbor."

"What's Westar?"

"Some kind of management business in Minneapolis."

"That all?"

"You got something better, smarty?" She stuck out her tongue.

"I talked to three witnesses. Each saw two men—out-of-towners—in a Blazer at the time Ferrall died."

"So, what does it prove?" she taunted. "There're lots of Blazers around."

"Touché."

"Does this add up to anything?"

She half-listened to his account of talking with Daly and Gantz, entranced by the sight of her dog lying beside him as he stroked his head. Jester was a rescue that didn't like men, yet he accepted Boston.

"Listen to this," he said and played the interview with Gantz.

She listened, still focused on Jester's cozy snuggle. Somewhere, she had read that dogs picked up the emotional vibes people gave off. If Jester trusted him… the idea gave her goosebumps, but she quickly backed away from thinking about what-ifs.

"Consider this," he said. "The strangers cut the trees to lure Ferrall into the woods and shoot him to frame Gantz. He's unknown outside the county, so the idea had to come from someone local."

"Yeah, well, I can see that," she agreed, squinting in concentration. "I don't get the connection between the trees and suicide."

"Me either. But get this… these guys couldn't find Ferrall's woods and got their directions from Gantz not knowing he's the guy they're supposed to frame. It would be funnier if it weren't murder."

She laughed and then turned serious. "So, we've got a boat-load of 'ifs.' How does it fit together?"

"Here are some new facts. We know third parties are involved. They aren't local. That means someone hired them. They cut the trees to replicate Gantz's earlier theft. That idea had to come from a local. Strutt saw them at Ferrall's house on the afternoon he died. All this undermines Jack's suicide theory."

"Anything new about Peder?"

"That requires speculation. Jack will agree he was murdered—but privately. I suspect they wanted to get Peder before school started. So, they probably staked out the parsonage and followed him. Then they captured him somewhere outside St. Ansgar." He paused and exhaled. "I found footprints at the farm. Could've been theirs but no sign that Peder was there."

"So, they killed him and dumped him on their way to kill Ferrall?"

"The timing fits."

"I don't understand about cutting the trees," she said, crossing her arms.

"Gantz gave them directions on Thursday. Maybe they cut the trees that night, thinking Strutt would tell Eliot in the morning, like before. They waited to shoot him on Friday when he came to check it out."

"Get Ferrall first, then Peder?"

"Yeah. But Strutt didn't report the trees until Saturday. They lost a day, so they went after Peder and then went for Ferrall at his house. They probably killed him there and improvised a suicide in the woods. It's a guess," he said, stroking Jester. "Meanwhile, someone local floated the rumor Ferrall was using Peder for sex."

"It makes sense," she agreed, releasing her arms. "Here's another tidbit. A colleague at the newspaper association told me all candidates must file reports with the state campaign finance board. I checked for the heck of it." She paused to tease him. "I know who is giving to the sheriff's campaigns and how much."

"What's this got to do with the murders?"

"I'll tell you but… oh, let me freshen your drink." She took his glass and left him hanging in suspense as she waltzed into the kitchen. It was flirting but safe enough—for now.

"Quit stalling, tell me."

"The shitheads in the Chamber gave Jack twenty bucks but gave Jager anywhere from one to five hundred. Jack's kitty has barely eighteen hundred, all local. Jager has nearly twelve grand. Five of that came from Minneapolis donors."

Boston whistled. "He's got some rich friends."

"The five grand came in just after Peder's death."

"Coincidence? I'd think a pay-off would be under the table."

She shrugged. "You think Jager's involved?"

He shook his head. "No, not directly. But I think he'd look the other way to gain from it. Say, I'm going to call it a day," he said, rising from the sofa. "Let's keep this between us for now. Thanks for the Coke. G' night."

Ginger saw him out the door, then leaned against it and listened to the sound of the Jeep fade in the distance. Her melancholia crept out of its hiding places and scurried about. What does he think of you, she wondered. Or does he? You're close now but still distant. You were in love once. God, help me get over that. Then she whispered the serenity prayer, lifted the phone and called her sponsor.

CHAPTER 26

Westar stuck in the back of Boston's mind like a bit of beef between his teeth. He had just seen Westar somewhere. Maybe on a letterhead or a bill or a card. It was on white paper with a *sans serif* font. The more he worked at recalling where he saw it, the more it stayed out of sight. Maybe it would come to him later when he wasn't trying to recall it. He peeled off his shirt and stuffed it in the Ever-Clean laundry bag.

"That's where I saw it," he said aloud. A Westar business form lay on the laundry counter. Ketcham must have seen him look at it because he whisked it out of sight. He must know something. Maybe it's something he doesn't want to disclose.

Lying in bed, he considered how to get Ketcham talking about Westar. You'll have to do it without making him suspicious or defensive. He's garrulous and probably lonely. He likes to talk man-to-man. More than once, Ketcham told him, "Go to Vegas if you want to get laid good. The hookers give the best blow jobs, too, lemme tell ya." He's such an improbable player. How does he fit into the scheme? But on the other hand, what's more interesting than the improbable?

A bell dinged as Boston entered the Ever-Clean Laundry. Ketcham limped to the counter and rasped out good morning around the cigarette in the corner of his mouth. He never seemed without one. "You can pick 'em up tomorrow afternoon," he said, taking the bag of shirts.

"Say, Ernie, how about a drink after work?" he asked. "I'd like to talk business with you."

Ketcham's mood brightened. "How 'bout the Post House Lounge? Say, five-thirty?"

"See you there," Boston said. He left hoping Ketcham's knowledge of Westar was greater than his acquaintance with Vegas hookers. Back in the office, he gazed at his father's photo on the wall and wondered what the old man might have made of the evidence at hand. Making sense of it had him stumped. A shortage of evidence had stalled Jack's investigation. Now the glut in his hand left him assembling a 1,000-piece puzzle without a box cover picture to guide him. Some of it was probably clutter. Dad was always good at finding truth amid the clutter.

He set a newsprint tablet on an easel and drew a timeline from 1893, when Breuer bought his farm, to 1984 and Ferrall's death. Proven events went above the timeline, such as Breuer's foreclosure, Kaplan's visits and the recent murders. Possible but undocumented events went below the line, such as Breuer's bootlegging, Filbert's obsession with Emma and the anonymous threats. After an hour, he had no more clarity than he had before. Next, he made a Venn diagram of three interlocking circles. As he filled each with names, dates, events and locations, he looked for congruences. Kaplan overlapped in time with Ferrall, Filbert and Emma; Peder was contemporaneous with Ferrall and Filbert. He added the rest of the evidence, but the picture still looked muddled. He left the office to clear his mind over lunch.

The critical evidence around Peder's death consisted of the footprints at Breuer's farm, his missing pack, clay on the bike tires but not on his shoes and the information in the three-ring binder. Maybe the men in the Blazer made the footprints at Breuer's farm. He wished Ginger was in the office because she was good at cutting through the clutter. Maybe tomorrow.

Boston arrived at the Post House just as Jorgenson pulled up next to him in a new Buick. They greeted each other, and the dealer complimented the *Statesman*'s series on the farm crisis. "Damned good reporting," he said.

"Thanks," Boston said. "Give Dub Willard the kudos. It was his idea."

"Low grain prices are killing me. New car sales are down. A lot of owners can't make their payments. I've held off on repos, but I don't know for how much longer. Hate to do it but…" he wagged his head. "Oh, by the way, I meant to call you. Patty wasn't going out with Peder."

"Okay, thanks," he said, suspecting it was a lie. He had looked through the library's collection of high school yearbooks. Patty Jorgenson was the only Patty in Peder's class. He recalled how sneaky and private he was at that age. Even if Jorgenson knew, he wouldn't admit it, especially if the death seemed suspicious. They entered the Post House together.

The cocktail lounge had seen better days. Besides the threadbare carpeting, the 1960s décor appeared tired. Its feeble air conditioning couldn't clear the smoky haze that made Boston's eyes itch. He took a booth and ordered scotch with a side of water. Mindful of the promise to Ginger, he watered the drink even more.

Ketcham arrived, and Boston ordered the double Jim Beam neat that he requested. Then the little man lit a cigarette. They talked about sports until the drink arrived. Up close, Boston noticed the magenta tint in Ketcham's nose. Burst blood vessels. Probably from habitual drinking. The swigs of liquor loosened Ketcham's tongue, and Boston sensed the time had come for his questions.

"Ernie, I want to run some stories about successful businesses starting with yours."

"Why?" he asked, leaning back with a squinty, sidelong look.

"You're a successful, essential service." Boston swirled the ice in his glass. "Readers want to know how you do it."

"Well, I guess that won't hurt nothin'. Might be good for business, *huh*?" Ketcham lit another unfiltered Camel. "Okay, but I don't have to answer questions I don't like."

"No. Of course not. Just tell me how you got into business. Tell it as it comes to you." He set a notebook by his drink.

Ketcham slurped some whiskey, sucked on the cigarette and blew a cloud of smoke toward the ceiling. "I bought the shop after three hitches in the Navy. That's how I got the limp." Dragging deeply on his cigarette, he wandered into stories about the miseries of cleaning clothes. "I was getting by but not getting ahead… know what I mean? Had a big note due at Commerce Bank. Daniels was about to close me down. Tight-fisted old fart. Didn't know how I was going to pay the fucker off. Then I got a silent partner."

"Explain that," Boston asked, rubbing his mouth to hide his surprise.

"Well, one day, this guy stops by and says, 'I've got a proposition for you.' And I tell him, 'I got enough trouble.' And he says, 'The town needs you. I want to help.' So, I ask him, 'What's your deal?' And he says, 'I'll give you money to pay off your note. You'll still own the business free and clear, but I'll be a silent partner.' 'Sounds fishy to me,' I say. 'Why do you want to be a silent partner? What's the catch?' He says, 'I'm doing good. It's important to help others, too. Everyone wins. I don't want anyone to know I'm doing this,' he says. 'This only works if I'm anonymous.' So, I tell him, 'Well, lemme think it over.'"

Ketcham stubbed out his cigarette, sipped the drink and tapped the pack of Camels against his thumb. He stuck one in the corner of his mouth and lit it. "Well, the way I figured it, I could lose my shirt dealing with Daniels or chance it with this guy. I know him. So, I threw in." He dragged deeply and then blew more smoke.

"And he helped you?"

"Help me? Fuck yes. Give me the cash to pay off my note. He says, 'Ernie, you don't owe me until you turn a profit. If you don't make a profit, you don't owe me a thing.' All I have to do is never let on who he is. After that, he got me a business expert." Ketcham sucked at his cigarette. "Didn't cost me, neither. I live good now. Life's easy. You know the best part? I don't do the fucking books." He slapped the tabletop and grinned. "Always hated that. No good at numbers."

"Well, who does them?" Something about this reminded Boston of a set-up in Illinois. One of his colleagues broke that story.

"The management company does 'em," Ketcham beamed. All I hafta do is put the money in a drop safe. A company agent deposits the money every Friday, and I get a receipt. Every month, I get a statement of receipts and expenses." Ketcham blew smoke upward.

"Made a profit every year. It's a good deal all around. Hell, I'm so well-managed I make a profit on low prices. Easy money."

"And what about your silent partner?"

"He's a saint. Don't want much. Don't want nobody to know it."

"I'll do a story on him if you give me his name."

Ketcham chuckled and waved a finger. "Can't help you. I promised. He's helped a lot of other guys, too. Maybe the company could help your paper. Ever think of that?"

"Hey, that's an idea, Ernie. What's the company called?"

"Westar. A Minneapolis outfit. The Post House uses 'em. So does the lumber yard, House of Truth, Zippy Car Wash and a couple of others."

Boston held himself in check though he could hardly wait to get away. What a break. A bonanza for the price of a couple of drinks. However, he feigned interest in Ketcham's adventures with Vegas hookers and blow jobs while he thought about ways to uncover the silent partner. He bought Ketcham another double before saying thanks for his story. Now it felt as if the wind behind him was blowing up a gale. It was so good he had to share it with Ginger.

The moment she opened her door, he saw the strain in her face. He remembered she had spent the afternoon arranging better care for Mama. "Hi. I was going to—oh, I can see this isn't a good time to talk about evidence."

"No, no. It's alright. Come in. I really need company," she said, holding tight to his arm and hustling him into the living room. "I want something to get my mind off Mama. Is that okay?"

"Of course, if it helps," he said, settling on the couch. "How are you… and Mama?"

"I'm moving her into the Franciscan Villas. It's better care for the money. And it's Catholic. But… ugh, the paperwork. I'm fine. Mama is… still Mama." She bounced lightly up and down in the chair. "You've got *noo-ooze*," she sang, "I hear it in your *voy-oyce.*"

"Yeah, I think so. Kaplan was after money laundering."

"Tell me—tell me everything." She crossed her arms under her breasts and smiled.

He told her what he learned from Ketcham. Then he backtracked to say Daniels guessed Kaplan was investigating the Minneapolis mob. He thought they might be laundering money through small-town businesses.

"But that was thirty, forty years ago. What's the connection?"

"Criminal organizations evolve like legal ones." He said they even had something equivalent to markets, product lines and customers. Peder's research binder outlined the mobsters' progression from bootleg liquor to protection rackets, black markets to liquor, gambling and prostitution. It might be drugs, now. "Whatever they do requires money laundering," he said. "Ernie may be in this up to his neck."

"You don't mean the killings?"

"No. He can't manage what's in a paper sack. I doubt he has any idea what he's doing." As he talked, he saw the strain fading from her face. He covertly admired her profile as light from the corner lamp accentuated her straight nose, firm chin and round breasts. He said the Westar agent probably added illicit money to Ketcham's receipts, put it in a bank account and adjusted the books. "Ernie lives well, dumb and happy."

"So, how'd he hook up with Westar?"

"*Ah*, excellent question, my dear Watson." Boston patted the couch. Jester jumped up beside him. "A silent partner brought in Westar," he said, stroking the dog's ears.

"Who?"

He paused until she asked "who" again.

"I hear an owl," he said and then ducked when she threw a small pillow. "He won't say, but he's local."

"Back to Kaplan," she said without the playful tone. "The killer must be dead."

"Then who has something to lose by exposing him?"

"A friend, a relative."

"Or an organization. Crime syndicates often outlive their founders. Anyway, we're getting somewhere. Well, that's it. I'm tired," he said and started to rise.

CHAPTER 27

Watching Boston and Jester snuggle reminded Ginger of something she had always wanted but rarely had—domestic harmony. Too many childhood memories were filled with parental quarrels, Catholic strictures and Mama's frigid silences when displeased. She grew up hungering for tender gestures, loving words and kind acts. Those were rare at home. Was that too much to expect? Boston's visit hinted at a possibility. She sensed something was happening between them—like yeast in dough. But for how long? He would eventually return to Chicago and, after that, what? A solitary life seemed less fulfilling now in ways it hadn't before. She didn't want him to leave.

"You look beat," she said before he could rise from the couch. She pushed gently to keep him in the seat. Then she climbed onto his lap, straddled his legs, removed his glasses and started to massage his scalp. As her fingers worked, she felt him relax beneath her. His sigh sounded like an affirmation. Is compassion the same as affection, she wondered. The distinction doesn't matter. Both feel alike and good and fulfilling. With his eyes closed, she thought he wore the same contented face Jester had when he stroked his head. Then she felt his arms encircle her waist. He pulled her closer and kissed her mouth. She kissed back passionately. He stroked her sides, and she caressed his neck. They wriggled against each other, giggling. Then he rolled onto his back with Ginger on top.

"I've missed that," she sighed, rubbing her lips on his. "You've improved."

"I hope so. You have too."

"Let's make sure," she whispered.

She spread her legs around him as his hands slipped under the sweatshirt. He unhooked the bra and caressed her breasts. Through her jeans, she felt his erection pressing against her. She shivered in anticipation of magical intimacy—something holy—maybe... Trembling, she sat up and pulled off her sweatshirt. Then she fumbled with his zipper and opened his pants. As she did, she felt him tremble as if in a spasm.

"*No*. We can't do this," he gasped, blinking as if awakened from a deep slumber. He tried to sit up. "This is all wrong. We have boundaries."

She rolled off him onto the floor, her face twisted with anguish. Tears streamed down her cheeks and dripped onto her breasts.

"It's not you," he cried as he zipped up. "It's my fault. I shouldn't have done it—"

"Why?" she screamed.

"I'm divorced."

"Oh bullshit," she bellowed, spraying droplets of spit. "Divorce... ha! It doesn't stop you from fucking Daphne. I know about that," she cried, her voice hoarse. "You say you need me. Then you use me. Then you drop me—just like before," she screamed. Now on fire, she stoked the rage she had nurtured since that humiliating, long-ago August night before he returned to college. The night he sneered, "Marriage? Get real. You're not my only piece of ass." She hadn't known her strength until her fist wearing his class ring broke his glasses and opened a gash in his temple. She never saw him after that until she applied for the job.

"You don't care about me—only you," she yelled, getting off the floor. She pulled the sweatshirt over her bare bosom. His silence infuriated her, and she flayed him again. "If you were half a man, you'd fuck me now and say, 'thank you, ma'am,' and go home. I could live with that. But you don't have the balls to show your feelings. Quit pretending to be a man. You're still... still the weak, fucking... asshole..." and then ran out of air. She gasped for breath. "Professional boundaries. What a load." She stalked into the kitchen and slammed her glass on the counter. It shattered. "You're right. It's a bad idea. I quit."

He followed her. "I'm sorry," he stuttered. "I don't understand."

"Damn you. Why'd you hire *me*?" She waited for an answer, but he stood mute with his hands hanging at his sides. After a couple of deep breaths, she felt her rage ebbing like air escaping from a balloon. He's as clueless as a child, she thought. "I know you don't understand," she said, glowering but controlled. She wiped her eyes with the back of her hands. "I hoped we were over the past. But we're not. Some things don't change, do they?" She knit her brows into a scowl.

"You surprised me," he said. "The massage felt like old times. I wanted, I thought I was over… I couldn't help kissing you. It seemed right," he said and then looked at his hands.

"Alright. We aren't over each other. We're still in the past. So, what are we going to do about it?" Why do you have to figure this out, she wondered. Why do women always have to make things right?

"I don't want to start a… then go to Chicago and… I don't want to start something, we can't—"

"So, you aren't over me but… but what?" Ginger put her hands on her hips. "What's unsettled isn't important to you, is it? Out of sight, out of mind. Just go to Chicago. Leave this unsettled. Leave me wondering… Our personal relationship isn't that important—is it?" Her words snapped like firecrackers, and she felt the rage rising again in her throat. "Your indifference hurts."

"No, yes… but—"

"You're gutless. I can't work for you. I won't work for you. It hurts too much." She grabbed his arm, spun him around and shoved him out the door.

"I can't help it."

"Can't help it," she sneered as he walked toward the Jeep. "You're pa-*thetic*. Go home—go to Chicago—go to hell—I quit!" she screamed into the darkness and slammed the door so hard its force made the kitchen window rattle in the sash. Then she leaned against the door, gasping for breath and listened to the sound of his car fade away and take her future with it. A moment later, she threw herself face down across the bed, feeling as worthless as a used Kleenex. "Why can't I forget him?" she blubbered. "Why?"

Before sobriety, heartaches used to remind her she was still very much alive. Misery had a purpose, but it needed company. She rifled her subconscious, calling out memories of other old hurts and invited them to join her. Self-pity and pain were two good companions for a drink. This hurt enough for a round, she told herself. Just one—if you can stop. If not…

She drove a mile beyond San Juan Lane to a grubby rural bar called The House of Truth. The location at a crossroad seemed metaphorically perfect, somehow. Yes, a crossroad. Which way will you go? she wondered as she pulled in. A sputtering neon sign outlined a highball glass, but its broken stem tube made the glass into a "vee"—for vice. Or maybe for victim. A sign in the window flashed Grain Belt Beer. The parking lot was empty. Good, she thought. You can drink alone. Entering, she breathed in the familiar aromas of stale tobacco, beer and despair. The barkeep was a stranger absorbed in the televised ballgame. With her buttock perched on a stool, she ordered Johnny Walker Black over ice. He brought the drink without a word and turned back to the TV.

She picked up the small glass and studied it in the dim light with its promise of liquid comfort. A false promise to be sure, but still better than his promise. She shook the glass, delighting in the tinkle of the ice cubes—like Christmas chimes.

"Well, here's to what can't be," she whispered, raising the glass to her image in the cloudy mirror. The sardonic toast froze in mid-salute when she saw a sad, haggard face looking back from the mirror. She knew the face. Not hers—not yet—but it could be hers after a couple years of drinking.

"Mother of God, what am I…" She shuddered. "Oh God, help me. I'm better than… he's not worth… worth… *this*." She set the untouched drink on the bar and bolted out the door. Leaning against her car, she gagged as waves of nausea convulsed her. The vile odor of vomit rose to her nostrils. Her knees wobbled until she finished retching and spitting. Then her head cleared. "You're the editor of his goddamn newspaper," she said through clenched teeth. "Mama needs you to have that job. You're gonna get it back. If you can't have him the way you want him, then… well, you'll be rid of him once he leaves. Yes. This might work out."

CHAPTER 28

Boston stumbled on a porch step and felt an urgent need for something besides the rail to steady him. A drink. Just the thing, he thought. You've just fucked up your life. It took only a second. And you knew better. But no, you were feeling instead of thinking. You're back at square one. Now what? He rubbed the scar and collapsed into a wing chair.

Is there some way to work this out? he wondered. There will be a cost, of course. An apology, at least. Not that she forgives or forgets. Even if you could go back, she'd find a way to get even. She always does. It's her way. She said, "I quit," and meant it. So, what do you tell the staff on Monday? They won't buy a story that it was by mutual agreement. It'll hurt your credibility. Robin can manage the *Statesman* as well as Ginger, but she has three kids. Call her in the morning. You're screwed if she says no. And she probably will.

He went to the buffet before he remembered there was no liquor in the house. "Goddamnit." He returned to the chair, twisting to ease the sudden pain beneath his ribs. You had a good thing going. Then you fucking blew it. Without Ginger, you don't have a partner. How are you going to challenge Jack or find Peder's killer? Braydon is running out of patience. Finding another editor will take… Fierce hammering on the front door broke up the pity party. "Who in the hell…?" he muttered on his way to the door.

"I'm not done talking to you," Ginger roared the moment he opened it. "You really pissed me off." Her eyes blazed with the anger he remembered. He backed up, but she advanced like a lioness until they stood nose to nose. "I've changed. Have you?" She poked him in the chest. "Have you? Have you changed?" She poked again, harder. Her voice echoed in the foyer.

He put up his palms as if surrendering but couldn't get away. Jesus, she's gone off the rails, he thought.

"I've grown up. Have you?" she demanded through lips curled into a hard line.

"Well, of course, you know… *uh*—"

"No, I don't know. I don't see a change. You're still the self-centered asshole I remember. You're all talk. Empty promises. I loved you once. I wanted a life with you. I was serious. Were you?" She stepped closer.

"Don't," he said. "This'll only hurt you more."

"I don't believe you. Mama loved me when she thought I'd marry you. Then she'd be somebody. She blamed me—not you—*me*—for breaking up. You could've… you… you never… never committed to…" she gasped, swallowed and wiped her eyes.

"Don't," he said, feeling her words close around him like a trap. He didn't have retorts or defenses against the salvo of accusations. This was the Ginger he remembered. The one he feared. The one he broke up with. She never admitted being wrong. Never at fault. Always turning his words back on him. "This is—"

"Shut up! Shut the fuck up and listen. I want you to listen," she thundered as another wave of ire rolled in. "I drank in high school but hid it. Drank more after we broke up. Drank even more after the divorce. Drank until I knew that I'd die unless I got help." She paused. "I almost drank tonight," she whispered.

Almost drank? What did that mean? The admission hit him in the gut. "Let's sit down and start over," he urged, grabbing the initiative while she gasped for breath. They sat at opposite ends of the couch with an awkward silence between them. Each waited for the other to say something, anything.

"We can't leave this unsettled," she said, regaining some composure. "For both our sakes, we need to understand what happened and why."

He nodded, looked into his hands and waited for her next words.

"It was simple for me. I haven't gotten laid in a long, long time. But I was ready for you—I've always wanted you. Being close to you, feeling your breath on my face, my fingers in your hair… your hands on my boobs, your hard-on… I got… I got hot all over. At last, and…"

He swallowed, nodded, but didn't know what to say.

"And then you said no. I felt you didn't want me—like before. I felt rejected again. When you didn't understand, I got mad. It's an old habit. But I think you know that. I blamed myself. Then I went to a bar. Old habits are hard to break."

"I'm sorry, it's on me. Double sorry because you went to the bar."

"Look, we grew up together," she continued, shifting into her common-sense tone of voice. "I feel close to you… want to be close to you, but there's this… this wall between us. I don't understand it. Why do you hide the best part of yourself from me? It's visible when you're with others. It's beautiful. Why do you hide it from me?"

He continued to look into his hands, uncertain how to answer that.

"Your reserve, your mask keeps us apart. I don't know why. I might be wrong, but I think you're lonely. That saddens me."

He heard the worry in her voice and compassion, too. A quick glance at her and then he shook his head. "I don't know. I'm attracted to you like before, but I don't trust myself."

"You're risking a career because of Peder and Jack. I admire you for that. But you're so much more—if only you knew it. We fell into our old habits. Are you willing to start over?"

Start over? He shivered at her words and felt the heavy stone leave his belly. He nodded as gratitude surged through him at receiving something he didn't deserve. He nodded again.

"You've been there for me with Mama. I want to be there for you."

He wagged his head, speechless, lost in the twists of their history. She showed up just when you needed an editor. She kept you from drinking, backed you to the hilt, quit, now she wants to start over and be there for you. But that's not it—not entirely. She's a force of nature. A rebel. Can you really start over, or is this wishful thinking?

He looked her in the eyes and absently rubbed the scar. "It's like this. You keep me grounded, sober, on course, so I can deal with what's on my plate." He swallowed. "I'm grateful for all you've done for me. I do need you. And I want you, too. But I want you when my head's clear. I can't trust myself with intimacy. Not yet. That's what I meant."

She glanced away. A moment later, she turned back with an impish smile twitching about her lips. "I think I understand," she said and reached for his hand. "You are who you are. And it's good. I don't want you to be different. I have things to learn, too. But remember, I'm like Mama—I want what I want in the way that I want it. I still find it hard to accept what I can't change. I know I can't change you. I don't want to change you, and I won't try. I promise."

He thanked her with a smile. They sat on the couch holding hands for a few minutes, then she squeezed and released.

"I'll see you Monday," she said and rose from the couch.

CHAPTER 29

Carson relished Sunday evenings when the week's masses, confessions and consultations were behind him. Tonight's dinner was at Boston's house, and the wine was his contribution. What an unlikely but enriching friendship, he thought while he looked for just the right wine. He thought of the many lessons in human motivation he learned as a stockbroker and then as a priest. Of late, he noticed that Boston talked less about his career and more about the paper. More and more, he spoke about what he felt and feared more than what he thought. Carson chose a bottle of *Riesling* to complement tonight's roast pork. Maybe this is a good time to mention the changes you have seen in him. But only over brandy after eating dinner and playing a couple of games of chess.

"Did you catch the presidential debate?" Carson asked as they sat before the fire. "I thought Reagan did well, don't you? He makes his point simply." Carson wasn't a Reagan supporter but said it to draw Boston out from behind whatever was going on inside him.

"Simplistic," he replied. "Mondale is truthful. Unfortunately, the truth isn't selling."

"None of us likes a difficult truth," Carson said and got up to stand at a turret window. "You can get crucified for it. By the way, how do you like this view," he asked, pointing at the city's lights.

"A lot more than I used to. That's why I hate to sell the house. But unfortunately, I don't have another choice. I'm going to miss the paper, too."

"Why?"

"It's a family legacy. I see the results of my work. Cause and effect. The *Statesman* is my weapon to get justice for Peder."

"All good reasons, but they don't answer my question, why is it hard to let go?"

"I'm trying to sort out some stuff with Ginger."

"Well, well," he said and turned from the window.

"Like I told you, Frank, we have a bitter and complicated past."

"I know. Before you hired her, you worried it wouldn't work out. So, why did you hire her?" Carson asked, sensing his question had touched a nerve.

"She was the best candidate. Knows more about newspapers than I do. We work together alright but… then there's our past. In the end, we're just not right for each other."

"You're sure about that?" Carson stroked his beard

"Hell, Frank, I'm not sure about anything anymore," and threw up his hands.

"Before you hired her, you told me about your complications with Ginger. Remember?"

Boston looked at him but didn't respond.

"And after reciting your history, I asked whether you wanted an editor or a lover. You didn't answer me then. But I think you've decided. Before you say anything, let me tell you a personal story." Carson stood with his back to the fire and recounted his career as a Wall Street trader. At the age of thirty-five, he had a fiancé, a couple million and a path to partnership. Back then, he focused all his energy on making money and gaining partnerships. His fiancé felt so neglected she broke the engagement and soon married someone else.

"I didn't know that."

"It hurt, but I kept working until the emptiness set in," he continued. "That's when I said, 'To hell with it.' I left, just like that." He snapped his fingers. "I was so scared for myself that I stayed at a monastery with a prep school friend. That's where God was waiting for me to wake up," he said and rubbed his backside. "After ordination, the bishop was hot to have me manage the church's investments. I said no. For my disobedience, he assigned me to a dying parish. I couldn't have been happier. Together, the members and I reversed the decline. A new bishop came in, and I transferred to Holy Name. Now here's my point," he said. "Your destiny, your true self, will remain obscure if you listen only to your head. What does your heart tell you about Ginger?"

"I don't know. She wants a commitment. I failed at marriage. Don't want to fail again."

"Is this about failing or about risking pain?"

"I'm going to Chicago soon."

"I hear words. I don't hear conviction. Look," Carson said in a lower voice. "It's time you came home."

"Home?"

"Home—your heart. It's the place you ran from. You'll return to it when you're ready to resolve the contradictions in your life. When you're ready to be the person you're meant to be."

"You learned that in seminary?"

"No, painful experience. And I think you're already aware of it."

Carson saw Boston's jaw tighten and suspected he was annoyed. A log collapsed into the hearth and sent a shower of sparks up the chimney. It seemed like a cue to leave. "Trust your heart, my friend," he said as he put on his jacket. "It's always right."

CHAPTER 30

Sully Drawz thought the Sunday traffic on the four-lane seemed heavier than normal. He alternated hands as he drove while he clenched and released his fists to loosen the stiff fingers. Either nerves or arthritis. Neither felt good. Otherwise, he was a fit, reticent man with a soldier's bearing. He owned a one-man security consultancy in a Minneapolis strip mall of franchise shops. His principal client had a dozen business associates scattered in various towns and required security. His client sent him to Featherstone because the associate there panicked over the newspaper's interest in an old murder. The associate turned out to be a meddling prick who complicated the project. Then it went haywire, and Drawz had to improvise. Now the newspaper has been picking at loose ends, and the associate had his undies in a bunch over it. The client wants him to clean up the mess with another rushed project. Drawz liked it even less.

"Here's the deal, Nix," he said to the short, younger man with acned cheeks. "We're taking out the newspaper owner and the editor." He blew out his breath. "It'll be trickier than last time. It's gotta be airtight."

Nix grunted but kept his eyes on the *Penthouse* centerfold.

Drawz thought the kid had limited talents, but that was alright because his line of work didn't need two masterminds. But he's a little over-eager to use a gun. Otherwise, he's a good sideman who doesn't think beyond my orders. And if he does, well, he's expendable. He yawned but kept his eyes on the stream of traffic. Killing men didn't bother him, but he regretted killing the kid. At least you tried to make it instantaneous, but you haven't slept well since. Well, you don't get to pick the targets in this business.

In this case, it was two targets at once. Big risk of failure. Nothing went as planned, he thought. You had to improvise the accidents on-the-fly. This do-over is because the associate thought he knew more about your specialty than you did. Each death is tailored to look like a run-of-the-mill accident. Deceiving the eye requires attention to detail. It's like that French phrase you can't pronounce, *trompe l'oeil*. The army taught you the art of camouflage and made you an instructor. Later, as an insurance investigator, you learned the art of subterfuge common to insurance fraud. You've got a good record of removing threats without triggering deep investigations. Fixing this fuck-up is going to take careful planning, imagination and patience—not to mention luck.

"Check out the packet, Nix. It's got background on the targets, their routines, cars, license numbers and a map to their houses. We're under pressure."

"Shit, why not shoot 'em, be done with it?" the kid pouted and rolled up the magazine.

"The sheriff's brother is one of the targets. We want to avoid investigation." This rush job has greater odds of a snafu, he thought, as he considered the possibilities of creating two ordinary accidents. In his ideal world, the subjects would die together, driving off a cliff. This wasn't an ideal world. However, September was the time of year when people turned on their furnaces. A lot of house fires start with faulty burners. An explosion would do. Or maybe carbon monoxide.

They checked into the Featherstone Best Western on the east side of town. Nix returned to groping his crotch while ogling the magazine's Pet of the Month. Drawz studied the information in the packet. Both targets had regular routines, and both lived alone outside the city's limits. The challenge lay in finding a way to hit them at home or some isolated spot in or outside the city.

The hitmen spent several hours on Monday morning scouting alleys and side streets in search of likely locations but found nothing suitable. The vacant lots along the railroad tracks were too exposed to view. Later, as Drawz sat on a bench in the Green, he saw the associate walk by. They made fleeting eye contact without acknowledging each other. He loathed the man because he was a demanding prick who didn't appreciate difficulties. When he got up, he bumped into a man wearing tortoise-shell glasses. They excused each other and went their separate ways. Drawz watched him go, certain he had just met his principal target. After a few minutes, he sauntered into the alley behind the *Statesman*. The licenses on the Jeep and the green Subaru matched the associate's notes. With both targets at their office, he could scope out their houses.

He slowed as they approached the Egg Lady's house, but he didn't stop because it was too close to the road. Anyone passing by would see their car. He slowed for the realtor's sign at San Juan Lane and then drove as far as the House of Truth. Nix wanted a drink, but Drawz said no. He drove up San Juan Lane and stopped at the house. If the owner returned, he could say they were interested in buying it.

Nix got out of the Blazer, lit a cigarette and dragged deeply with relief because Drawz wouldn't let him smoke in his vehicle. He took several good puffs and then joined Drawz in circling the house. They took care not to trample the flowers or leave tracks as they checked the potential entry points. "Jeez-us, he must have a big dog," Nix muttered, staring at the immense doghouse built into the back wall of the house.

"It doesn't look used," Drawz said. He turned and lifted the lid covering the pressure gauge and controls on the propane tank. "This'll work."

They circled the house again, peered in the windows and tried the doors with gloved hands. Meade was careful when he locked up, Drawz thought, but the old-style locks were easy to pick when the time came.

"Well, what do we do?" Nix asked, lighting another cigarette.

"Pick up that butt when you're done," Drawz ordered. "This house is ripe for a gas explosion. With the right design, it'll happen when we're not around. I still need to get a couple things from the hardware store."

Drawz stopped on the road next to a cornfield near the Egg Lady's house. With corn as their cover, they walked down the rows to the end of the field. The back porch was a hundred feet away across an open lawn. He studied it through his pocket binoculars. Satisfied there was no one inside, they hopped the wire fence and approached the house. Then he stopped at the sound of barking inside.

"Hold it. Go back," Drawz said. "We'll have to figure a mutt in our plans."

They returned to the motel. Nix opened his magazine, and Drawz took a shower. Afterward, he hummed while he worked out a plan at the room's tiny desk. "Here's the idea," he said. "We can fill the house with gas. The trick is touching it off when the target is there, and we aren't. It's so far from town there won't be anything left by the time the fire trucks arrive."

"Sounds good. How ya gonna rig the other house," Nix asked, now preoccupied with his automatic pistol.

"I'm not. We'll have to get her another way. Two explosions… that's too suspicious."

"We could follow 'em sometime, then take 'em, like we did the boy."

"Maybe." Drawz didn't like that. Damned near impossible to improvise an accident when you don't know where they might be or when. He hated this assignment.

Nix took apart the .41 caliber pistol. The gun was powerful, fast and he thought it was the most beautiful piece ever made. He cleaned each part daily. Though Drawz carried a small automatic, Nix knew he didn't like shooting people. Why, he couldn't understand. It was simpler than setting up accidents. He thought his boss was smart but rather odd. Though Nix liked him well enough, he considered the .41 his only true friend.

"Hey, Sully, if nothin' else works, there's this," he said, racking a cartridge into the chamber.

Sobriety had taught Ginger the value of disciplined living. She habitually rose at daybreak to pray under the oak behind the house. She recited the rosary, offered petitions for Mama and finished with the serenity prayer. After devotions, she practiced yoga, followed by breakfast. Today was Monday, and she rushed the prayers, skipped yoga and breakfast, and arrived at the *Statesman* well before the staff. Twilight filled the newsroom, where a phone rang at an empty desk, followed by a click of the voicemail machine. The fax machine squealed behind a divider and then spat out pages. She retrieved Peder's binder in hopes of finding something Boston had missed. The idea made her smile. For now, at least, a light-hearted intellectual competition was the only foreplay she trusted. After reviewing all of Peder's binder, she knew Boston hadn't overlooked anything.

Reporters and editors trickled in, filling the newsroom with chatter about the Falcon's football win on Friday night, the latest episodes of *Dynasty*, *Cheers* or the interviews on *60 Minutes*. The serenity of daybreak ebbed, and she felt hungry and left the building for breakfast.

From time to time, she had overheard scraps of stairwell chatter about Boston and Daphne. Though tantalizing, she felt listening to prurient gossip was beneath her. She couldn't ignore it now. Not after Friday night's brouhaha and truce. Whatever his relations with Daphne, they mattered now. She lingered outside the Streamliner for a moment, then swallowed her uncertainty and entered. Her first visit since returning.

Early morning regulars at the counter glanced her way and then continued talking and stuffing their faces with eggs, ham and toast. The unchanged décor stirred memories of hanging out there with Boston. Daphne was then mama's little helper and a pesky brat who hung around with the seniors.

She settled into a booth, caught sight of Daphne and wished she hadn't come. Watching her easy banter with the men at the counter, she understood why Boston—or any man—might be attracted to her. She flirts, she's suggestive, flashes a little cleavage bending over. *Stop it*, she scolded herself. You're being catty. You did the same thing the other night. No, Daphne's success comes from something more than great tits and a round ass. She's that and more. But what is she like? It mattered if Daphne and Boston were serious. But you shouldn't be here. You're a voyeur, a snoop prying into his private life. She gathered her purse and prepared to leave.

"Good morning," Daphne said, standing by the booth with a coffee pot and a cup. "Coffee?" she asked, setting the cup in front of Ginger and filling it. "I've been hoping you'd came in someday," she said. "I haven't seen you in years. You look fabulous."

"Oh, hi," Ginger replied hesitantly. "I've been busy. Haven't had the time. This is marvelous. Just as I remember. And you, you've changed—fantastic."

"Thanks, may I?" Daphne asked, and then sat without waiting for an answer.

"Please do," she said, feeling trapped by the "other" woman as she now thought of her. The moment felt like a scene ripped from the romance novels she read as a girl.

"Are you still freelancing?" Daphne asked. "I loved your pieces in *Family Life*. Especially the ones about caring for parents at the end of life. It struck a chord because of my mom. I like the way you think."

"I don't have time to freelance now," she said, wishing Daphne would leave. "The paper and my mom take up my time. How long have you—"

"Mom left it to me. She died when I was seventeen. Chiara managed it until I finished college. *Uh…* well, gotta get back to my regulars," she said with a wink. "The guys pay a lot of the bills. Come in later next time when it will be easier to talk."

Ginger watched her return to the counter and resume her role as the sassy, light-hearted host. She never mentioned Boston, she thought. Does that mean you're not her rival or what? If she's your rival, then she's a formidable one. That buxom figure and sassy talk hide a shrewdly intelligent woman. And honest, too. That's probably what attracts him. He values honesty. So, in this game, you'll have to outdo her in honesty.

Chiara brought her breakfast. She ate it in a hurry and then rushed to the office. After that encounter, she wanted to spend a few minutes with Boston. He was on the phone, so she waited in her office. Then Robin corralled her to look at the mock-up for the paper's new masthead. The women were about the same age and had bonded during Ginger's transition as editor. Since then, they enjoyed several girls-night-out over dinner and theater in Rochester. She fidgeted as they worked, debating whether to talk to Robin about Boston, woman-to-woman. After all, what's a gal-pal for? She decided against it until she had something more concrete. They finished their review, and she went looking for Boston. Maybe that would flush Daphne from her mind.

CHAPTER 31

The siren wailed from the city power station as it did every noon. Boston slipped into his jacket and stuck his head into Ginger's office. "If you're free, I'd like your company on a trip to the Breuer farm."

"Okay, I'm free. It looks like a good afternoon to get out of town," she said, warmed at the prospect of spending time with him. "Oh, by the way, the only gray clay is near St. Ansgar."

"Thanks for checking. That's why we're going. I need a sample. It's a hunch," he said on the way downstairs to the Jeep.

He pulled into Buddy's A & W, one of their high school hangouts, and ordered lunch. The carhop brought the order on a tray that hung from his car window. Ginger remembered the days when they sat in his chromed 52 Chevy Belair eating burgers, drinking malts and listening to the radio. Buddy's was his idea. She hoped it was his attempt to weave a happy strand from their past into the present, if not the future. Was that because of Friday night? She hoped so.

As they passed the road running south to Lake Iosco, it reminded her of carefree summer picnics at Sioux Point before the Ferralls bought it. Back then, they lay on the beach by a small fire, swigged beer she filched from her dad and explored sex. You lived in the moment then, she recalled. That was all that existed at seventeen. You didn't see the pitfalls of adult love—you didn't care. She felt a remnant of that carefree feeling and held it, inviting images of…

"I met with Calvin this morning," he said, interrupting her reverie. "I said I was interested in further investments. It was a trick to find out about Dominion Properties."

"So, how'd it go?" she asked absently, reluctant to leave the memories.

"Better for me than him," he said with a grin. "We got on well while he gave me all the B.S. about the investments. Then I said we ran across Dominion Properties while researching Eliot's obituary and noticed he was a director until 1950. I asked what that was about."

"What did he say?"

"His face froze when I said Dominion—you know, froze like you see in horror flicks. I swear, he got pale and then red in the face. Then he yelled it was none of my business. He called me a rumormonger, a disgrace to dad's memory and all but threw me out. All in all, it went better than I'd hoped."

"Think it's linked to Westar."

"Of course. If he'd said Dominion was a real estate company, a routine business, I might've dropped it. This tells me it's worth digging into."

"*Hmm*." She thought it was interesting but bit her lip while reordering her thoughts. Then she waited a few minutes more. "I ate breakfast at the Streamliner. I'm glad it hasn't changed."

"Best food around."

A sidelong glance revealed he was listening but looking straight ahead. "Daphne stopped by to chat. She had a lot of ideas for articles focused on professional women."

"*Un-huh.*"

"Don't worry, we didn't talk about you." she snapped. He said nothing more, and his silence irked her. That hadn't changed. You're rushing things, she thought and then gazed out the window to salvage as much of the moment's happiness as possible.

Nix and Drawz started the day parked in the alley behind the *Statesman* and watched the Jeep and the Subaru. If either car left, they would follow it and grab the driver outside the city limits. If they were lucky, the targets might leave together in one car. The morning dragged on. By noon, Nix's bowels were in full revolt against last night's chilidog supper. Lowering the car windows to let out the stink wasn't enough. He groaned and wanted the motel toilet and a change of underwear. Plans can never account for something like this, Drawz thought sourly on the drive to the motel. While Nix went inside, he went to the drugstore for some Imodium. Then he walked to Brekke's hardware for the items needed to rig an explosion.

"Here's the plan," Drawz said on their way back to the alley. "The man is easier to take than the woman. We can't touch her unless we get rid of the dog. Killing it will draw suspicion. And I don't like killing dogs."

"That's fine with me, but the boss wants 'em both."

"The man is calling the shots. If we take him out, she'll drop the whole thing."

"Well, whatever you say, Sully. I just follow your orders."

"There's always a chance we can get 'em together, either at his house or in a car. But that depends on luck. His house is isolated. I can make it go up with nothing pointing to us."

Drawz pulled into the alley and noticed the Jeep was gone, but the Subaru remained. He checked his watch. He might be at lunch. An hour passed and the Jeep didn't return. Now Drawz felt sick in his gut. No matter what you do, your project is already fucked beyond repair. And killing the sheriff's brother is a stupid idea. No matter how you do it, it'll be thoroughly investigated. Nix is pragmatic, at least. He would just shoot the targets. But shooting is a last resort. Much better to rig the house for an explosion.

"We can't go to his house 'til we know where he's at," Drawz said, feeling time running out. He returned to the motel, called the *Statesman*, and asked for Boston. While he talked to someone, he jotted notes on a pad. "Okay. That's very helpful. Thank you so much. I'll meet him there. I think we got a break," Drawz said as they left the motel. "They both went to the farm where we caught the kid."

⁂

Ginger's chat with Daphne rankled Boston. Imagining them together made him twitchy. An invasion of his privacy. Daphne was none of her business and vice versa. Since he couldn't do anything about it, he said nothing and let the matter die.

"Did you know Peder worked up a history of St. Ansgar?" he asked as they approached the village. She didn't know, so he told her how the Norwegian settlers set up a cooperative factory that turned clay into drainage tiles. At its peak, the co-op sold tiles throughout the region. The factory closed in the 1950s, then the railroad pulled up steel and the village started dying. "Edmund Ferrall owned the general store from 1913 to 1931."

"I didn't know that either," she said. "It wasn't in Peder's notebook."

"That was a separate assignment. You think it's relevant?"

"At this point, everything seems relevant," she said, happy to see him relaxed again. "Let's keep track of that."

Minutes later, he drove down the long grassy slope and stopped at the stone foundation near the creek. The sky had clouded over, and the humid breeze carried the scent of on-coming rain that added an extra measure of dreariness to the wrecked farmstead.

"I'll hike up the slope and take some pictures while you play in the mud," she cracked. "Then let's go. This place is creepy." She stood by the Jeep as he waded through waist-high grass and goldenrod to the bank of Clay Creek. Then she started up the knoll along a faint trail. She walked backward through the grass and raspberry canes, snapping photos as she went. Then she stumbled and landed on her butt. She gasped at the sight of the knapsack at her feet. Jumping to her feet, she hollered Boston's name at the top of her lungs.

His head popped above the creek's bank, and she held the pack aloft. He clambered out of the creek, sprinting and stumbling through the grass toward her. "I'm too old for this," he gasped, bending over to catch his breath. "Where… where was it?"

"There, in the raspberries. I tripped over it."

He noticed a tremor in his hands as he opened the pack. It held a bottle of water, a notebook, a camera and two rolls of exposed film.

"Peder's. No doubt about it. So, he *was* here," he gasped. Then he swiveled to look around the pasture.

As he did, she saw his expression morph rapidly from surprise to disbelief to something like an aura of revelation. "This is it," he whispered. "I had a dream. Peder was riding a county road but vanished in the dust. Then he showed up in a patch of raspberries and waved to me. Then he appeared in the ravine on his back with his eyes open. Smiling. It's weird. I must've known he was here, somehow. But how?"

"Dreams will tell you what you didn't know you knew. Trust your dreams—and don't think so much."

"I hope his film tells us something."

They followed the faint trail of trampled grass toward the woods. "What do you think happened," she asked when they came to a large patch of flattened grass.

"They killed him here—here—here where no one could see it," he said with a throb in his voice. "They must've followed him from town and showed up while he was here, in the raspberries. His bike would've been by the foundation. That told them he was here—somewhere. I saw their tracks the day Peder vanished. He probably sensed trouble. Likely, he started crawling to the woods and ditched the pack to move faster. This will change the investigation."

The pack's discovery sucked the nostalgic joy from the outing. Boston teetered between exultation and grief. Yes, the investigation can move forward again. Yes, that's important but… then he heard a vehicle on the road beyond the woods. Its sound changed from a steady speed to slowing, followed by silence. He guessed it stopped at the head of the lane. He and Ginger were almost to the Jeep when he heard it drive away.

"Let's go," he snapped, opening the Jeep's door.

"You're jumpy."

"It's late. I think it's going to rain."

"I don't like this place."

"Me neither."

CHAPTER 32

"We're getting close," Boston said as they drove away from the farm. "I can feel it. I read something about a psychic link between wolves and caribou. It sounded kind of woo-woo, but the science is real. I've felt something like it in the last week. It's like I share a psychic current with the killer."

"Oh, and which are you—the predator or the prey?"

"Probably both. But I know how the killer thinks," he said. "And I better start watching my back. And yours, too."

"*Hmm*," she shivered.

They entered St. Ansgar, and it seemed livelier at dusk than in daylight. The lights were on at the café-beer bar attached to the general store, and he noticed a dozen cars and pick-ups parked beside it, including two Blazers. Both looked black, but any dark color would appear black in the twilight. After a quarter mile, Boston decided to go back and get the license numbers. Glancing into the rearview before turning, he saw one of the Blazers was on the road behind him.

Don't panic, he cautioned. It's a local going home; it will take a side road in a mile or two. If not, then… he continued driving toward Featherstone while pondering the psychic link with the killers—if that's what it was. They killed by staging accidents.

After two miles, the Blazer remained a quarter mile behind them. What kind of lethal accidents can you rig in this open countryside, he wondered. The first flicker of fear prickled in his neck. It wasn't fear because he could imagine an accident but because he couldn't. If you can't imagine it, you can't prepare for it.

Ginger rode in silence, surprised he hadn't connected Ferrall's time at the St. Ansgar's general store to their investigation. The elder Ferrall must have known Breuer. Calvin and Eliot probably met him, too. Ferrall must have leased the farm to him. Was it friendships or something else? Maybe Breuer sold him bootleg liquor. And maybe the elder Ferrall sold it to gangsters. It might be significant. Would Calvin and Eliot know that? However, she didn't mention it. She wanted to preserve the remnants of the day's carefree feeling.

"Watch for deer," he said and switched on the headlights. The twilight wasn't yet dark enough for the lights to have real effect. He rolled his shoulders to loosen them. The Blazer remained a quarter mile back. What were "they" up to?

"Are we being followed?"

"I don't know."

She turned to look back. "You think it's—"

"*I don't know.* You look for deer. I'll watch the Blazer." He said it sharper than he intended. "Sorry, I'm edgy."

Darkness fell as Boston turned onto the causeway across the Tatanka River. Beyond the reach of headlights, the road's shoulders plunged into an inky abyss. He slowed as they crossed the bridge and the Blazer caught up until it was nearly on his bumper. If they were the killers, how would they do it? Then he saw the memorial cross on the bridge.

"Hold on," he warned, downshifting to engage the four-wheel drive. They crossed the one-lane bridge, and the Blazer pulled abreast as if to pass. It sideswiped the Jeep. The Wagoneer skidded sideways with a metal-on-metal shriek. Its right wheels slipped off the asphalt. Then it tilted. The Blazer dropped back for another hit, and Boston wrenched the Jeep onto the highway.

"C'mon, c'mon, you son-of-a-bitch," he whispered, waiting for the Blazer to pull abreast. When it did, he swerved into it and accelerated, shoving the pursuers to the causeway's brink before the

Chevy braked and disengaged. The cars left the causeway and raced in tandem on the wider, level road. Boston watched the Blazer pull almost even, saw its passenger window open, saw Nix aim—

"*Deeer*," Ginger screamed as a large buck leaped from the ditch. Boston stood on the brakes. The Blazer passed them and struck the deer. Chevy and corpse pirouetted a quarter turn and stopped. Boston glimpsed the driver staring at the deer's head as he swerved around the wreck and raced up the long hill. Over the crest, he switched off the headlights, took his foot off the gas and downshifted.

"Are you… are you okay?" he gasped as if he had sprinted.

"Well… yeah. I'm okay, but… I feel shaky."

"Me too," he said, noticing the tremor in his hands from the fear he hadn't felt a moment ago. The highway curved from east to southeast at the bottom of the hill, but he turned north onto a gravel road. Then he let the Jeep roll forward through the darkness at fifteen miles per hour.

"Why are we going so slow?"

"I don't want to raise dust. It might show up in the headlights if they follow," he answered in a matching whisper. Then he laughed. "Why are we whispering?" He pulled off the road behind a clump of trees where they could watch the highway half a mile away.

"That poor deer," she said.

"Yeah, it saved our hides."

They listened to their breathing in the dark. Then Ginger felt a flutter in her belly. She giggled. Then giggled again. When she couldn't hold it in, she threw back her head and laughed and laughed until she gasped and giggled and had hiccups.

"You sure showed me a good time," she howled and slugged his arm as another jag of laughter took her breath.

"Let's do it again someti—" but laughter cut off his words. His guffaws triggered hers until they giggled and hooted like children telling potty jokes. They sniggered and snorted until they gasped for breath. Until laughter expelled their fear.

Afterward, in a moment of silence, she knew they had experienced something beyond survival. It's too raw, too primal to understand, she thought. But something profound has happened to us. You and he will never be the same. Your past is dead. This is a reset. Whatever happens, life or death, will happen to both of you. You're living this together. Knowing that, she felt at peace.

"There they are," she said, pointing to the yellow fog lights creeping over the hill. The car moved slowly, as if feeling its way down the slope as carefully as a blind man with a cane. It followed the highway to the southeast and vanished in the darkness. Then they saw its brake lights flash as it stopped, turned around and headed for the intersection with mismatched fog lights.

"Oh, shit," he hissed. "We've got to get farther away." He shifted into gear and drove along the gravel road at the same dawdling speed.

"It's okay," she said, squeezing his arm. "I'm with you. Whatever happens, I'm with you all the way." Hearing herself say it aloud, she recognized it as a commitment. Yes. All the way. You mean it. You mean it with your heart. You mean it to last.

He glanced at her, nodded and turned his attention to the road. His visibility barely exceeded a hundred feet. Only the murky darkness and distance shielded them. As he drove, he recalled the times when he traveled with the Marines in Viet Nam. He had shared their food, their camps and their risks. That was their bond. Now he felt the same with Ginger. Our lives are at risk, and we're like Marines fighting for each other.

"They've turned on this road," she said, looking back. "I think they're going faster than we are. Can we speed up?"

"No. They don't know we're here. Dust will give us away. Sit tight. There's a crossroad ahead. That'll give us three escape routes. They'll have to choose one."

"But they're gaining on us."

"Don't worry." The road curved around a knoll that briefly blocked the line of sight to the Blazer. He glanced at the standing corn verging both sides of the road and made his plan. "Hang on," he said, "we're going to disappear." Then he made an abrupt right turn onto a tractor lane between two cornfields as the Jeep bounced and bucked along the ruts for a quarter mile. He drove it into the corn at the field's far end. They got out. He took her hand, and they walked back toward the road and hid in the corn.

The damp breeze rustled the cornstalks. Ginger shivered, and Boston put his windbreaker over her shoulders. Then he stood behind her and wrapped his arms around her. She crossed her arms over his. Leaning against him, she tried to make sense of the chase, the ramming, the gun and the deer. It happened so fast, but it happened. It didn't just happen to you, she told herself. It happened to *us*. She shivered and drew his arms tighter. "Thank you. I feel warmer."

The Blazer's rattle reached them before the crumpled wreck hobbled into view behind misaligned fog lights. It passed them without headlights and vanished out of earshot. It returned a few minutes later. They heard the men's voices as they passed but couldn't make out the words.

"They'll try again, won't they," she said, certain they would.

"Yeah, but not tonight. They'll have to get a new car. Let's go," he said as a light rain pattered on the corn. They reached the Jeep, damp and cold. He started the engine and turned on the heater while they waited for what felt like a long time before the Chevy got off the road. To be safe, he drove the backroads to Featherstone and the Statesman Building. Ginger got into her car. He followed her home and then pulled into her yard. Getting out of the Jeep in the rain, he drew her to him. They stood in the headlight beams, wrapped in each other's arms, while the rain matted their hair and ran into their eyes. The sound of her breathing comforted him. Neither said anything, but he felt the silence said everything. At least, he hoped it did.

"Thank you—for everything," she said at last.

"Everything?"

"Yeah, everything. Especially today."

"I'll see you tomorrow," he said, giving her a final squeeze and then got into the Jeep.

Ginger's tears of gratitude mingled with the rain. She felt blessed. Something terrible but wonderful just happened—to *us*. She sat on the back porch in wet clothes and watched the Jeep's headlights crawl along the road and up San Juan Hill. She felt tired but not sleepy. Jester nudged her, and she stroked his ears. Then she laughed at herself. We just survived attempted murder, and you were worried about Daphne. *Ha, silly girl.*

CHAPTER 33

Boston felt a prickle along his spine as if every cell in his body carried high voltage. It was painfully clear. Though he didn't have all the answers, what he knew threatened someone. It might be Calvin, though he wasn't certain. If not him, then someone close to him wanted them dead. His wish almost came true tonight, he thought. These killers are creative. They improvised an accident on the spot. What next? Maybe they did it already. He unlocked the front door, stepped aside and then pushed the door open. Nothing happened. He turned on the foyer light and entered. Then let out a breath he didn't know he had been holding. Everything seemed in order except his sense of security. His death had moved a possibility closer to a probability.

He phoned Jack, and Kris answered. His brother was campaigning for the evening. The killers were God-knows-where by now. The highway patrol would catch them if they stayed on the highways, but he doubted they would. If he called the sheriff's office, they would send a deputy to make a report, and Jager was in charge of that unit. Better to keep this to himself until tomorrow. The killers might try again, and he might not be so lucky the next time.

More pieces came together in his sleep. In the morning, while he shaved, he recalled something Daniels said in passing. It was almost a question, and at the time, it seemed odd he said it. Something along the lines of, "How did a St. Ansgar storekeeper earn enough to buy a bank during the Depression?" How *did* Ferrall buy the bank? It was more than an idle question, but it was deniable as an accusation. He rinsed the razor and slapped bracer on his skin. *Ahh.*

His mind felt as if popping with possible but unproven connections. They began with Breuer and ran through the elder Ferrall to Citizen's State Bank to Kaplan to Dominion to Westar to Peder. Eliot and Calvin are the only people who tie all that together, he thought. Did they also have a link to Kid Cann? Daniels hinted that someone backed the elder Ferrall's purchase of the bank.

It was still early, but he phoned Ginger at home, something he had never done at this hour. She answered in an annoyed tone that all but asked, "Do you know what time it is?" He apologized. Then he outlined the idea that was burning inside him. She agreed.

He locked the house after breakfast and inspected the Jeep. The damage to the driver's side was more severe than it appeared in the dark. Jousting had stripped off the trim, sheared off the side mirror and buckled the left front and rear panels. A lot of work for the body shop. He gave the hood an affectionate pat as if it were a dog. Its size, weight and power kept them from plunging into the Tatanka. If anyone asked him, he would say he hit a tree.

Hazel Watkins was talking to a few reporters when he arrived. As the paper's business manager, she was his father's right hand. Now she was Ginger's. The petite, fiftyish, bleach-blond wore pendant earrings, many bracelets and matching cat's-eye glasses. He greeted the staff, took Hazel by the elbow and gently guided her into his office. Then he closed the door.

"What's this about," she asked, somewhere between anger and alarm.

"You're not in trouble," he said. "This is confidential. Did anyone call me yesterday?"

"You had eight or ten calls. Nothing urgent. I knew all the callers but one."

"Did he leave his name?"

"No. But he's interested in your house. He wanted to see you right away. Asked where he could find you. I told him you were in St. Ansgar at the Breuer farm."

"He called," he said. Then he told her.

"Oh-my-God," Hazel gasped and blanched to a paler shade. "I'm sorry," she said over trembling lips.

"Not your fault. But don't mention it. This is about Peder's death. From now on, don't tell anyone where I am. Or Ginger either. Keep this between us until I talk to Jack." He gave her a tissue and then Peder's binder. "Please make a copy right away."

When Ginger arrived, they reviewed their evidence behind his closed door. "We've got stuff Jack doesn't have," he said. "I don't know how he'll react. Or even if he'll use it."

"Let me photograph it," she said. "If he sits on it, the photos will give us leverage."

"I hope it doesn't come to that. If he doesn't use it, I might not forgive him. Before I invite him for coffee, let's figure out how to introduce our loot. It's got to be a sequence of facts. No explanations, no theories. In the right sequence, I think he'll see what we see and reach a conclusion he feels is his."

"Go on," she said, raising her left eyebrow while skewing her mouth to the right.

"First, we show him the evidence that undermines his theory. Then we produce the evidence that suggests a better theory. We'll play good cop-bad cop if we have to. You're the good cop—sweet and reasonable. If he needs a push, I'll be the heavy."

"No, let me be the bad cop," she giggled.

"That's how he's always seen you. You'll play against type. I know sweet and reasonable is a heavy lift for you but—"

"*Ha-ha*, yeah, whatever you say," she snickered. "Let's draw it out. That'll make him more curious. Maybe open his thick—"

"Okay, okay. I know you want to stick it to him, but this isn't a joke. He's proud, scared and defensive. We can't humiliate him. He needs to feel we're on his side. Our lives depend on it. He'll come around if he thinks he's figured it out."

"You're right," she nodded as her grin receded. "I'll behave."

Hazel laid Peder's binder and its duplicate on Boston's table. Then he and Ginger rehearsed the presentation one more time. It felt like a practical joke—except it wasn't. Yet, they giggled.

He picked up the phone. "Hey, good morning, brother. Say, we found something interesting yesterday. We're not sure how it fits, but you might want to look at it. How about coffee at my office? Say, half an hour?"

CHAPTER 34

Jack had given up on good news. Then, Boston's chipper tone stirred his hopes of something like evidence or leads. Anything, as long as it didn't involve Kaplan. He reordered his schedule and entered Boston's office with high expectations. Then he saw Ginger. Looking from one to the other, he thought at once of adolescents who were up to something. Whatever it was, it better be good and not waste his time. He unbuttoned his jacket and took a chair. When Ginger handed him a mug of fresh coffee, he felt certain he was being set up.

"C'mon, guys. Whaddya got? I don't have all day."

"This, for one thing," Boston said as he lifted the nylon pack from under the table. Ginger found it."

"Ho-lee shit! Peder's pack. Where was it?"

"Under some bushes in Breuer's pasture," he said. "It's got a notebook, camera and two rolls of film."

Jack slapped the table. "Damn. Now that *is* something. The deputies said they combed that place. How in the hell did they miss it? Well, I intend to find out."

Then Boston described the path of trampled grass that Peder made as he crawled away.

"That explains the grass stains on his knees," Jack said as he zipped open the pack, looked at the camera and put it back. "We'll develop the film. See what it tells us. Also, the notebook. This is great. Anything else?"

"Yeah, clay." Boston tossed him a plastic bag. "Bet you a bottle of Jameson it matches the stuff on Peder's bike and Ferrall's porch."

"I don't see what it proves." Here we go again, he thought. "That clay could've come from anywhere."

"No," Ginger said. "The Soil Conservation guy says the only deposit is near St. Ansgar."

"Eliot's shoes didn't have any," Boston added. "Neither did Peder's. I'll come back to Peder in a second. There's a witness who says Peder wasn't at Eliot's that day."

"Okay. Peder wasn't at Ferrall's," Jack conceded, unhappy because intuition told him where the discussion was heading. He crossed his arms.

"This is Peder's research," Ginger said and pushed the duplicated binder toward him. "Something in it, something he found, must threaten someone."

He read a page, ran a hand over his curly hair and turned another page. Goddamnit, he's back to Kaplan, he thought. "Interesting stuff, but it doesn't give me a name. If this is your Kaplan theory, I'm not buying it." He waved away the papers.

"We've still got a few more things," Boston interrupted as Jack stood to leave. "Three local witnesses saw the same two strangers in a dark Chevy around Hennessey just before the deaths." Then he recounted his conversations with Daly, Gantz and Strutt. "Strutt didn't see Peder at Eliot's that day, but he saw the Blazer pull in just after noon. Remember the footprints I saw at Breuer's the day Peder vanished?"

"Yeah. You think it was whoever snatched Peder?"

"Exactly. The tracks were in clay. They must have left it on Ferrall's porch. The timing fits when you consider when Peder and Ferrall died."

Jack scowled. "Okay, so they grabbed Peder at Breuer's. Probably killed him there. Easier to handle. That accounts for the bruises on his wrists. Then they dropped him in the ravine to look like an accident. So, you think they went to Ferrall's, and that's when Strutt saw them?"

"It fits the timeline. Here's another piece," Boston said. He played his recording of Gantz. "I don't think he cut those trees. In fact, I'm sure of it. I think you are, too. And he didn't kill Ferrall."

"Okay, I'll buy that," Jack said, still irritated. "But it doesn't look like anyone local is involved. It's still a bunch of suppositions." He waved his arm over the evidence. "I can't be sure it's fact. I've heard enough. I'm gonna do this my way," he huffed as he stood to leave.

"Sit," Boston ordered. "There's more."

He froze as Ginger recapped the contributions to Jager's campaign. "These donors want something from Jager that you're too honest to give," she said.

"Goddamn right. Who are these donors? I'll get to the—"

Boston held up his hand. He recounted the conversation with Ketcham. "See the pattern," he said. "Ketcham and the others aren't particularly astute businessmen. I'm sure they're unwitting players in a money-laundering scheme." He handed Jack a list of the Westar-managed businesses Ketcham mentioned.

"Money-laundering. *Hmm*. Is that why Kaplan was here?" he asked, feeling his temples throb. "No one's going to believe that. I can't do this until after the election."

"We both know Peder's death was intentional. So was Ferrall's," Boston said, trying to hose down his five-alarm anger. If he pooh-poohs you again… he thought, now ready to grab him by the ears. "Both were interested in Kaplan. Someone was afraid of what they knew. Someone Kaplan investigated. Someone here."

"Like who?" Jack growled. He thought his temples were going to explode. "Gimme a name or stop wasting my time. As it is, I won't investigate before the election."

Boston stood and leaned across the table until he and Jack were nose-to-nose. "Damn you, look at the whole picture. Finding and reporting facts is our job—including the inconvenient facts you want to ignore. If you ignore them… if you stick to a theory… one you know is weak… I'll take the evidence we have to Mercer. And that will make news in the *Statesman*, too."

"You son of a bitch," he sputtered, jumping to his feet. He swept the binder, pack and bag of clay into his arms. "I'm impounding this… this evidence."

"Good," Boston said. "We want you to have it. And we want you to use it. We've photographed everything. If you don't use it soon, we won't be silent. You've got a job to do. Don't lose my respect."

Ginger looked from one man to the other, her mouth open in disbelief. The once inseparable brothers were locked in a stony-faced stare-down. My God, she thought, they're really at odds. Boston just put brotherhood on the line. That's incredible. Then the tension broke as suddenly as it started. Jack eased his butt into the chair. Boston exhaled and sat down.

"Here are the last pieces," Boston said and recounted the conversations with Daniels in a calm voice. "All along, he's been nudging me with hints and bits of information. He believed Kaplan was looking for local connections to the Minneapolis mob. He said Kaplan spent more time with Edmund Ferrall than anyone else."

"Well, Emery is a shrewd old bird," Jack said, pulling on his lower lip. "He doesn't gossip but does he know something for sure or is he guessing?" Then he answered his own question. "He knows what goes on out of sight. If it was money laundering, then anyone involved would certainly kill to protect it. But Calvin?" Jack shook his head. "Calvin."

"Then there's this piece," Boston said.

Jack felt his eyes bug out as Boston recounted the run-in on the Tatanka causeway. He felt the words as if they were body blows from a Vikings lineman. "Jesus," he cried. "Now I see it. I see it. It sounds so far-fetched, but it makes sense. Calvin hired killers who staged accidents that don't raise suspicion." He rubbed his hands together and grinned. "Now we have a motive and a suspect. If it's money laundering, then it's certainly more than a local crime."

"Well, there you are," Boston said. "That's all we have for you."

"That's all?" Jack laughed from his belly. "That's all… *ha-ha-ha*! You have made my day, my week, my month. Thanks. Both of you." As he stood to leave, he felt as if he had just shed thirty pounds.

"Take the Jeep to the courthouse. We'll comb it for evidence." Then, gathering the clay, the pack and the binder in his arms, he waltzed to the stairway giving silent thanks for the brother who had his back.

As he vanished down the stairs, Boston and Ginger turned to each other and gave themselves high-fives.

"That was a gutsy bluff—threatening to give Mercer the evidence," she said.

"I wasn't bluffing."

"Whaaat?" Her eyebrows shot up. "Man, I underestimated you."

"I didn't want to do it. Thank God he came around." He met her eyes and smiled.

"I better get to work," she said. "You too, rookie," and nudged him.

Boston settled behind his desk. With Jack squared away, he felt certain the case would end soon. For the first time in weeks, he thought of returning to Chicago. You've dreamed of this day, the news of your promotion, the congratulations and then… why doesn't that excite you now? But you have to do it. Braydon nominated you. He delayed his retirement so you could stay. And you promised to return. The job you always wanted is waiting. Is this what you want?

He put off the question. The case wasn't over yet. Late that afternoon, he walked to the courthouse and picked up the Jeep. It was already twilight when he pulled onto the main street. Two blocks farther and he pulled over for a patrol unit with flashing red-blue lights. The cruiser stopped behind him, and an officer approached. From the silhouette, he knew it wasn't Jack. He must have forgotten something at the courthouse and rolled down the window.

"Your taillight is out," Jager barked, not as a favor but as an infraction.

"Thanks. I know. I'm taking it to the body shop."

"I want your license and insurance."

Annoyed, Boston handed over the documents.

"Out of the car, now!"

"What's this about?"

"I'll decide that," Jager said. In a swift, well-practiced move, he grabbed Boston's arm, spun him around and cuffed his wrists behind him. Then he slammed him against the Jeep. "It's time you give officers the respect they're due," he said, his voice low and cold. Then he lifted Boston's wrists until he gasped in pain.

Pressed against the Jeep with his head turned toward the cruiser, he saw a car stop behind it. Ginger got out. He heard the click of heels as she walked toward them. Jager must have heard them because he quickly released the cuffs.

"That's all there is to it," he said crisply. "Thanks for asking how it's done."

"Let me do you a favor in return," Boston said, rubbing his wrists as Ginger stood nearby. "I tracked down rumors connected to a Minneapolis PD internal investigation," he said. "Your name came up in excessive use of force—"

"Watch it," Jager snarled as he stumbled backward.

"A Minneapolis newspaper contact sent me a file. It includes memos and interviews. Naturally, I'll call you for comment before we run a story."

"You watch it," Jager growled as he regained his balance. "You'll be hearing from me," he said over his shoulder as he returned to the car.

"What's with the handcuffs," Ginger asked. "Nothing kinky, I hope."

"It's not what you think," he laughed. "Intimidation. Jager's desperate. Now he knows I've got a file on the internal investigation. I let him think we might run a story."

"Clever of you," she said with an appraising smile. "You're even more ruthless than I thought. Now that your thumb is on the scale—keep it there." Then she walked to her car.

CHAPTER 35

Daphne wondered if it was time to come clean with Boston. It wasn't what she knew that bothered her as much as what might happen after she told him. It meant naming names. Though the names might help the investigation, her life could be difficult if people knew she was the source. Telling him would be a relief. Maybe then she would feel cleaner than if she continued listening to the rumors in silence.

She called his office and invited him to lunch at her house. He accepted though she thought he sounded preoccupied. For the rest of the morning, she tried to distract herself by checking employee time cards, paying monthly bills and writing a want-ad seeking part-time kitchen staff. Even that wasn't enough to keep her mind off what she needed to tell him. The investigation has come between us, she thought. It's not like him to say anything, but you feel the change. Maybe he thinks things are fine. Women usually pick up on changes before men do… if they do. His obsession with Peder is like an odor. You've got to clear the air.

She left Chiara in charge, went home and slapped together a salad with some sandwiches. As she worked, she twitched at the smallest sounds. Her anxiety felt a second skin. It's all in your head, she told herself, but that didn't work. Everything isn't okay anymore.

Boston arrived in body, but she knew instantly that the most important part of him wasn't with her. His soul was somewhere else. Worse, she knew it wouldn't return anytime soon—if ever. He gave off tension the way a cast-iron stove radiated heat. He seemed preoccupied and said little over lunch.

"I heard about your accident," she said to draw him out of his cone of silence.

"Yeah. It involved another car and a deer."

"I worry about you," she said softly. "I don't know what I'd do if…" but she checked herself. They said no commitments. Neither ate much. She picked at the salad; he nibbled on a sandwich. They made fleeting eye contact, but he invariably looked away. Our relations have changed, she told herself. If they haven't, they will once you tell him.

"Let's sit on the couch," she said, taking his hand. "There's something I've been keeping from you. It's about the Ferralls."

"The Ferralls?"

She seated herself to look at him and drew a breath. "Eliot was my father."

"Your father," he gulped. "Your father. I'm sorry. I had no idea."

"Chiara knows… you and she… you're the only ones," she said in small gusts of breath. "I had to tell you. All day I hear trash talk about him. It's driving me crazy. I guess Dora, Calvin and Nelson are my closest relatives. How weird is that?" She made a grotesque face. "Mom told me just before she died. Chiara knows everything."

"I'm sorry for your losses," he said. "And in so many ways."

"I feel better telling you. It's bitter-sweet. We weren't close like fathers and daughters are. He was thoughtful and loyal but not what you'd call affectionate. I missed that. But he looked after me from a distance. He paid for my college, helped me finance this house and upgrade the Streamliner. We met a few times a year in Rochester or Winona or in Wisconsin." She wiped away a tear.

"I'm glad you told me. Thank you," he said, and his arm drew her to him. "You know, I got suspicious when you referred to him as Mister Ferrall."

"Oh, you noticed that. It was hard to mourn him and keep the secret after his death. There's more I need to tell you." She said the elder Ferrall got the Streamliner through foreclosure. He gave it to Eliot after the war, but he didn't want it and hired a woman to run it. Meanwhile, he fell in love with Emma. Their affair was a secret, but her pregnancy became the scandal of 1949. It happened just as he bought the farm. Eliot directed the woman to train Emma in the restaurant business before Daphne's birth. Two years later, he sold her the Streamliner for a dollar.

"That clears up a lot," he said. "When you told me about life as a love child, I took it as candor. Later, I realized you skipped over how your mom got the restaurant. You told me the salacious stuff as a distraction." He smiled and put his finger under her chin.

"Oh. You noticed that, too," she laughed. "Eliot—I always called him that—he worried his father would make trouble for mom. That's why my paternity was a secret." Daphne wiped a tear and smeared some mascara. "You know about the Kaplan rumor, of course."

"Why didn't they marry?"

"Eliot knew his father and Calvin were involved in something illegal. He expected to end up in prison with them. He didn't want my mom and me to bear that, too. That was their secret." Daphne went to the bedroom and returned with a manila packet. "This came by courier last week. Will you give it to Jack and keep my name out of it?"

He turned the packet in his hands. The return address was a Rochester law firm. The notarized cover memo inside it described the documents sealed inside another envelope marked, "To be opened after my death."

"I've read the cover memo," she said. "I'm shocked."

"Why didn't you give it to Jack?"

"It's evidence against a relative. He's powerful, mean and has lots of friends," she said, sitting erect. "Who are people going to believe—me or Calvin? In case you missed it, bad news messengers don't live long. Folks will hate me if my name is connected to it. I know this is connected to your investigation. So, now you know the truth."

As he read the memo, his excitement became something approaching joy, even triumph. "This is incredible," he gushed, "just incredible. With this evidence, I think Jack can make arrests. Thank you for trusting me. I'll see that he keeps your name out of it." He started to rise, but she pulled him back onto the sofa.

"Wait. There's something more," she said, looking into his eyes. "We've always been honest with each other… well, mostly honest."

"Yeah, we have. That's something I admire about you."

She smiled though it hurt. This will hurt you more after you say it, she thought. You hoped to avoid this conversation, but it's not possible. Partial honesty isn't honesty. She sat up straight. "It's time to end our affair. I can tell it's already over for you, but you're too kind to break it off."

"What are you saying?"

"Ginger has your heart."

"No, that's not—"

"Oh, for Pete's sake!" She rolled her eyes in disbelief. "I knew this moment would come. I knew it a week after you hired her. What took you so long to figure it out? When I sat with her the other day, I sensed she was very uncomfortable. She loves you, you know."

"How do you know?

"Trust me, I know," she said, putting her hand over his. "We've had lots of fun, though. Great evenings and unforgettable desserts. I'll miss them. You are a gentle lover. But your heart hasn't been in it since Peder died. I know it's not because of me. You're over the divorce. You're in a new place." She put a finger on his chin, leaned forward and kissed him. "I'm glad I was here for you, but you've moved on, even if you don't realize it."

His shoulders sagged as he sighed. "I'm sorry that—"

"Don't. I'm not hurt. Not angry. We gave each other what we could. I was willing to take the risk. I am who I am. We'd be miserable if you pretended or tried to change for me."

How she knew that, he hadn't a clue, but he knew she was right. They stood in her doorway for a moment. Then he bent down and kissed her softly on the cheek. "Thank you. You're a rare and honest friend. I'll never forget you."

She watched him walk away. For the first time, she ended an affair with regret. Living life without a commitment didn't feel as liberating as it used to. You wanted him when you were a sixth grader, but he had Ginger. You had him for the summer; now Ginger has him again. She sniffled, wiped her cheek and closed the door.

CHAPTER 36

Boston walked to the rental car feeling both elation and sadness. She ended the affair and let you off the hook, he thought. How do you repay a kindness like that? Even if the affair was her idea, you all but abandoned her after you started the investigation—with Ginger. She was unselfish to end it without guilt or drama. He got behind the wheel. You're a cad, he thought.

Then he sat in the car and read the cover memo again. If the sealed packet held what Jack needed, he hoped the pages confirmed the evidence he had gathered. Then there would be justice for Peder and Eliot. It seemed Kaplan was probably investigating Edmund or Calvin for links to the Minneapolis underworld. What a break. He thought of sharing the news with Ginger. She would be irked if he bypassed her. However, he promised Daphne to keep her name out of it. He returned to the *Statesman* and was pleased that Ginger had left for the day.

He called Jack and then walked to the courthouse with the packet. He felt as excited as a bird-dog on the opening day of hunting.

"This is for you," Jack said with gusto before Boston could give him the packet. It was a gift box of Jameson whiskey. "The clay tested out. Identical to stuff on Ferrall's porch and the bike. Peder's film had artsy photos of the school, some distant shots of a dark Blazer and two men. They match your description. Now, what else ya got?"

Jack's eagerness cheered him. He sounded like his old self, the confident captain of a winning team. "Daphne just told me Eliot was her father."

"Ho-lee shit!" he gasped, eyes wide open. "No kidding?"

"No kidding. She gave me this." He passed him the packet. "She and I read the cover memo, but the rest is sealed. Figured you'd want it that way."

"Wow, wow," he said, shaking his head and pulling on his lower lip. "The cover memo alone is a gold mine. My God, Calvin and his old man were behind this. Hard to believe. I never would've guessed." He stared at the memo. "All these years, he and his old man laundered money for the mob. Had a hand in Kaplan's murder. Jesus—it fits." He emitted grunts of satisfaction as he read the memo again.

"Keep Daphne's name out of it, will you? She's scared of the Ferralls."

"Of course. By the way, we found Calvin and Nelson are silent partners tied to Westar."

"I'm not surprised now. But Calvin covered his tracks. What about Nelson?"

"I don't know. If these documents bear out, he's at least on the hook for money laundering. Beyond that… But this," and he slapped the cover memo with the back of his hand. "This is a map to several crimes. Mercer and the grand jury will have a Thanksgiving feast. I'll hold a press conference tomorrow. So, give me good coverage. Let's see who calls the tip line."

"You look and sound like your old self," Boston said.

"I feel it, thanks to you. I owe you big time."

"No, you owe Ginger and Daphne big time."

Ginger and Boston stood together in the courthouse rotunda during Jack's press conference. When he stepped to the rostrum, she realized he was a naturally good-looking man and even more so in his uniform. He's not really the big lug who got between you and Boston that you thought he was. You were wrong to think so.

"Good morning," he began, speaking without notes. "Significant new information has come to light in the deaths of Eliot Ferrall and Peder Norgaard. We now know both were murdered in connection with their interest in detective Kaplan. This is a complex case. It involves several individuals living within and outside the county." He paused when the rotunda erupted in a buzz of murmurs. Then he resumed, saying it was a complex crime and the investigation would involve other state and federal agencies. After he finished speaking, he deflected all questions about the suspects and promised an update in a few days as the investigation progressed. After that, the small scrum of reporters broke up to file reports.

Ginger gave Boston a side-long glance. Yes, he has changed, she thought. You know it in your heart. He's not the man who interviewed you. In two months, he's shed the aloofness, big ego and self-centered ambition that you've hated. He's risked his career for Peder and Jack. Maybe now he'll find peace, if not redemption.

But what does it mean going forward? He'll leave for Chicago as soon as the case is closed, she thought as they walked toward the office. That will be in a couple of weeks or maybe a few days. You don't want him to go, do you? Not now. Not when you've turned to a new page. You've known your feelings for him ever since the Tatanka. Does he feel it? He hasn't said how he feels. As they walked, she felt his fingers lightly touching hers. On this sunny October morning, with the air as crisp as a McIntosh apple, life seemed too short not to stretch the moment as long as possible.

"I'm surprised he hasn't made an arrest," she said, firmly lacing her fingers with his. "He's got suspects. Is this part of his re-election plan, like a TV teaser?"

"No. Self-protection. Miz Mercer wants all the 'eyes' dotted and 'tees' crossed before she indicts anyone. She and the grand jury must be feasting on the evidence. The charges will be icing on the cake. Our coverage will keep the county in thrall. It'll be like Watergate."

"But will people believe Calvin is behind it?"

"I think Jack's holding off—he's revealing a little at a time so people can digest the idea. That will make a conviction more likely."

"When it happens, it's because of you," she said, squeezing his hand and holding it tight. "Let's take a turn around the Green," she said. "I'm not ready to let go of you yet."

"Yeah, let's," he said. They took their time sauntering around the park while holding hands. He suggested expanding the press conference story to include a recap of everything known about the deaths. That might help prepare the public for what lay ahead.

"That's okay with me," she said with a wry smile. "Just remember, I still get the last word." Then she elbowed him. "You—get to work."

FERRALL-NORGAARD DEATHS LINKED TO KAPLAN MURDER appeared in the next morning's edition. In it, Boston drew parallels between the detective's murder and those of Peder and Ferrall. COLD CASE LINKED TO ALTON COUNTY CRIME the next day covered Kaplan's investigation of the Minneapolis mob. A flurry of phone calls followed each story. Letters to the editor were generally positive with a few anonymous threats. He read them carefully, parsing the phrases for the identity of their authors.

The stories stirred the city. Corey Luedtke collared Boston as he entered Rexall Drug. "There ain't no gangsters around here," he said. "This ain't Chicago, ya know."

"I'm as surprised as you are, Corey. As far as I know, it's all true."

"I dunno," Luedtke said as he walked away. "Pretty far-fetched, you ask me, though."

"You," Heistad bellowed as Boston left the drugstore. "Primus isn't locating here. It's because of your witch hunt over Kaplan. All the same, Jack's going down."

He looked Heistad in the eye. "Arne, you're a hypocrite. According to state campaign reports, you gave Jack twenty bucks and Jager a hundred."

"So?"

"It's public information. I think readers will be interested in the way their civic leaders play both sides," he said, enjoying Heistad's discomfort. "All I have to do is report it." Then he walked away. Damn, that felt good.

Later that afternoon, he took a phone call and recognized the gruff voice. "Excellent reporting, excellent," Daniels said and then cleared his throat. "You and the sheriff are on the right track. Keep going." Then he hung up.

CHAPTER 37

Nelson believed good luck had always stuck to him like his mustache. He took over the bank at thirty, built a house by the golf course and bought a condo in the Virgin Islands. With his salary and a baby on the way, he had the whole package. Lucky. No other word for it. This morning, like every other, he checked his tie in the front hall mirror and brushed the mustache with his fingers. He called the 'stache his "babe magnet." In eight years of marriage, Karen had never seen him with a clean upper lip. She put his hand on her belly to feel their baby move. He smiled and then turned to look in the mirror one last time. Once the baby came, he hoped Karen could restore her figure and continue giving him what he expected of a wife. Most of all, he hoped she would stop complaining.

"You won't travel anymore, will you?" she begged. "I need you here in case—"

"I'm not going anywhere," he said, thinking of the pert Iowa cashier he often saw in a town only an hour away. "Well, bye honey. See ya later." Then he was out the door.

The lucky feeling had waned since the sheriff's press conference. Lately, it seemed everyone in town, even his fellow Chamber leaders, spoke cautiously and indirectly. They were careful who they talked to. All because of Meade's crusade, he thought. Nelson parked behind the bank, picked up copies of the *Statesman* and the *Wall Street Journal* and walked to the Streamliner. Fortunately, some things hadn't changed. Like Daphne. He sat in a booth and fantasized about a night with her as he pretended to read the paper. My God, he thought, stroking his crotch. She's built like an amusement park with great rides. And she owes you a favor, too. Once Meade is gone—

"Good morning, Nelson. Coffee?" Chiara asked, quashing his erotic daydream. "So, how's Karen doing? She's about due now, isn't she?"

"Oh yeah, any day now," he said, disappointed that Chiara waited on him. He folded the *Journal* and picked up the *Statesman*. ARRESTS EXPECTED SOON led today's issue. *Arrests?* The word made him sick to his stomach.

"You look pale," Chiara said as she set down his coffee and Danish. "Are you alright?"

"Just heartburn," he said. "I'm alright." After a couple sips of coffee and a bite of Danish, he slipped a five spot under the saucer and left. Calm down and think, he told himself as he scurried to the bank. You've got a plan for this.

The bank didn't open for business until 9:00 a.m. Its lobby and offices were still empty. He locked his office door behind him though it felt stuffy, and his shirt was damp under the arms. Then he speed-dialed and heard the call ring three times before anyone answered. "Have you seen today's *Statesman*?" he squeaked. He wiped his face as he listened. "We need to get out of here. Now. I'll pick you up. Okay? We'll be there by tomorrow." He chewed his mustache as he listened. "You're staying? Why? What do you mean, stick it out? I won't." He slammed down the phone. "I knew it … I knew it," he blubbered, feeling exposed as if Meade had already printed his name.

He called Karen and said something had just come up. He would be gone overnight. "Now, don't worry, honey. Call my mom if you need anything. Love ya, babe," he said as he put his "just in case" plan into motion. He made it a week after he became president and learned in detail what kind of business the bank was doing. Calvin told him a coffin was the only way out. Well, you're not waiting for that, he thought as he removed a leather briefcase from his personal safe. It was already packed with cash in large bills, four passports—

each with a different name—and two clean shirts. After several phone calls, he transferred funds from his accounts in a Florida bank to one in Panama.

It was only 8:15 by his watch. If you leave now, he thought, you can catch a noon flight out of Minneapolis and be in Argentina by midnight. He took a last look around. The phone rang and he jumped. After a moment's hesitation, he answered. A friend. While they talked, he said, "*uh-huh, uh-huh,*" and scribbled on a pad. "Okay. Thanks, I owe you," he said. "I'll wire the rest in a couple days." Then he hung up, grabbed the briefcase and left.

Dora ignored the ringing phone while she made her breakfast—orange juice with vodka. No one called her at this hour. Calvin picked it up. She half-listened to his side of the conversation. It was as cryptic as usual. She rarely knew who he was talking to or what it was about. He had stopped telling her long ago.

"Who was that?"

"Nelson."

"Oh. Something about Karen?"

"No. He wants me to go to a meeting in Minneapolis. I am staying here."

Dora glanced at Calvin. He seemed more and more a stranger than her husband for thirty-five years. His brown hair had grayed over the summer. The creases from the nostrils were deeper. His tailored suits seemed too large. She thought he had aged years in only three months.

"Have you seen today's paper?" she asked and took it off the kitchen table. "The sheriff is going to make some arrests."

"I saw it. It's nothing. Meade is turning Kaplan into gold. It sells papers," he snorted. "That and prop up his brother's campaign."

"Oh, yes, dear," she said and strode across the kitchen, holding the drink and the paper. "You know there's more to this, don't you? Don't you?" She shook the paper in his face. In her belly, she knew he was implicated, somehow. And if he is, what does it mean for you?

"Shut up," he bellowed. "*Shut up*." His backhand made her head snap. The tumbler of juice flew from her hand and shattered on the tile floor. "Fix yourself another," he snarled on his way down the corridor to his home office.

Dora propped herself against the counter. She put a hand to her cheek where the skin felt hot. He was sometimes cold and distant but had never hit her. Never. Why did he do that? He's not the man you married, she thought. Deep in her belly, she knew the truth. Their union is, was, and had been one of habit or convenience or symbiosis more than love. You must look out for yourself now, she told herself as she swept up the broken glass.

CHAPTER 38

Boston hung up the phone feeling the end was near. He slipped into his jacket, paused at Ginger's door and said he was joining Jack to serve papers on the Ferralls.

"Are you asking for permission," she asked with a laugh.

"Well, you said I worked for you."

"Go have fun with your brother—and take good notes."

Thomas, Kasson and Mercer were waiting for him in Jack's office when he arrived. Mercer stood at the window, hands behind her back, gazing at Citizen's State Bank. Boston thought of Napoleon in skirts sizing up the enemy.

"We're serving search warrants on Nelson and Calvin," Jack said, slapping them against his large palm. "We'll bring them here for questioning."

"Why don't you arrest them?" Boston interjected. "You've got all the proof you need,"

"Not yet," Mercer said, still gazing out the window. "There's evidence against Calvin."

"Why not arrest him now?"

"He's a local player in a bigger game. We want his higher-ups too."

"Oh, and Calvin talks in return for a deal?" He bit his tongue, feeling his temper slipping its leash. Don't blow it; it's too important, he thought.

"Hold on," Mercer ordered and then laid into him like a sergeant flaying a recruit. "For your information, I've got grand jury indictments." She listed first- and second-degree murder, conspiracy to commit murder, racketeering, money laundering and a few other things. Even if she pled down a charge or two, Calvin and Nelson would get more than a slap. "You satisfied?"

Before he could answer, Jack cleared his throat. "You are here as a reporter. And only that. I know you have strong feelings. We all do. But… you will keep your mouth shut," he ordered in the voice of a sheriff and not of a brother. "Is that clear?"

"Whatever you say," he said, embarrassed at this verbal spanking in front of the others. The walk to the bank seemed dream-like. Despite all the evidence, it seemed beyond credence that a city benefactor had committed murder to cover a money-laundering operation for the mob, an operation that had suckered many in the city as his unwitting accomplices.

Jack told the bank's receptionist he wanted to see Nelson. In her practiced courtesy, she said he had gone to Iowa. "Shall I make an appointment for tomorrow?"

"No, thanks. I'll catch him later. Meanwhile, these deputies will execute a search warrant. Please call whoever is now in charge," he ordered.

The receptionist lost her composure, wiped her eyes and then picked up the phone. Jack and the others huddled in the lobby out of earshot. Thomas left them to alert the highway patrol and airport security in Minneapolis, Des Moines, Chicago and other places. Boston followed Jack up the stairs to Calvin's office. His assistant said he was at home, ill. Jack handed her the search warrant and ordered the deputies to secure the records. He also ordered her not to call Calvin.

"Let's make a house call," Jack said on the way to the lobby. "I've always gone by the book on arrests," he said as they got into the Suburban. "This has to be better than that. They're civic leaders. When the shit hits the fan—and it will—I don't want it on me because of sloppy procedures." He was silent for a moment. "Nelson is Jager's campaign manager. You don't suppose the charges will reflect badly on him, do you?" His teeth glowed in his grin.

Deputy Larson and two other officers waited for them at the end of Calvin's driveway. Jack sent the deputies around the house and then rang the bell. He tapped the warrant against his wrist while he waited.

"Good morning, Sheriff," Dora said in a husky voice. "Come in. What may I do for you?"

"I want to see Calvin," he said. Then he saw the red welt on her cheek. You better ask her about it, he thought. Ask after you serve the warrant.

"I don't think he's expecting you," she said and led them down the corridor.

"I'll only be a minute."

"Who is it? I do not want to be bothered."

Jack stepped into the home office. Its décor matched the other rooms. Calvin sat hunched at his desk. The paper shredder beside him churned out confetti that overflowed the wastebasket.

"I am busy. What do you want?"

Jack extended the warrant in its blue wrapper. "Calvin Ferrall," he said in his official tone of voice, "I have a warrant to search your house, your car and your office. Please come with us. We want to ask you some questions."

"Question me? Not at the courthouse. I will not do that."

"You will," he said. Then he reminded him of his right to remain silent. "Deputy, cuff Mister Ferrall if he refuses to cooperate."

Calvin yelled at Dora to call his attorney as the deputy hustled him out the door.

"There, done by the book," Jack said. "Now for the hard part."

"What's that?"

"Convicting the son of a bitch."

Glenda Mercer had a courtroom reputation for a gruff, I've-seen-this-movie-before demeanor. When she read through Eliot Ferrall's documents, she felt gob-smacked at the men and the crimes she was about to prosecute. It was a gold mine of facts and connections that allowed the grand jury to bring a formal case against the Ferralls—

father and son. The law is a cruel mistress, and she was grateful it could still surprise her. You're not as jaded as you feared, she told herself.

Calvin and his attorney waited in the courthouse basement's interrogation room. Its fluorescent lights, stone walls and folding metal chairs seemed designed for discomfort to prevent suspects from dragging out the interrogations. Kasson peered at them through one-way glass like a baker checking cookies in an oven. She waited until Calvin fidgeted.

Will he say anything you don't already know? she wondered as she entered. Or will he stonewall? Either way, you have enough evidence to convict him. Kasson introduced herself, and her first questions went over basic, non-incriminating facts. Did you grow up St. Ansgar? Did your father buy the bank in 1932? Were you president of the bank before Nelson? The first hour went as she expected. It wasn't tedious because she listened for evasions that suggested lies. As her questioning focused on the here and now, Calvin said he didn't clearly recollect certain dates and events. He denied knowing Kaplan or anything about money laundering. He was no longer involved in banking, but Nelson might know something useful. As she probed deeper into the business, he relied more on his attorney. Then the interrogation ended.

"Learn anything new?" Mercer asked when Kasson briefed her and Jack.

"He admitted to being a silent partner trying to help struggling business owners. He didn't know anything about money laundering. That's something he thought Nelson could explain. Nelson has left town."

"Then what do we have?" Mercer asked in a sharp voice.

"I doubt we'll learn anything more until he's in a cell," Kasson said. "Maybe then he'll cooperate in hopes of a deal. If we catch Nelson, he might cooperate when he understands he's been set up to take the fall."

"I think we have solid evidence for a conviction," Mercer said. "We can prove the Ferralls were silent partners of businesses managed by Westar. The Feds already have their eye on Westar for drug-related money laundering in several small cities. I won't charge the local businesses. They seem unaware of being conduits for laundering mob funds through the bank.

"It's your show now, Glenda," Jack said. "What next?"

"Post deputies close by his house so he can't leave town. I'll get the arrest warrants," she said. Her phone rang. She answered it and handed the receiver to Jack. "It's for you, Sheriff."

He listened and nodded. "Thanks for your help," he said. "We'll send a car." He turned to Mercer with a grin. "The Dakota County sheriff has Nelson in custody."

Nelson waited alone in the courthouse interrogation room. He felt afraid and embarrassed and wondered what went wrong. The getaway plan was simple. Keep the briefcase packed with money and passports, tell the receptionist you're going to Iowa—he went often—and fly out of Minneapolis to a smaller airport like Chicago-Midway. From there, fly to Miami for a Pan Am flight to Buenos Aires or Montevideo. With the passports and cash, you can create a new identity and avoid extradition. Karen and the baby can follow later. It was smooth sailing. You could see the airport, and then the state trooper pulled you over at the Mendota Bridge.

"Wha-wha-what's going on?" he stuttered as Jack entered with Kasson behind him. "Why am I here?" His voice pitched higher than usual. He quivered like a rabbit facing a coyote. Then he wiped his mustache and flashed his best salesman's smile as if to say, "c'mon, you know me, give me a break."

"Why so much cash and so many passports?" Jack asked. "The secretary said you went to Iowa. What happened? Make a wrong turn?" He smiled without friendliness.

"Iowa? No, that's next week."

"Cut the bullshit, Nelson. We know the whole story, so work with us."

"I don't know anything. Honest."

"Your uncle Eliot gave us all ten yards," Jack said. Then he said they could prove Edmund bought liquor from Breuer, sold it to Kid Cann and the mob helped him buy the bank as part of their operation. His father arranged to hide Kaplan's body in Breuer's farmhouse. The bank had been laundering mob money for nearly fifty years, and his father invested it. "We also know you hired hit men to take out your uncle, Peder Norgaard and Boston Meade."

"No. Never, I swear," he cried as his mustache fluttered. "I don't know anything. I don't." Nelson felt his stomach heave as if he was about to throw up.

"Your old man says you're the one to ask about money laundering."

"He wouldn't—he's my father."

"You don't know your old man. You're expendable."

"You're just saying that because… because I'm backing Dwayne. It's payback."

Jack grinned. "When you go to prison at Oak Park Heights," he said in a satin voice, "You can forget parole. No golf. No nooky on the side. It'll be hard time. That's for the state crimes. There're Federal charges, too. So, a good-looking guy like you will be quite a catch for some of the harder cases in Federal prison."

"I want a lawyer," Nelson said and shivered. Wait a sec, he thought. You might still have a way out. Jager's sure to win next week's election. My lawyer can stall the case until he takes office. He can muddle the evidence. Then Mercer will drop the unwinnable case. Maybe you can throw Jack a bone now, something minor that looks like cooperation. Get released.

"Here's what I know, but it's not much," he said. He said Kaplan met his grandfather. He was following up on some marked bills the Barker gang stole. The money went through the bank without their knowledge. That was all he knew about money laundering. "Honest."

"I thought I knew you," Jack said and leaned into Nelson while the banker leaned as far back as he could. "You're lying, you little prick. I'm not talking about the thirties or the Barkers. I'm talking about today—*today*. You're in it. You and your old man."

Nelson shrank in the chair. Lies and charm aren't working, he realized. There's nothing to stop you from going under. If you do, so will everything you love—the bank presidency, money, political influence, Karen and the perky Iowa cashier. What are your options? Maybe a plea deal. Yeah, maybe a plea in return for testimony. A few months in jail and then probation and community service.

"It's not my fault," he whined. "Father forced me into it. I didn't have a choice."

Jack waved in two deputies. "Let him call his lawyer. Then take him to a cell."

CHAPTER 39

Boston hummed as he smashed the garlic, shelled the shrimp and set the balsamic rice on the burner. Preparing this meal pleased him because Ginger was going to share it. He enjoyed cooking when he was married, but after Vicky left him, it reminded him of spousal failure. This was different. He knew Ginger appreciated a candlelight dinner with sparkling cider. Tonight, if all went well, they might talk about a future—if there was to be one.

Ginger burst into the house without knocking. He met her gaze and held it, transfixed by the teased hair, bold lipstick and more eye shadow than she used at the office. He saw that her clothes were tight in all the right places.

"*Bienvenu a chez Meade*," he said in his limited French. "Come," he said, taking her hand and leading her to the great room, where a fire blazed in the hearth, and sparkling cider cooled in an ice bucket next to a plate of brie and crackers. "For you."

"*Por moi? C'est beau. Merci*," she said, squeezing his hand.

They sat close together on the couch with glasses of cider. He asked about Mama and her reaction to the new quarters at Franciscan Villas.

"She loves it. I even saw her smile. The place is teeming with nuns," she said and laughed with real joy. "Mama may never speak to me," she said, "but I accept that. And she may never forgive me, either, but I can forgive myself. Seeing to her comfort is my part of the reconciliation. I'll leave her end of it to God. Now—tell me about the warrants," she demanded, bouncing with excitement.

He recounted the verbal spanking from Jack and Mercer, and she threw back her head and laughed. Her effervescent mirth assured him their chemistry was real. What had been leaden was now golden. He guessed that last week's blow-up set off an emotional chain reaction that climaxed on the Tatanka causeway. She's not the cunning girl you dumped years ago, he thought. And you're no longer the man you were in June. You can talk of a future.

He led her to the dining room table. "Oh my God. You did this for me?" she cried in surprise and then *ooh*-ed and *ahh*-ed at the setting of good linen, China, flatware and crystal. When he brought out the entrees, she gushed over the fact he liked to cook and cooked well. Dinner went as he hoped, seasoned with smiles and coy glances in her amber eyes.

"I'm thinking about the future, if there is one," he said. "Before we talk about that, I need to clear up a couple things." He laid his fork and knife on the plate. "The divorce, Dad's death and Peder's murder have changed my priorities. The high-profile life I lived in Chicago doesn't excite me now."

"Really, how's that?" she asked in surprise, resting her chin on folded hands.

"I used to compare myself to dad because it felt like I was supposed to be like him—be as good as he was. Except I didn't feel I was. So, I faked it. That's the person you knew. When I left for college, I didn't know who I was or where I belonged, except it wasn't here. After a couple promotions at the *Outlook,* I still felt pressed to prove my ability. I don't feel that pressure now. Not here."

She lifted her chin from her hands and smiled. "Thank you for telling me."

He swallowed and readied himself to tell her a harder truth. "Years ago… when we… well, I left you because you planned my life. I was to take over the paper, we'd have money, status and a lot of kids in this house." He paused, looking for a sign of disagreement. "I suppose it looked ideal to you. Honestly, it looked like suffocation to me. Always a prisoner of dad's fame… prisoner of others' expectations. You're forceful when you want something… you don't like 'no' as an answer. Your dream was my nightmare." He paused for a moment. "After I hired you, I realized I was still afraid to tell you 'no' and make it stick."

She sipped cider, pursed her lips and drew a breath. "Well, you're right. Marrying you would've been a dream come true. After that first year at Columbia… you were so full of yourself. I hated you for it, but I couldn't let you go." She paused. "I wanted to get away from Mama. Marriage was the way out. I'd be a Meade and not a drunken switchman's daughter. Mama thought she'd be somebody, too. Then you said…" She drew a breath that caught in her throat. "Then you sneered at marriage. You crushed my dreams… so I slugged you."

Her confession filled his belly with butterflies. Not from the words as much as her grit in saying them. My God, fearless honesty. Nothing to fear from that. Nothing at all.

"But here we are," she said, beaming. "We're working together a little like I dreamed. We see each other every day and talk about the paper. Sure, we differ, but we support each other. Seeing you with Peder, I sort of imagined he was ours. You were a good father figure to him. Like it or not, we're joined at the hip, aren't we?" She raised her plucked brows.

He nodded. "I would've liked Peder as a son."

"There's something else," she said, rising and standing by him. "I hated you for breaking up. Blamed you for everything else, especially my drinking. I still held that grudge when you hired me. And then, after a couple weeks, I realized you weren't the guy I hated. That was someone I invented to avoid owning my failures. Your actions have revealed you since Peder's death. I truly know you." She grasped his hand, fished something from the pocket of her skirt and put it in his palm.

He gulped in recognition. His lips moved without words. In his palm lay the large, high school class ring he gave her. His promise of an engagement. The ring that had scarred his temple. He looked into her eyes.

"I know, I know," she said, throwing up her hands. "God knows why I kept it. I suppose it was a promise with no place to go. Maybe it reminded me why I hated you. Now it reminds me why I love you." She bent down and put her lips to the scar. "I'm truly sorry."

He sat still, slowly absorbing her confession. Is this an apology or a reconciliation or both? He couldn't remember her apologizing before. It was always his fault. He gazed at the ring, stupefied at the sight. Once it united them, then it parted them, and now it reconciled them. He felt overawed as if looking at the Milky Way on a clear winter's night. Her moist lips salved an old wound. Apologies—the stuff of miracles.

"Enough confessions," she said. "Play the piano. Some of our favorites."

"What do you want to sing?" he asked as he led her to the Steinway. He used to accompany her when she rehearsed for the high school musicals. He riffled the keys.

"How about... *uh*... 'Put Your Head on My Shoulder.'" She hummed a bar.

He picked out the melody by ear, and her contralto filled the room. Then he reprised "Broken-Hearted Melody," "Will You Still Love Me Tomorrow" and other favorites from their puppy love years.

"I want a Patsy Cline number," she begged. "How about 'Crazy'?"

"After all you've been through, you want *that* one?"

"I've been singing it for years. All right, how about 'I Fall to Pieces'?"

He shook his head. "Don't know it."

"Okay, how about 'I'm Back in Baby's Arms'?"

"Now you're talking."

As he played, she stood behind him with her hands resting on his shoulders. He wondered if she expected an invitation to spend the night in baby's arms. He hoped not. It was too soon to say "yes" to sex, and all that followed from it. You've got something good going, he reflected. Don't fuck it up. The mantle clock chimed ten. He felt relieved when she said it was time to go home. They hugged, and she left.

The ringing phone jolted Boston out of a deep, restful sleep. He stumbled getting out of bed and then picked it up and mumbled, "hello."

"Hey, good morning," Jack said. "Glad I caught you. Want to cover an arrest? I'll pick you up at nine."

"Yeah… but why are you calling at six-thirty, asshole?"

"Just to make certain you're ready, mister detective."

The word "arrest" brought him instantly awake. He moaned but got up. It's about time, he thought, as he washed his face in cold water. Yesterday, he felt bummed when Jack didn't invite him to cover Calvin's interrogation. He felt left out when he heard secondhand that Nelson was in jail. Jack didn't call him about that, either. His brother's habit of going by the book left no space for an interested sidekick. When he grumbled about it last night, Ginger took Jack's side for once. She thought his absence from the scene would protect Jack from charges of favoritism.

He made coffee and waited until 7:00 a.m. to call Ginger with an invitation to breakfast at 8:00. She arrived early, as eager as he was. They chatted about the next stories over scrambled eggs, toast and coffee.

"What do you think Calvin will do?"

"I don't know. There'll be deputies. He'll fight when he gets to court. Chances are, I'll be a witness at the trial. That means your job is assuring objectivity—remember?"

She stuck out her tongue, and he laughed. "Of course. Go," she urged. "It's too important. If it weren't for you—"

The Suburban's arrival interrupted their talk. Boston went onto the veranda and Ginger followed. Jack waved and she waved back, hesitantly. Boston was about to step off the porch, but she grabbed his arm and kissed him fiercely on the mouth.

"Wow, what's that about—as if I didn't know?" Jack said in his low voice as Boston got in the Suburban. "Whatever it's about, I'm all for it."

"It's not what you think it is. I asked her to breakfast to plan the story."

"*Uh-huh*. Breakfast. What time did she arrive last night?"

"Damn-it. I'm not sleeping with her. Or Daphne, now. I don't want anyone hurt."

"Most of all, you." Jack glanced at him and then looked ahead.

"We've moved beyond the past," he said as he watched a farmer plowing stubble. He was momentarily mesmerized by the ribbon of soil rolling off the moldboard. That's what you did last night, he thought. You plowed under the stubble to plant something new. "Surviving the Tatanka put things in perspective." He paused. "We've got something solid now, like you and Kris."

"Good," he grunted. "I was afraid you'd repeat the past… maybe get a matching scar."

He glanced at his brother again. "I don't feel a need to prove anything."

"*Uh-huh*. Especially to yourself."

"Yeah. Especially to myself. I'm not going back to Chicago. Not permanently."

"I know," he said softly as he swerved around a tractor towing a grain wagon. "I haven't seen you this happy in years. I know you're at home here."

"It shows?"

He made a hissing sound with his lips. "Shows? You must be blind. I knew you and Ginger had something going again. Besides that, your focus on Peder's death showed me you're one of us."

"Thanks for telling me. Sometimes, I feel like a fool."

"That's what friends are for. They show you what you can't see."

"You're the second one to tell me that."

"Who's the first?"

"Daphne."

CHAPTER 40

Calvin sat on the edge of his bed after another rotten night. His mind just wouldn't rest. He stood and broke wind. Then, stretching, he shuffled to his bedroom window. A roaring wind beneath the leaden clouds whipped spume off the waves on Lake Iosco. A foul day. He turned from the window to take a shower.

The pulsing water on his shoulders soothed him enough to think about his situation. Mercer can't convict you without Nelson's testimony, he thought. Running to Argentina puts the spotlight on him. He looks guilty. Just as well he left. He is weak and too prone to crack under pressure. Let him take the rap. Mercer is not likely to come after you, especially if you express surprise and regret over Nelson's crimes.

The more he thought about it, the better he felt. You have Jager as an ally, a source of inside information. He had told Nelson the case rested on circumstantial evidence. In that case, your attorney will argue that Eliot killed Peder and committed suicide. There is enough ambiguity in that for acquittal. And if the case drags on, Mercer might drop it. Without Nelson, who is left to testify against me? No one. And no one will ever believe it. If they do, the organization can always find a hold-out to create a hung jury. No, you will be alright.

Then he thought of life after a trial and acquittal. The organization might not have any use for your bank or financial services or you. You are too old to continue the risks and the strain. Meade will make certain the paper covers every allegation. Even if acquitted, people will avoid you like a contagious disease. He thought of the money he had quietly put in offshore accounts. It was money the organization didn't know about. More than enough money to live comfortably somewhere warm. He buttoned his shirt and noticed his hands trembled when he knotted the tie. You will be fine, he thought, unable to fully overcome the doubt that had wormed its way in overnight.

Dora woke completely sober after closing yesterday with a pot of chamomile tea instead of brandy. Stretching her arms, she thought it was the best night's sleep in years. Then she heard Calvin moving about in the adjacent bedroom. The sheriff is going to arrest him today, she guessed. If not today, tomorrow. Soon anyway. Once he's arrested, you can start life over. You'll be free to leave Featherstone and go abroad. Maybe look for Claudio in Madrid or find a man like him. This marriage is over. You married for love but sold out for money. You have no one to blame but yourself. Now he's doing something criminal. Possibly murder.

Her second-floor room was a retreat in pastel colors with an attached bath and a walk-in closet. The king-size bed had a matching nightstand; its other wall had an armchair and desk. She examined herself in the full-length mirror and liked what she saw. Regular spa sessions kept her figure looking forty-four instead of fifty-four. If she could keep her face and figure, she might have another shot at romance or even love. As usual, she took care making up her face and then dressed in a loose cashmere sweater and wool slacks. Dora felt younger than her years when dressed in chic clothing. She strode down the stairs and into the kitchen. Calvin sat hunched at the marble countertop. From the look on his face, she guessed he had barely slept.

"Good morning," she said with a bright smile. "I hope you slept well."

He growled something inaudible around a mouth filled with toast and marmalade.

"I wonder if the sheriff will come back," she said, pouring a glass of orange juice without adding vodka. "He'll probably question me too."

"Shut up. Fix your drink and shut up. I need to think."

"Oh, I'm not drinking today. I want to be clear-headed. Who knows, he might ask me questions, too," she said, spreading her arms in a gesture of possibility.

"They don't question wives," he snarled. Then he pushed away from the counter. "Besides, you don't know anything."

"I can testify if I choose."

"My attorney will make a fool of you," he said and lumbered to his office.

Dora let out her breath, suddenly trapped between loving the man he used to be and longing to leave the man he had become. Leaving seemed easier when she woke up. Now she realized love—even one-sided love—didn't let go easily. She walked the corridor to his office, where he scribbled notes with a trembling hand.

He sensed her presence and looked up. She stood with her arms folded under her breasts. Yes, he thought, she is still a beautiful woman, and it reflects well on you, too. Men notice her, and she likes their attention. You do not mind as long as they just look.

"Oh, Calvin, I know more than you think," she said, her voice full of sadness. "I'm a lush. Probably a fool. But I'm not stupid. Something troubles you. I've known it a long time."

He detested that soft, rueful tone that made it harder to deny her wish. Mother had that voice, too, he recalled. A diabolical trap. He felt like an ungrateful heel when he refused Mother's wishes. But he loathed himself when he gave in to Dora's.

"Leave me alone," he growled. "I am busy." He turned his attention to some papers. This is no time to talk about what she does or does not know.

"Listen," she begged. "I've tried to ignore what I've overheard. I ignored it to protect you. You and Nelson. Because of what we mean to each other. That's what's important. That might be why I drank… to forget my suspicions."

"What you think—is *nothing*. What you know—is *nothing*," he snapped. You have to shut her up, he realized. Send her away, commit her to… even if—

"You've destroyed yourself, Calvin. Destroyed everything I loved in you," she continued in a plaintive voice.

"You know nothing. You were always drinking," he said, realizing she was a bigger threat sober than drunk and hoped she would retreat and mix a drink. When she didn't, he saw something new in her refusal—defiance. She was not backing down.

"I wasn't always drunk. I've stood by you a long time," she cried. "I'll stand by you if you tell Jack what you know. I can't pretend anymore."

"You know nothing," he roared, terrified. "It is too late. Talk and I will be dead in a week. And you, too. We have to see it through." Yes, he thought, include her, so she realizes there is no way out but to go along.

"You know who wanted Eliot and the boy killed, don't you? Don't you?"

Her words sent a tremor through him. His fingers trembled. She knows too much to be trusted, he thought, as his mind raced through his options. Get her committed to rehab, a mental hospital and—

"You know who did it," she whispered. "I overheard you… you were…"

He shot out of the chair. One hand closed around her throat. She gasped as he squeezed. Her knee hit him in the groin. He wheezed and let go. As she turned to run, he grabbed a handful of the sweater. She bent over, extended her arms and backed out of the sweater. It slipped over her head. She ran upstairs and locked the door to her room. He followed, lumbering up the stairs with labored breathing. His kick shattered the lock, and the door slammed open. Dora stood at the nightstand with the phone in her hand.

"I cannot let you talk," he said in an impassive voice. "You will ruin my life. Nelson's life. Your life. We must stay together. Be silent. Talk and we are all dead."

Too late, she realized the depth of his anger, his fear. It was always there but hidden. Now it transformed his appearance. He glowered at her, the arms limp at the sides, the head sunk into the shoulders, the narrowed eyes ablaze with feral violence. He moved clumsily, a monster on the loose.

"Give up," she cried. "Make a deal. I'd rather die than live this way."

"Nelson will take the blame," he said, taking another step.

"No. Not Nelson. Not my baby."

"He went to Argentina. Running is a confession. I cannot do anything."

"Goddamn you."

"Shut up. We will be all right. They cannot pin it on me. They cannot touch him. Don't talk. We will be alright," he growled and stepped closer.

"I won't," she seethed between clenched teeth. "I won't be a party to murder."

"I am in too deep. They will kill you, too."

"I don't care. I won't have this on my conscience."

"Too bad," he muttered. "Too bad." His backhand sent Dora cartwheeling across the wide bed, onto the floor and into the corner. Her fall knocked over a table lamp. He picked it up, yanked the cord from the outlet and ripped off the shade. The lamp's long, brass stem fit his hand like a baton. He plodded like a robot around the bed toward her. Spittle clung to his chin. The wheeze of his breathing filled the room. With each step, he slapped the baton against his palm. Step, slap-slap, step, slap-slap.

Dora scrambled to her feet, flexed her knees and pressed her hands against the wall. Calvin has killed before, she realized. Now, he's going to kill again. She watched his eyes. He was only a step away. Then he lifted the baton and roared as he swung the baton toward her. She vaulted across the bed before the baton sank into the sheetrock wall. While Calvin yanked at it, Dora's scrabbled in the nightstand drawer for a letter opener, a nail file, anything for a weapon.

Deputy Thomas sat in his cruiser at the end of Calvin's driveway. The deputies who had stayed all night were in another. When Jack arrived, they followed the Suburban to the house. The trees on the point weren't close enough to break the raw wind off Lake Iosco, but a pair of chickadees flitted between the trees and a feeder outside Calvin's house.

"I want his arrest by the book," Jack told them, scowling to reinforce the point. "Treat him with courtesy but no favors." Two deputies went to the other sides of the house. Jack was about to ring the bell when he raised his hand. "Listen—hear that?" Muffled voices from inside the house rose and fell. "I think they're arguing." Then a *crash*, silence, a shriek and the dull *thud* of something heavy. Jack yanked open the front door and rushed into the foyer. It was silent inside the house except for a clock ticking in another room.

Standing at the bottom of the stairs, he cocked his head, puzzled by the rhythmic slapping sound. Then *bang-bang*. Silence. *Bang*. Several heavy objects hit the floor at once. Jack and Thomas drew their pistols. The odor of nitro drifted down the stairs.

"Calvin—Dora? It's Sheriff Meade."

"Up here," Dora called in an even voice. "Top of the stairs."

They raced up the stairs single file and stopped abruptly in the bedroom doorway. Calvin Eugene Ferrall, city leader, public benefactor and killer lay face-down on the taffy carpet. "Oh, sweet Jesus," Jack moaned. He squatted to press a finger on Calvin's neck. "He's dead," he said, rising to his feet, careful to avoid the pool of blood. "What happened?"

"I shot him—but he's been dead for years," she said from the window seat. She drew the cashmere Afghan closely about her bare torso while looking at Calvin. He died long ago, she thought. Died a little each day. Died of fear and greed that squeezed the goodness out of him. He's gone. You've never hated him. Now you're free but alone.

"Do you want to call your attorney," Jack asked.

"That's alright," she said. "I know my rights. I'll call him if you arrest me. Otherwise, let me talk while I have the nerve." Thomas left the room to call the crime scene unit, the coroner and an ambulance. Boston sat on the end of the bed to write notes.

"Take your time. Tell me what happened," Jack coaxed. "Can I get you anything?"

"No. I haven't been this sober in years. Now, let me talk," she said, believing the truth was the only way out. But how much truth?

Everything you suspect or only what you know? She started with this morning's attack. After that, she couldn't stop talking. "I don't know much about his business… finance doesn't interest me… but it's something illegal. We were newly married when I overheard his father tell someone Kaplan was gone forever. It meant nothing until the *Statesman* ran the stories."

"And lately, the other deaths?"

"Kaplan's discovery didn't bother Calvin. Not until he heard that Peder met Eliot. After that, I overheard him talking to someone about a research project. It made sense after Peder and Eliot died. I didn't want to believe it."

She stood, gathered the robe like a royal cape and pointed out the window. "This view… building the house cost a bundle. I don't know where he got the money. I didn't care. Even if I suspected something, the bank had audits, so it had to be alright. But audits and conscience aren't the same. A conscience doesn't let you sleep."

"Anything else?"

"He went crazy when I begged him to give up. Turn in the others. He wouldn't. Said he was in too deep." Then she began weeping, and her shoulders shook.

"Those marks on your neck—did he attack you? Hit you?"

"Yes. And then he came after me with that lamp. I threw reading glasses, a Bible and—"

"Yours?" Jack lifted the Beretta .380 from the bed.

She nodded. "It was at the back of the drawer. I forgot I had it. He bought it years ago for my protection," she said with a wry smile. "Will anything happen to Nelson? He said you can't touch him in Argentina."

"He's in jail. We picked him up yesterday."

"*Nooo*. Not my baby. What's he done? I want to see him. Please?"

"Maybe later, after we're done questioning you and him. That's enough for now," Jack said. "We'll step out while you get dressed. A deputy will take you to the courthouse for a statement. We'll question you some more later."

CHAPTER 41

Jack started the Suburban but let the engine idle while the heater battled the wintry chill in the oncoming rain. Calvin's crimes, his sudden death and Dora's coolness rattled him. Though he had no part in Calvin's death, it weighed on him. Was there anything you could have done to prevent it? Arrive a few minutes earlier? No, he thought. You couldn't foresee that. It's not on you, just as Peder's death isn't on Boston. It played out the way it was supposed to.

"Aw, shit," Boston groused.

"Aw, shit, what?"

"This isn't what I had in mind."

"You wanted days of humiliating public trial with a conviction?"

"Goddamn right, I did."

"That's vengeance. Dead or alive, his reputation is the same. You can get your revenge with an article about his crimes. And another about whatever Mercer does with Nelson. It won't be what you wanted, but it will be justice."

"What about Nelson?"

"Mercer will charge him with bank fraud and money laundering."

Boston sniffed and then exhaled as if conceding defeat. It was that kind of a day.

"What?" Jack looked at him.

"Just remembering this place as it was…" but his voice trailed off for a moment. "The old fishing shacks… summer bonfires… our duck blind. Life was pure. Now…" He shrugged.

"We grew up. What's next for you?"

"I'm going to visit the Norgaards and make peace with myself."

"It's about time," he said, patting his brother's shoulder. They sat a while longer and talked of the good times long past as the spumy waves broke on the sandy point.

"Are you going to charge her?"

"Depends. Murder, manslaughter or self-defense? You heard the story. Her lawyer will call you as a witness."

"You don't want to charge her, do you?"

"It's my job to gather the facts. It's Glenda's job to convict her. She doesn't like to lose. I doubt she'll charge unless she has an abundance of evidence."

"And you're not going to dig for it, are you?"

Jack pursed his lips as he shifted the Suburban into gear. "Justice is more than the abstract letter of the law. Justice is balance. Community harmony. After what Calvin did to her, some might say she delivered perfect justice."

"Is that your argument?"

He didn't reply at first. The roaring wind off Lake Iosco wasn't the only storm in the county. Jack knew the word of Calvin's death would run through Featherstone like a tornado. It would upend the city by nightfall. A civic leader killed by his wife. Another leader in jail. And he knew the next arrest would definitely affect the election. How will the voters react to it on Tuesday, he worried. It's in everyone's interest to put out all the facts right now.

"There's something else you need to know," Jack said.

"What else?"

"Nelson left telephone and bank numbers on his desk pad. We traced them. Guess who got paid for alerting him to the warrants?"

Boston caught Jack's note of glee. "You mean—"

"Nelson transferred money to Jager's account yesterday. His arrest is at noon."

"I want to be there when you do it."

"Oh, not me. That's Thomas's job. He'll do it just before Jager speaks at the Chamber luncheon. I'll be at home taking a nap."

"Do you have enough to convict him?"

"Yeah, but his trial won't happen until after the election."

"You know, it's possible he can win the election while in jail."

"I think Nelson will help us. Once he's charged with murder, he'll shit his pants and ask for a deal. He might get it if he fingers Jager and confirms his old man's crimes."

Boston laughed. "You've been reading Machiavelli."

"No. I've been listening to you." He put a big hand on Boston's shoulder. "You saw what I couldn't… didn't want to see because I was scared of losing. My head was so far up my ass I didn't see anything but shit."

"Ginger did a lot of this."

"Yeah, but you stood by me when you didn't have to," he added in a husky voice. "I owe my life to you."

"You stood by me, too. That's what brothers do."

"That's a fact."

Ginger went to the office, cleared her calendar for the day and waited by the phone. When Boston didn't return, she went to lunch at Hanson's Coffee Shop. Her salad arrived followed by Hazel, a moment later. "What?"

"Boston wants you. Right now," she said. "He's really worked up."

"Tell him I'll be along in a minute," she said, annoyed and then excited. Something big must have happened if he sent Hazel to find her. She forked the salad into a take-out carton and rushed to the office in the cold rain. "What's going on?"

"Sharpen your pencils, gal. It's a blockbuster."

She disliked being called gal but bit her tongue. He closed the door to his office. Whatever happened had put a gleam in his eyes and a ring in his voice. She listened as he spoke in staccato bursts, like a Tommy gun spitting bullets.

"She shot him? Incredible!"

He hopped about as giddy as a cub reporter with his first scoop as he repeated what Dora told them.

"Alright, alright, Ahab, you've harpooned the whale," she said, laughing. "Pull yourself together. I need you cool and detached." The story enthralled her. It might be the biggest of her career. She envisioned an entire issue about a crime family in a small Minnesota city. "Now—how many stories? I think I hear three or maybe four. You talk and I'll type."

Her fingers flicked across the computer keys as he laid out the sequence of events. Then they went over it, connecting Calvin and Nelson to pieces of accumulated evidence. Rolling her shoulders, she realized there might be more material than they could squeeze into a regular edition. Two hours passed as they wrote, read their text and moved paragraphs to shape and reshape the stories. He went over the evidence while she chose the details for the narrative.

This is what you dreamed of in high school, she thought. You're together, working in concert, like dancers expecting each other's moves. A chill ran down her spine. At last, maybe our lives will… His phone interrupted her thoughts.

He listened, hung up and slapped the desk, grinning from ear to ear.

"Well, spit it out," she ordered, falling for his tease.

"That was Ellen," he said. "I asked her to cover Jager's talk at the Chamber luncheon. I didn't tell her the deputies were going to arrest him." Then he explained why. The phone rang again. He listened and hung up. "That was Jack. Nelson will cooperate with the investigation. We'll have more stories tomorrow. And maybe the day after."

"Okay, down, boy, down. Let's figure out how to lay out this story."

Hazel was a *Statesman* veteran, the right hand to London, then Boston and now Ginger. She was discrete and rarely entered their offices without knocking. Today, however, she abandoned discretion and put her ear to Boston's office door. Whatever it was, it was a big story. She overheard Ginger and Boston debating where and how to place the stories. It sounded as if neither was inclined to give ground to the other. Through the door, she heard Boston say:

"Put the crime stories on the front page. Let people see the whole picture. That includes the Jager piece."

Ginger: "No. That might trigger sympathy."

"That doesn't make sense."

"You listen to me," she said, in a sharp, don't mess-with-me tone. "We endorsed Jack. I don't want Jager's story to look political. He's in jail but on the ballot. He can still win."

Hazel smiled, thinking, good for you, Ginger. Don't back down.

"Well, let's make sure he doesn't win," Boston said. "I'm the owner. I say it's front page."

Hazel shook her head. *Uh-oh*, Boston. You pulled rank. Big mistake.

"We agreed… I have the last word. It goes on page three."

"Oh, all right," he conceded. "But I don't agree."

Meanwhile, the other editors had crept to the door and heard Boston say, "You like to fight, don't you?"

Ginger laughed. "Yeah, but I like making up even more."

"Remind me to fight with you more often."

"Any time. Do you want to make up tonight?"

"Only if you do."

Hazel put a finger to her lips and waved the curious eavesdroppers back to their desks, snickering at what they overheard.

CHAPTER 42

Boston looked out the turret window at the rainy dusk, content to simply be in the moment and grateful it was all he possessed. Tomorrow wasn't his. Not yet. When it came, it would be a gift. His place in the world and his purpose in life never looked so clear as it did now. He couldn't recall ever feeling like this. You're as real as sunlight or rain or air without reference to anything else, he thought. You're free to be yourself. How long has it been since you consulted a memory of dad to decide what to do? It's been weeks. Now you know you aren't him. And so does everyone else. That's reconciliation. It must be what Father Frank meant. You're home at last.

He looked at the town, gray in the rain. By tomorrow morning, word of Calvin's death will have burned across Featherstone like a grassfire before the spring wind. Everyone would have heard a version of the story. Tomorrow, they could feast on the details in the *Statesman.*

CALVIN FERRALL KILLED IN DOMESTIC QUARREL. LOCAL LEADERS HAD MOB TIES. That was a three-column story detailing the Ferrall's crimes, from bootlegging to money laundering to the deaths of Kaplan, Eliot and Peder. FEATHERSTONE BANKER NABBED ran below the fold. It covered Nelson's arrest. Ginger put COUNTY DEPUTY ARRESTED where it would be visible at the top of page three. Besides reporting on the bribe, the story added information about the internal investigation for excessive use of force.

Boston drove into town but detoured away from the courthouse. It was lined with a scrum of reporters and television vans setting up for Jack's press conference. He knew Curt and Ellen would be there. Ginger and Robin, too.

He entered the *Statesman*'s newsroom to the sudden applause of editors, reporters and pressmen. They surprised him, and he felt his face warm with embarrassment over the attention. But it pleased him, too. He felt their affection and knew he belonged with them.

"Yesterday, I was an unpaid reporter," he told them as they ate a celebratory coffee cake. "Today, I'm merely the paper's owner, a publisher with nothing to do. But you, you are an incredible team. I'm proud to be one of you."

His office phone rang constantly, but he ignored it until the voicemail filled with messages. He ignored them, too. Then Hazel put a crisp, white business envelope on his desk. She said it was hand-delivered. The Commerce Bank return address told him who wrote it. The short letter, penned in a sharp, slanting hand, got right to the point. "Boston. Congratulations! I salute you and the *Statesman*. You have confirmed something I long suspected but didn't know how to expose. Thank you. Most respectfully, Emery Daniels."

"Thank you, Emery Daniels," he whispered. "Without you, there wouldn't be a story."

After an hour, he returned home to escape the phone, but the house phone rang and the voicemail filled with messages. Sooner or later, a reporter—or a gaggle of them—would show up for a comment he didn't want to make. He laced up his hiking shoes and left the house for a long afternoon hike at Limestone State Park. Always a good place to think.

He went to the *Statesman* in the morning, knowing there was little for him to do at the paper except get in the way. He went on his customary midmorning walk around the Green beneath clearing skies and a chilly wind. As he passed the Emporium, Pinky waved from the show window. He waved back with a strange tingle down his spine. It appeared they now accepted him as one of them.

Heistad was leaving his office when Boston passed and gave him a flustered greeting with the embarrassed expression of a dog that had wet the floor. "*Uh*… you know, I'm sorry for the things I said," he began. "You did something… well, incredible. I saw Nelson every day… never had any idea that… well…" He offered his hand. "No hard feelings, I hope."

"None," he assured him and continued walking. Everyone knows who you are, he thought, not as they imagine you are. Your place is here.

⁂

Boston sifted through the voicemails at the office, noting which ones to return either by phone or in person. Then Jack called. He sounded worried.

"I don't think you're out of danger," he said. "Nelson doesn't know the killers' names, so we don't know who's on the loose. We better assume someone in the mob sees you and Ginger as threats because of what you know. So, watch your backs."

Jack's right, he thought. You better be careful, and he took note of the vehicles in the alley when he arrived at the *Statesman.* Then he checked at noon and each evening when he left by the loading dock door. It was easy to match vehicles to the businesses they served. As he left for the evening, he noticed the Dodge pick-up and the box truck hadn't moved since noon, but the dark Ford Crown Victoria was new. It was parked up the alley. Because of the twilight, he couldn't see if anyone was in it. He lingered in the dock doorway for a moment, then got into the Jeep and started the engine. The Crown Vic remained parked when he pulled away.

He stopped at the mailbox and looked up San Juan Lane at the dark shape against the evening sky. The house had seemed as invincible as a castle when he was a boy. Now its isolation made it vulnerable to an ambush. This realization, once planted, made him uneasy and fear took root.

He unlocked the front door, entered the house and flipped on the foyer light switch. He jumped at the flash-*POP*. Just a light bulb, he thought and then noticed the rasp in his breathing. He caught a whiff of propane on his way to the kitchen or thought he did. The burners were in working order. You're getting jumpy, he realized, as he replaced the foyer light. Just relax and use your brain. Then he set about making supper.

While he ate, he tried to re-enter the killer's mind so he wouldn't be the prey. This killer murders by staging everyday accidents. He's opportunistic and resourceful. That's how he nearly ran you into the Tatanka. The alley is the only place in town where he is likely to abduct or shoot you. You're the most vulnerable here at the house or on the road to it.

While washing the dishes, he thought about how they might get to him. They could blow up the house while I'm at the office. But that's pointless without me in it. They could easily pick the locks and get into the house. Then open the burners and fill it with gas. But they need to make sure you're in the house when it blows up.

He put away the dishes, thinking about how to set off a remote explosion. A timer won't do because they can't predict my return. What they need is an ignition that you set off—*a lightbulb*. That might work. Just rewire a switch to cause a short circuit. The spark would ignite the gas. When you come home and turn on a light and *BOOM,* you and the house go up like a Roman candle. Afterward, the evidence will point to a faulty stove. If you can think of it, you can bet they have, too. He slept poorly.

Before leaving for the office, he raised all the windows an inch to cross-ventilate the house. Then he plugged a table lamp into the foyer circuit and left it burning. He recorded the pressure on the propane tank and shut off the gas to the house. His defensive preparations guaranteed nothing. There was more than one way to blow up a house.

Office chores didn't distract him for long from his antsy worries about the house. Ginger took him to lunch, and he told her about the risk they faced. Then he returned home. Getting out of the Jeep, he saw the crushed cigarette butt. He picked it up and sniffed. Still fresh. He felt a chill. Then he remembered the Crown Vic wasn't in the alley when he arrived this morning, but it was there when he left after lunch. They are watching, he thought, as he circled the outside of the house. All of the windows were closed. Peering inside, he saw the table lamp was still burning, but it had been plugged into a different circuit. The propane valve was turned on. That meant gas to the house. He shut it off.

Sweat dripped from his armpits, and his heart pounded audibly in his chest. He wiped sweaty palms against his slacks. You've entered the killer's mind, he thought. He pushed up on a window. Thank God, they didn't lock them. The window released the stink of propane. He pushed open all the ground-floor windows. When he no longer smelled gas, he propped open the back and front doors, so the breeze swept through the house. When he felt it was safe, he entered and shut off the burners. Then he switched on the foyer light. The bulb popped, and he felt a strange affirmation that he thought like the killer.

CHAPTER 43

Boston spent the afternoon airing the house. As he did, he played mind games to predict the killers' next moves. It reminded him of playing chess. They were professionals, so their boss must have been Calvin's boss. They would wait to see if the booby trap worked. When it didn't, they would try something else. Maybe break in at night, lock him in a closet and torch the house. Or it might be something he hadn't thought of or couldn't imagine. Or they might go after Ginger. The exercise drove him to desire a drink.

He called Ginger at the office and told her what he had discovered. "Keep it to yourself but be cautious entering your house."

"Jester always barks when I arrive," she said. "If he doesn't, I'll know. Then I'll call you. Are you going to call Jack?"

"No. He'll tell me to move into town with him. I won't do it unless he takes you, too."

She laughed long and loud. "Yeah, right. Some household." Then laughed some more.

"I'm staying here until these goons are caught or dead. Either is fine with me."

The mild afternoon air gave way that night to a Canadian cold front that dragged in low clouds and lower temperatures. Instead of a trip to the office, Boston unpacked several cartons until he found the .357 revolver his father carried as an Army Air Force pilot. An uncle told him he killed two Germans after he was shot down. If so, his father had never spoken of it. Boston took it to Viet Nam as a reporter, where a Marine gunny taught him to shoot expertly. That was fifteen years ago. He hadn't fired it since. However, on this cold, gray day, he felt better preparing for a fight than waiting for it. The Smith & Wesson in its shoulder holster had a reassuring heft.

He set three cans atop some fence posts behind the carriage barn. They didn't look like killers and couldn't shoot back. He loaded the chambers and snapped the cylinder in place. This is silly, he thought. You're overreacting. Playing cops and robbers. Except, the killers aren't playing. No, this isn't silly.

The first three shots missed. "Shit," he groused, thinking of the gunny's instructions. Then he recalled the stance, the two-handed grip and looked at the target beyond the sights. A squeeze of the trigger and the can sailed away with a gaping hole. He did it again and again and again until he could knock off three cans with three quick shots. Satisfied, he reloaded and slipped the pistol into the holster. They've avoided gunplay for accidents, but it's good to be prepared. At least you can defend yourself if it came to that and shrugged off his worries about their next trick.

He stacked the lawn chairs in the carriage barn, inspected the storm windows and split a short cord of fireplace wood. He stacked the wood in a lean-to next to the carriage barn. The afternoon passed quickly as he buttoned up the house and yard for the winter. Querulous honking overhead drew his attention to long skeins of migrating geese streaming south across the continent beneath the low clouds. An awesome sight of creatures free of jurisdictions. He and Jack used to hunt them from a blind off Sioux Point. He was a hunter then; now he was prey.

Jack's invitation to supper offered a respite from sitting alone in the drafty house while the wind moaned about the eaves. For a few cozy hours, he lapsed comfortably into the web of familial love woven into decades of shared history. After eating, the brothers went to the rec room. Jack poured drinks and they settled into the beanbag chairs.

"I feel the campaign is coming together," he said. "People are coming back to me. Jager seemed on edge a few days before his arrest, like maybe someone was about to reveal something. You don't know about that, do you?" he said with a sideways roll of his eyes.

"Who, me?"

"Yeah, you…" and then he laughed from his belly. "An' I don't wanna know."

As Boston laughed with him, he debated whether to mention the booby trap. If Kris overheard him, she would hound him until he moved in with them. He decided to risk it after he swore Jack to secrecy.

"Goddamn it, why didn't you tell me last night?" he growled. "I could've sent a crew out for evidence. You might not be so lucky the next time. Let me park a deputy at the lane."

"No, not there. Put one on the road between my house and Ginger's."

Jack agreed and called the office. He returned, shaking his head with Kris right behind him. "They're no extra deputies tonight. Best I can do is have a patrol swing by your place and hers every hour."

"I heard all of that," Kris said, standing in front of Boston, her hands planted on the hips. "Now, you listen here," she began, shaking her finger. "You're staying with us. We've got the room. You'll be safe here. I don't want to hear 'no' and a lot of excuses."

"Thanks, sis, but I can't do that. If I'm at risk, so is Ginger. I won't take the easy way out," he said. "If you take me, you take Ginger, too."

Then they argued with proposals and counter-proposals. "Oh, alright, have it your way," she said. "Honestly, Boston, you're more pig-headed than Jack. At least promise you'll be careful," she begged, putting her hand on his arm.

Seeing a smile lurking behind her frown, he kissed her cheek. "I love you, too," he said.

It was nearly 10:00 p.m. when he backed out of the driveway. A small voice at the back of his head urged him to stay. He ignored it. Ginger's house was dark when he passed it. The gale bullied the Jeep, and in the headlight beams, wind-borne leaves scuttled across the road like mice fleeing a cat. He tried not to see it as an omen. Then he stopped at the bottom of his lane. He saw the foyer window aglow from the lamp he left burning. The small voice said they might be waiting for him inside the house. If so, they probably parked nearby and walked in. He drove to the crossroad at the House of Truth. The

Crown Vic wasn't along the road or in the bar's lot, but its absence wasn't as reassuring as he had hoped. He drove into his yard without headlights and parked next to the carriage barn. Getting out, he crouched in the dark but felt as if he stood in a spotlight. He flinched at the rustle of leaves. From his cover, he studied the windows looking for faint shadows cast by someone moving inside. Nothing. He tossed a pebble toward the porch. It bounced twice down the steps with sharp clicks. Wind gusts followed. Another pebble. Of course, they would wait for him to enter.

Running at a crouch from cover to cover, he went to the propane tank. The controls were as he left them. The windows he cracked open were still ajar. The backdoor was still locked. Drawing a breath, he crawled into the doghouse and pushed on its hinged back wall. It swung inward, and he crawled through the short tunnel into a mudroom cabinet. Generations of dogs used it to go in and out at night. Rusty was the last. As teens, he and Jack sometimes snuck in that way after late nights out.

Seated on the mudroom floor, he turned his head this way and that, listening for unfamiliar sounds. It took a moment to recognize the furnace blower, refrigerator compressor and mantle clock. No human sounds. He sniffed but didn't detect hints of aftershave, tobacco or sweat—only cooking odors, dirty dishes and the garbage pail under the sink. Satisfied, he locked the windows, turned out the table lamp and went upstairs. He realized the revolver was useless hanging from the bedpost and its presence seemed less reassuring now.

CHAPTER 44

The wind screeched and roared through the oaks all night. Small sounds wakened Boston with a start. He turned his head to winnow the source of the sound. Was it a limb brushing the roof or leaves whirling against a windowpane or the wind keening about the eaves? Or were they picking the lock, jimmying a window or something else? The wind gave them the perfect cover for a break-in. A thump woke him from a light sleep. He crept down the back stairs to the kitchen gripping the revolver. The stove's clock read 2:10 a.m. He glided from room to room, feeling more vulnerable than he ever felt in Viet Nam. But that was war, and you were with the Marines. This is different. "It's murder, you're alone, and you're scaring yourself shitless," he whispered in disgust and returned to his bed.

The fitful night ended shortly after 5:00 a.m. The gale had blown itself out and the overcast with it. Morning stars twinkled through the bedroom window. He shivered in the cold and pulled on jeans, a sweatshirt and running shoes. Then he descended the main stairway lit by the moonlight pouring through the great room windows. He stopped at a turret window for a view of Venus rising in the east. Tattered bits of clouds drifted by the half moon, and frost glistened on the lawn.

A form moved furtively down the hill among the trees along the lane. It was one shadow among many and too dark to see clearly. The animal moved carefully, never far from the trees, as if sensing danger. It was probably a buck in search of a doe. As it trotted closer, he noticed the uneven gait as though it had been injured. He watched it leave the cover of trees near the top of his lane and angle across the grassy slope. Then he saw it wasn't an injured deer but two men jogging toward the house.

He whirled about and took the stairs two at a time. Snatching the holstered revolver and a mackinaw, he bounded down the back stairs to the mudroom. He closed the electrical main, dropped to the floor and then crawled through the hinged cabinet to the doghouse. Drawing a breath, he dashed to the carriage barn. A moment later, he saw flashlight beams sweeping through the great room.

He grasped the Jeep's door. Then remembered the keys were in the house. Ambush them as they leave the house, he thought. No, that won't work. Too easy for one to go around the house and catch you in a crossfire. You've got the initiative as long as you keep moving. If you have to face them, do it on ground you choose. Someplace unexpected. He jogged downhill through the trees that edged the lane. Then he came to a Ford Crown Victoria parked in the trees where his lane joined the county road.

Got you now, he thought, though he wasn't thinking but following an instinct more basic than thought. He let the air out of the left front tire. Take them when they change it. He crouched behind some hazel bushes to wait. His sense of time slowed. He heard cows bawl in the distance. Then he heard the wingbeats of a crow overhead. He flinched at catching a shadow in his peripheral vision. He shivered. Whether it was cold, fear or anticipation, he couldn't tell. Waiting stretched on dream-like. What are you doing here? Is this justice or something else? Calvin's dead but these two killed Peder. He waited, nursing his rage with memories of Peder until his mouth burned with the acrid taste of bile.

It was nearly sunup when he heard them talking as they walked down the lane. "…an' how the fuck did he get away," one of them asked in a nasal voice. "His car's still there."

"Just as well," the other drawled. "I don't want to shoot anyone in their house—"

"Well fuck that, we shoulda torched it—"

"Oh sure… we tried that, and he figured it out."

"The boss wanted him an' the bitch done last week," the nasal one whined. "Now what's-his-name is dead, and the heat's on us."

"Yeah, but it's our ass if there's a screw-up."

Boston crouched lower and gripped the revolver in both hands. His knuckles white in the dim light. Now you've got them, he told himself. *You're mine.*

Drawz started the car. It went ten feet and stopped. "C'mon, Nix. Get the spare," he ordered. The two men worked without speaking and made swift work jacking up the car. Nix grunted as he wrenched off the lug nuts. The last one stuck.

Boston crept forward and stood by a thick tree. His vision tunneled to only the men. *Take them now* roared in his head. "Stand up," he yelled and flinched at the sharp click when he cocked the revolver. "Hands on your heads." The men stood, raised their arms and looked over their shoulders toward him. His hands trembled in panic. He didn't know how to get their guns. Say something, a voice told him. Keep the initiative. "You, you in the tan jacket. Turn around. Slowly. Hands on your head."

Drawz turned toward him. He seemed so non-plussed, it gave Boston jitters.

"With your left hand, unbuckle your belt. Drop your pants."

He complied but seemed amused.

"Okay, you with the black pants. Turn and do the same."

But Nix spun about. His hand and pistol a blur. Two shots. Bark fragments stung Boston's cheek as he closed his fist. Nix pitched back against the car and then fell forward. Drawz pulled his automatic. Five shots fused into a long barrage before Drawz fell on his back with his feet tangled in his pants. Two red stains spread across his blue button-down shirt.

Boston stared at the bodies, gasping as if he had run sprints. Nix was dead, face down in the gravel. Drawz was still alive but bleeding. Boston picked up Drawz' pistol and then Nix's and tossed them into the car. Seeing a brick-sized mobile radiophone on the seat, he took it and punched in Jack's home number.

"It's Boston. I've got… one dead… one wounded… on my lane… hurry." Then he turned to Drawz whose narrowed eyes followed him.

He wasn't through with him. Not yet. Not until he satisfied something inside. The foul taste returned to his mouth as he approached.

"Did Ferrall… hire you," he asked, gasping. "I know the… basic facts. Give me… names. Lie and… I'll shoot…"

"You're not… a killer," Drawz whispered as blood bubbled through clenched teeth.

"Try me. Talk or… you can… bleed out," he wheezed, holding his side with one hand. "Did you… kill the boy?"

"I'm sorry… about that… not… my idea… you, you set him up. You… got him killed."

Something red and black, like a volcano, erupted inside Boston's chest. His fury came as a tidal wave of immense, godlike power over life and death. *Kill him. Kill him now*, the inner voice ordered. *You owe it to Peder. No one will know. They won't care. Do it now*. "Yes," he said to the voice and thumbed back the hammer.

You misjudged him, Drawz thought as he looked into the revolver's barrel scarcely eight feet away. He shivered and felt the aiming point was the gap between his eyebrows. He *is* a killer, he realized. Not stone cold like Nix. He's got a conscience. It'll kill him later. Drawz hoped he wouldn't miss.

Seeing fear replace Drawz's smirk aroused Boston. The sight gave him a sensation like erotic pleasure as he prolonged the man's terror while awaiting his end. He thought of the Gunny who said squeeze the trigger. Don't pull. Squeeze it gently. Just a little more pressure and…

"Drop the gun!"

He looked up and saw a deputy by the Suburban aiming his pistol.

"Drop it," Jack ordered from somewhere behind him.

Boston lowered his arm, and Jack took the revolver.

"You alright?"

"Okay. Little… out of… breath."

"You kill him?" Jack nodded toward Nix.

"Yeah. Guns are… in the car. Shot the oth—" and then he doubled over with a groan.

"You hit? Oh, Christ, no," Jack cried.

Boston came to on the ground as a medic slit the bloody sweatshirt up the side. He said something about one under the arm. A little more to the right and… and then Jack said something about the emergency room.

"You've been hit," Jack told him when he was fully conscious. "It's a flesh wound, but we're going to the hospital. I don't think the other one is going to make it."

An orderly in green scrubs eased Boston into a wheelchair and turned him over to a nurse he didn't know. She wasted no time cutting away the rest of the sweatshirt. With dispassionate efficiency, she cleaned his wounds and asked questions about his medical history. He couldn't remember anything. While she worked, Jack paced about the room fussing aloud and asking how serious the wounds were and if he would he be alright.

"Jack, sit down and shut up," she said. "He's going to be fine."

Boston didn't know the rotund Doctor Nielsen who looked at his wounds. "You're going to hurt for a while," he said. "You were shot twice. One bullet ripped the flesh under the left arm and broke the fourth rib. The other went through at the ninth rib. Fortunately, it didn't hit any organs. There are splinters in your cheek. You're lucky they didn't hit a major artery." Then Doctor Nielsen scribbled a prescription for painkillers and gave it to the nurse.

"Hold still," she ordered as she injected Boston with an anesthetic. A moment later, when the area numbed, she stitched the torn flesh as easily as sewing a button. "There. Now rest. Don't lift anything. Check in next week. If you don't, Kris will be all over your case." She smiled at him for the first time.

"Hey, look at this?" Jack wiggled his fingers through the bullet holes in the mackinaw.

"Oh, damn," he moaned. "I just bought it."

"Well, now you've got a tale to go with it."

"Screw you," he said, grimacing because cussing didn't hurt as much as laughing.

"Here, take this," the nurse said, holding out a painkiller and a cup of water.

"Not yet," Jack intervened. "I need his statement while his head is clear. I'll take him to my house for breakfast. Kris can administer the dose."

"Who do you think you are to—"

"I'm the sheriff, that's who," he said. "He is now my case."

Jack picked up the phone, called Kris and said he was bringing Boston to breakfast. And he was hungry. Ten minutes later, Kris opened the door unprepared to see him with his arm in a sling, a bandage around his torso, another band-aid on his cheek and a blood-stained jacket draped over bare shoulders. Jack sketched in what happened as they sat in the kitchen.

"You could have been killed," she cried, bursting into tears. "Ben and Lily would've been devasted. Honestly, Boston… What were you thinking?" she demanded, shaking a finger at him. "No, don't tell me. You weren't thinking. *Men.*" Then, gathering herself, she smothered him with non-stop chiding wrapped in tones of love as only a mother can do. As she continued scolding, Jack buttoned him into one of his large flannel shirts. Then they sat at the kitchen table with pancakes, eggs, bacon and coffee. "Jack, say grace."

"Grace? Oh yeah, grace," he said and recited the one they learned in catechism with an added thanks for his brother's life. Boston said little as he ate his way through the eggs and pancakes. When he revived, Jack got a pad and a pen. "Tell me what happened. Keep it simple."

He recounted the break-in and the escape but couldn't recall much of what happened in the shoot-out, except it seemed to have happened long ago to someone else. His fleeting memory of the details was already hazy. Nothing he said registered as something that involved him. It could have been a scene from a movie.

"That's enough," Jack said, slipping the notebook into his pocket. "One more question. This isn't for the report. As your brother, I have to know. Were you going to kill him? Something in your eyes… your face. It wasn't you… it scared the shit outta me."

"I don't know," he said, drawing out the words. "A voice told me to kill him. I wanted to… I guess… it said I had a right to… I don't know."

"Alright, enough." He rested his hand on Boston's good shoulder. "We'll notarize your statement at my office, then I'll bring you back here."

"No. Drop me at the office."

"You heard the doc. Rest."

"I'm okay for a while. There's not much pain. I want to outline the story while I can. Ginger can drive me home."

"You can't manage alone," Kris said. "You'll stay with us. I'll take care of you. Please?"

"Thanks, sis, but I'll be okay. If I need help, I'll call. Alright?"

"Alright, be that way," she conceded. "But I'll check on you." Then she kissed him.

"I love you, too, sis," he replied and winced as he slid his good arm into the mackinaw's sleeve. Jack buttoned it over the sling as he and Kris continued arguing over his care. Then he took the painkiller from her hand with a glass of water.

CHAPTER 45

Ginger dreamed she was following Boston through a tunnel toward a distant light. He vanished as she was about to touch him and reappeared farther on but still out of reach. The dream was full of Fourth of July fireworks and peals of thunder, followed by silence. An ambulance raced through her dream with its siren screaming. She woke for a moment, rolled over and lapsed into sleep.

Rising after sun-up, she bundled herself into a parka and prayed beneath the oak. In the crisp air, small clouds left her mouth as she recited the Our Father. She thought of clouds as *ruach*, the Hebrew word for spirit and wind. The *ruach* of God made life possible because *ruach* was also love. Facing the sun, she said, "Yes, Boston. I love you. I'll take you as you are."

She arrived early at the *Statesman* and entered an empty newsroom. Boston's car wasn't out back, so that meant the cleaning crew left the light burning in his office. Second time this month. If it happens again, she thought and entered to turn it off. She gasped at the sight of Boston hunched at the desk. His face seemed pinched in pain.

"*Uh*, good… morning. Are, are you sick?"

"No," he rasped. "Close the door."

She was certain he was sick. The room was warm enough, but he had a jacket buttoned over a flannel shirt. Then she noticed the empty left sleeve. "What happened to your arm? What's—?"

"They broke into my house," he said in a harsh voice. "I *shot* the sonsabitches. One's dead. Maybe both."

"You killed… Oh my God, oh, Boston…"

"Yeah." A pause. "I'm not proud of it, but—"

"But you're not okay."

"I got hit. Broke a couple ribs."

"You could've been killed!"

"Yeah, I might've. And you, too. Please, help me finish this story."

Oh God, she thought, he doesn't know when to quit. "Move over, I'll type. Just tell me what happened." Her fingers tapped out his words as he recounted the events. She asked a few questions and printed off an eight-paragraph story: ONE KILLED, TWO WOUNDED IN SHOOT-OUT.

"Look this over. I'll be right back," she said and rushed to the restroom. She flushed the vomit down the toilet and rinsed her mouth from the tap, but the vile aftertaste lingered. Seeing her pallid cheeks in the mirror, she pinched them to restore color. When she returned, Boston had redacted the article into four terse paragraphs that linked the killers to the deaths of Peder and Eliot. His excised version said only that he shot them when they broke into his house. Gone were her lines about laying ambush and being wounded.

"You can't take that out. People have a right to know."

"People have a right to the pertinent facts," he whispered. "I don't need to be glorified in my own newspaper. Just print it. Then take me home. I'm fading."

She took his arm and helped him down the stairs. "He's got the flu and a temperature," she told a reporter who had just arrived. Then she guided him to her car. She knew her lie would forestall questions only until Robin picked up the copy. It would come out in tomorrow's edition.

Boston dozed on the ride home, and Ginger steadied him going up the three steps to the veranda. Once inside the house, he asked to go upstairs to his bedroom.

"Not today," she said in a voice that wouldn't brook contradiction. "You're not ready for the stairs." She eased him into a great room chair and then crossed the foyer to the guestroom. It was as she remembered it, with an adjacent bathroom. There were folded sheets and blankets atop the queen-sized mattress.

This is more than an act of kindness, she thought, as she made up the bed. This is a commitment. You're giving yourself to his care. You're giving to him as he risked his life for yours. Is that love? You know the answer. There's no going back.

With a mother's patience, she helped him out of his clothes and into pajamas. She checked the bandages, relieved the wounds weren't bleeding through the gauze. These moments of intimacy aroused her, but she held that inside. It was enough to feel aroused. When he sat on the bed, she eased him onto a pillow though the movement made him gasp. Then, pulling the covers to his chin, she kissed him as if he were a child, but he was already asleep.

Ginger called Hazel, who said everyone wanted to know how he was feeling. Ginger said he was resting, that he had the flu and she was about to spend the afternoon with her mother.

"Oh, yes, I forgot," Hazel said. Then they laughed. Ginger hung up, certain that everyone knew where she was, if not why. She also suspected what they were imagining and found that wonderfully titillating. If only that were so.

The house always had lots of good books in the great room, but most of them were packed. All that remained were complete sets of leather-bound Harvard classics that looked good but were rarely read. She wasn't in the mood for *Little Women* or *Wuthering Heights* or *A Tale of Two Cities*. Then she came upon a stray paperback copy of *An Indecent Obsession*. The title struck her as apt for her circumstances. She curled up in the guestroom armchair.

"I don't want a life without you," she whispered and hoped his subconscious could hear the words, "What are we? Colleagues, friends, lovers—what?" Having spoken her feelings, she began reading.

"What are you doing here," he asked when he woke at midday, groggy from painkillers.

"Looking after you. Are you hungry?"

"Thanks, yeah. But you don't need to do that. I can—"

"No, you can't. Not today. Besides, it's my turn to help you."

He yelped when he tried to sit up. She put an arm behind his shoulders and pushed him upright. Pride more than muscle got him on his feet. Then he sat in the breakfast nook while she prepared vegetable soup, crackers and cheese.

What is he thinking? she wondered. Was he silent because of the painkillers or fatigue or the shock of killing a man—or was it two men? He said little while he ate. Then he went back to bed. But his silence didn't perturb her this time. She sat on the veranda with the book but gazed for a while at the rolling countryside. Autumn was full-on, with the crimson sumac flaring next to the bronze oaks. She returned to her teenage dream of living in this house. That was long ago when she was another person, but it was a beautiful dream.

"How do you feel now," she asked when he woke at sundown.

"I don't know. Still confused. It happened so fast. Most of it's hazy."

"I think it will get clearer as you talk about it."

"I thought… it's what they did to Peder… I wanted to kill them. Then I killed one or was it two? It just happened. A reflex. One of them said it was my fault. That's when I snapped. All of a sudden, I felt incredible power—like I was God. A voice told me to kill him because I had the right to do it. I was pulling the trigger when Jack stopped me."

"It's alright," she whispered, "you're alright." Her face was so close to his that their noses nearly touched. She put her hand on his cheek. He covered it with his. They spoke in whispers. Each felt the other's breath. Then knocking on the front door interrupted their prelude to a kiss. Ginger drew back, startled. She opened the door and faced a short, plump blue-eyed woman with curly brown hair wearing nurse's scrubs.

"You must be Ginger," the woman said. "I'm Kris."

"You're Jack's wife," she said, realizing she had never thought of Jack as married. "I'm glad to meet you," she said, extending her hand. She hoped Kris didn't come to replace her.

"I stopped by to check up on him. How's he doing?"

She gave Kris a droll smile and a "follow me" nod toward the guestroom. Then she stood back as Kris went to the bed.

"How're you feeling, Superman? I said I'd check on you." She kissed him. Then she turned to Ginger. "Mind if I check a couple vitals?"

"No. Be my guest."

She took his temperature, blood pressure and pulse. Then she opened the pajama top and inspected the bandages. "Well, everything seems normal except his judgment." She turned to face Ginger with a smile that he couldn't see. "Is he giving you any trouble?"

"No more than usual," she said, liking Kris. She's smart, sassy and strong—we could be friends.

"I think you're in good hands," Kris told him as she put away her instruments. "You don't need anything from me." Then she pointed at Ginger. "Now, you do *exactly* as she tells you—or else." Ginger walked her to the door. "I feel better knowing you're here," Kris said. "I know you'll keep him from doing something stupid."

"If I can't, I know who to call." Then they laughed together and said goodbye.

When she returned to the room, Boston wanted to practice getting out of bed.

"You can try, but it'll hurt."

"I've got to find a way. In case I need to take a leak in the night."

"Okay… try it, but it's going to hurt." She wished Superman would ask for help.

Instead of asking, he rolled onto his right side, dropped his right leg over the edge of the bed and used his right arm as a lever to push his body into a sitting position. After a brief gasp, he grinned, pleased he could do it.

He ate the simple but substantial supper she cooked. As they ate, his conversation maundered about from detail to detail before doubling back and repeating what he had said. He's rattled from killing a man or two, she guessed. It's his conscience talking, but maybe he's shocked that he can be violent. Is there honor in that? Maybe talking will purge a sense of guilt. She finished eating and helped him to bed.

Propped on pillows, he took her hands in his and looked into her eyes. "Thank you. From the bottom of my heart, thank you. I've never needed anyone the way I've needed you today. I know I will be okay, but please stay until I'm asleep. After that, lock me in. I'm sure I'll feel better tomorrow."

"Oh, I'm sure of it," she laughed. Then she fluffed his pillow and kissed him goodnight.

CHAPTER 46

Boston woke in the twilight of dawn in a strange room wondering, where am I? Then he remembered. You're in the guestroom. Then the sequence of yesterday's events settled into place. Ginger's goodnight kiss was the last thing he remembered.

Lying on his good side, he saw the room between the bed and the door. The book Ginger was reading lay on the armchair's seat. Then, he noticed her skirt, blouse and bra draped over the arm of the chair. It took a moment for this to register clearly. Behind him came the soft rise and fall of breathing. Easing onto his back, he saw her sleeping on the bed's far side, covered by the quilt his mother had pieced. In the morning light, her lustrous hair seemed even redder against the white pillowcase.

What if we spend the day in bed? The idea gave him a sudden hard-on. She won't do that anymore than you will, but he indulged this fantasy, exhaled softly and stared at the ceiling. You slept together, but nothing happened—nothing physical, anyway. But you slept together, and something has happened. He touched the scar on his temple. Something has happened. You are both living into a future. You can stay in bed with her if you choose, but you're not ready to plunge in, even if she is. You need clarity. Sex now will fuck it up. Someday—maybe soon, you will. So, what are you going to do? You can't just lie here with a hard-on.

Seeing the sun's rays sneak beneath through the drapes inspired him to get up. This was Saturday, and the draft of his November

Outlook column was due next week. All of the notes were at the office. Unlike the earlier columns, this one would be personal—a recap of the summer. The theme was clear in his mind, and he wanted to finish it now. He folded back the blankets, filled his lungs and held his breath to keep the broken ribs in place. They hurt. Then he rolled onto his good side and levered himself into a sitting position. The ribs flared for an instant but didn't throb. He glanced over his shoulder. Ginger was still asleep. Moving slowly, he crept to the staircase, grasped the banister and went to his room. He hurried as much as he could, but one-handed dressing took time. If Ginger woke before he left, he was certain they would have an argument over it.

Securing his arm in the sling, he crept down the back stairs and left the house by the back door. Shifting the Jeep into neutral, he gave it a little shove and hopped in as it coasted down the lane. He started the engine below the hill, pleased that he had just made a clean escape. The newsroom was usually deserted on Saturdays except for whoever was on call. But they rarely showed up before 10:00 a.m. As he entered, he saw a light on in Robin's office and paused at her door.

"You… you're…" she cried, as astonished as if he had risen from the dead.

"I'm okay. Just sore."

She was happy to see him and wanted to hear all about what had happened. "Tell you what," he said, fishing $20 from his wallet. "I'll give you an exclusive if you buy us some coffee and rolls. I don't want to talk to people right now." When she returned, they sat at his office table and ate strudel while he recounted the break-in, the shoot-out and Ginger's care.

"Where is she now?"

"I guess she's sleeping…" he said with a shrug.

"*Uh-huh*. I suppose she is," she said with a smirk. "You know, you two aren't fooling anybody. But we're all for you."

"Thanks," he said and blushed.

Then she told him about the talk on the street. Most of it was about his exploits. The rest was about Jack's success in busting a crime ring. She thought the election-year fence-sitters were now getting behind Jack.

"Why are you here," she asked. "You should be resting."

"I've got a column to finish. Why are you here?"

"My ex and I alternate weekends with the kids. It's easier to write poetry when I can't see dirty dishes."

"Poetry… why am I not surprised?"

"I've published two collections so far, and I'm working on a third."

They finished the coffee and strudel, and Robin returned to her verses. He closed his door and called Braydon. They spent an hour talking about his next steps, and, in the end, he told his boss about the shooting. Before signing off, he promised to avoid doing anything else so heroically stupid. An hour passed, and while he was reworking his column, the door flew open. Ginger stood there with a glow in her eyes that reminded him of a bride after the wedding night.

"You turkey," she said in a low voice. Then her cherry lips widened into a bright smile. She closed the door and kissed him on the mouth. "I knew you'd be here. Why didn't you wake me?"

"I didn't have the heart to," he said easily, kissing her back. "You looked so, *uh*… virginal in my bed. I… *uh*… thought if I let you sleep, you'd… *umm*, I did it to save your honor. Thank you for taking care of me."

"I wanted to. As for my honor—ha. It's Halloween. Do you want a trick or a treat?"

He exhaled. "Another good night's sleep will be a treat. My ribs aren't ready for a trick. How about a rain check? I promise to collect. Meantime, let's go out to dinner."

"You're on," she said and kissed him again. "I'm off to see Mama—for real this time."

It was already twilight when he pulled up to the Egg Lady's house in the BMW. He wore a navy blazer without a tie. Ginger stepped out of the house in an indigo dress with a strand of pearls and her hair teased into curls. She gawked at the car.

"The Jeep was camouflage," he said. "I got out the Beemer, so you'll know what kind of guy you're going out with."

"Oh, are we having a date… a real date?" She giggled.

"I hope so," he said. "It's about time."

They entered the country club and the buzz of conversations died as the guests turned toward them. The silent attention unsettled Boston. He felt as if they were celebrities, and he didn't know what to do or say. He didn't want to talk about the Ferralls or the shooting. Instead, he simply nodded to acquaintances and said thank you to well wishers. Taking Ginger's arm, they followed the waiter to a small table well apart from the others. It had the vase of fresh red roses he had ordered.

"We're celebrating," Ginger said to the waiter before Boston could order drinks. "I want a club soda over ice with lime. He wants Tullamore Dew—neat."

Boston started to protest.

"It's all right. You deserve it. It won't affect me. Or you—now."

They tapped their glasses. "To us."

"I want you to come to Mass with me tomorrow," she said. "It's All Saint's Day. I want you with me when I give thanks for your life."

"Well… okay," he said, uncomfortable because he hadn't gone in years but retained the guilt imparted in childhood. "I probably forgot how it goes."

"That's okay. I have a prayer book. Then, if you can manage, let's take your sporty car and have a picnic somewhere."

CHAPTER 47

"Thank God, that's over," Jack said, still in pajamas. He stirred cream into his coffee until it was whiter than he was. The election was over. His winning trend had set in early, but he stayed up until the end. Then he slept in. He was still amazed he carried all but six of the county's sixty-six precincts.

"See, you won big," Kris said. "Just like before." She refilled his cup.

"Yeah," he laughed. "Jailing my opponent guaranteed a landslide."

Boston phoned to congratulate him. He thought Jack's handling of the Ferrall case swung voters behind him.

"While we're talking," Jack said, "we're going celebrate on Sunday. We want you and... *uh, uh...* Ginger to come here to watch the Viking-Packer game. We'll have sloppy joes and all the trimmings. Will you come?"

"Of course, but I can't speak for Ginger."

"Well, ask her and let me know."

"Nope. Quit treating her like gum stuck to my shoe. I won't come unless you invite her."

"Aw, c'mon. Just ask her and—"

"No. It's time you two deal with each other like adults. Here's her number. What are you afraid of? You're the sheriff."

"Oh, all right," he grumbled. He put it off until noon. Then he didn't feel ready and postponed it again by telling himself she was busy. Besides, he had some chores.

"Is Ginger coming?" Kris asked at supper.

"I was just going to call her," he fibbed and slunk to the phone. He dialed and braced for the sarcasm that was sure to follow. She answered. Then he hemmed and hawed before blurting the invitation.

"Thank you. I'd love to come. I've met Kris, and Boston's told me about your kids."

"Good. See you soon." He hung up, relieved.

Sunday was cold and wet, but that couldn't overtake the homey aromas of sloppy joes in Jack's house. There was a chocolate cake on the dining table. The family room had a sideboard of bowls filled with baby carrots, cheese curds, potato chips, guacamoles and salsa. It also held beer, whiskey and sodas.

Jack wore his Vikings sweatshirt and waited at the window. When they pulled up, he whisked them out of the bone-chilling rain. "Welcome. I'm glad you're here," he said, giving Ginger a toothy smile that she returned with one of her own. Then he put his arm around her—a first. Kris hugged her. Boston wiped the rain off his glasses. Lily took to Ginger at once and wanted to show off her Barbies. Ben went to the family room with the men for the pregame show and opened a Coke. Jack handed Boston whiskey over ice and then made one for himself. The three males dropped into the bean bag chairs in front of the muted television.

"What a week," Jack sighed. "I won big thanks to you… oh, and Ginger. I got to thinking… you know, between banking, investments and silent partners, the Ferrall's managed to sucker nearly everyone into a web that abetted and covered their crimes."

"I suppose that includes us, too," Boston said.

"Yeah. Us too. Next week I'll hold another press conference and—"

"Don't tell me, tell Ginger. She's the editor."

"Okay, I'll tell her over supper. For now, just play dumb." He said that Nelson's cooperation had helped the Feds find a network that ran drug money through several other small city banks. For that, he might get a lighter sentence. There was no evidence he was involved in hiring the hitmen. "Oh, the one you wounded will pull through. He'll do time."

"Any charges against Dora?"

"No. Self-defense."

"I suppose Karen and Dora will lose their houses. A shame they'll suffer, too."

"Yeah. The law isn't perfect but… well, we do the best we can."

"It's still a shame."

"Karen's water broke yesterday while she visited Nelson," he said. "The contractions came on so fast that detective Kasson delivered the baby before the doctor arrived. I'm glad Nelson saw it all. We let him hold Baby Dora for a while. I figure she'll be six when he's up for parole."

"How funny, but how sad."

"I heard Dora plans to take Karen and the baby with her to Minneapolis. Her parents have money. I think they'll get by."

"Tell Ginger, not me."

"Yeah, I will. Another thing," Jack said, dropping his voice. "I know you felt invisible because of Dad's fame. For the record, you went far beyond anything he ever did. Or could've done. Yeah, he was a stylish writer and a great columnist. None better. But he and I didn't have your grit to buck the town and take on something like Kaplan's death. I want you to know that. And another thing…" Jack paused. "Dad told me about your last conversation with him. It hurt, but he understood. He didn't hold it against you. He said separation was best until you came to terms with yourself."

"Thanks. Since then, I've realized I made him into someone larger than life. Someone he wasn't. Now I feel like I have a place in this town."

"You do. And just between us, I'm going to start working on a master's in psychotherapy. Someday I'll open a practice. Good counseling might head off trouble before some other sheriff has to clean it up. So, what about you?" He got up and mixed two more whiskeys.

Before Boston could answer, they heard peals of feminine laughter in the living room above them.

"I know, I know. They're two of a kind," Jack said, shaking his head. "After Kris met Ginger, she talked her up to the sky. Said it's time we bring her into the family."

"Thanks for calling her."

"Thank you for insisting. It was worth it to hear her surprise. You know, I was kind of blind to the fact that she had changed, but my ideas about her hadn't. That's prejudice. And it can happen to anyone."

Giggles followed another burst of laughter.

"And another thing," Jack said with a laugh. "You and me, we better stick together. Those two are going to be more than we can manage."

"That's a fact." Boston raised his glass.

CHAPTER 48

It was Ginger's idea to throw a memorial gathering for those most deeply touched by Peder's death. In a perverse way, Boston thought it was a party for them, too. If it weren't for Peder's death, he knew they wouldn't be together now. His death had changed everything. Their guests would arrive in about an hour: Jack and Kris, the Norgaards (if they came), Thomas, Kasson, Hazel, Carson, Robin, Ellen and the other reporters. And Daphne. Ginger insisted on Daphne. He spent the morning cleaning and arranging the furniture in the great room. Ginger promised to help, but she hadn't showed up. He checked the time and tried not to be annoyed.

Ginger fretted at running late. That was because of the salon appointment. Fortunately, the tailor was on time, and the new clothes fit perfectly. She raced home in the snow flurries, showered and put on the new clothes. This must be how a debutant feels, she thought, gazing at herself in the mirror. We're a couple, however it works out.

November's first sloppy snowfall, with its omens of changing seasons, covered San Juan Hill in white. The snow meant Boston might migrate to Chicago, and there would be long months between his visits. She huffed the damp air ripe with the scent of woodsmoke. What's cozier than large flakes outside and a crackling fire inside?

Then she flung open the front door. Boston stood spellbound in the foyer holding a dishtowel. Then she swept past him into the great room like a diva, flung the woolen cape over a wingchair and twirled about in a dark green midi skirt with its matching bolero jacket.

"Like it," she asked, and her hands slid slowly down the bodice of her jacket. "Well?" Her lips twitched as if to say something. She watched his eyes travel from her face to her bust to her hips. Lust, she hoped.

"God—you turn me on," he said, twisting the towel.

"And?" she cocked an eyebrow.

He made a hungry sound in his throat.

"Come on. Tell me what you feel. Say it out loud."

"I think that, *uh*—"

"What? What do you think? C'mon, tell me." She wiggled her fingers.

He pushed her gently onto the sofa until they lay nose-to-nose. "I'm not over you," he whispered. "I don't ever want to be over you. I love you."

"I love you, too," she said, putting her lips to his ear. "I've waited months to hear it."

"Months?"

"You're the only guy I couldn't forget. So, can we be in love and work together?"

"Well, I kind of thought that's what we've been doing."

"Let's do it right," she said, kissing his mouth. "You need to know more about me. And there's more I want to know about you. Let's keep going a day at a time until we're comfortable being vulnerable." Then she thought of Chicago. He hadn't said anything lately. After another kiss, they sat up, and she straightened her clothes.

"I know, you're wondering about Chicago," he said. "Here's my latest column for the *Outlook*. What do you think?" He gave her two typed sheets from the coffee table.

She put on her glasses and read, "The View from Here – Boston Meade."

> The German poet and philosopher Frederick Schiller wrote: "It is not flesh and blood but the heart which makes us fathers and sons." Schiller knew that no man ever outgrows the example of his father. Whether for good or ill, a father is a yardstick by which each

son measures his life. Fathers are phantoms to some men, cautionary figures to others, and to others, a model of everything they want to become. Fathers are always with their sons, sometimes visibly, often unseen, but always a presence that guides them toward destinies they can scarcely see.

"Wow, what a beginning!"

I am the fortunate son of a country editor and have seen the good and the ill fathers do. Though I struggled to succeed beyond the orbit of my father's fame, I made his standards mine. Whether my assignment was Beirut, Saigon, Chicago or Washington, I mentally consulted the man who published the *Alton County Statesman*. I published my father's newspaper during five months of leave from this magazine. Taking on his role has made me more fully myself. A father's example lasts a lifetime, and I acknowledge a debt I can never repay. Therefore, I will continue publishing the local news essential to communal life. It is a task as necessary as breathing.

"It sounds like your valedictory," she said, meeting his eyes. "This is fabulous. I want to run it in the *Statesman*, too."

"I don't know. It sounds a lot like a gloss on Turgenev in *Fathers and Sons*. Those relationships are complicated. The deaths of Peder, Eliot and even Calvin came out of father-son relationships gone bad," he said softly.

"And your father-son relationship," she asked, putting her hand on his.

"That, too. Dad and I were loving but competitive. Close but guarded. I've learned to accept him as he was and not as I imagined him to be."

"I love your conclusion."

I love reporting the news for the good it does. After twenty years of covering national and international

> news, this column will shift its perspective to look more deeply at notable events through the lens of my community. Like my father before me, I will survey the world from Featherstone. It is from here, where I now live, that I will comment on the ways momentous events affect us at a community level. My father and his generation did much good, and I have a responsibility to pass that to coming generations.

"It's the best piece you've ever written," she said in a husky voice.

"I hope so." Then he got up and added a piece of oak to the fire. "I'm happier here than I ever was in Chicago. This is home. Father Frank told me home is the place you run from but return to when you're ready to reconcile the contradictions of your life."

"That sounds so right."

"Unfortunately, I have to go back to Chicago."

"*What*? *What do you mean*?" she cried, feeling the ground sink beneath her.

"I've got unfinished business in Chicago."

"What's unfinished? You just wrote that—"

"I've got to negotiate a contract with the *Outlook* so I can write my column from here. And I have to sell the condo and get rid of stuff I don't need. I'll be gone a month."

"And then?"

"I'll live and work from here. I might take an occasional project for the *Outlook*. After twenty years apart, is a month too long?"

"Some days, an hour is too long," she said with a pout that quickly turned into a smile. "No, I guess not."

"And what about this," he asked and then paused, weighing what he was about to say because he couldn't foresee how it might turn out. "Would you like to live here? That is, you take the guest room, I'll keep my room upstairs. We'll share the house so we can take things a day at a time until we think the time is right to—"

"Live in sin! Really?" she squealed, her eyes wide. "You mean it?" Then she gave him the brightest of smiles. "Yeah, well, I always dreamed of living here. Yes, yes, but on one condition."

"What's that?"
"Love me, love my dog."
"How does Jester feel about it?"
"The same way I do."

ACKNOWLEDGEMENTS

This novel would not be possible without the guidance and encouragement of Jill Swenson of Swenson Books, whose insight, friendship and advocacy kept me moving toward publication. Many thanks to Peter Hajinian, Geoff Barnard, Garland West and Ralph Winklemeyer, critical readers whose precise, often blunt, but insightful observations and suggestions shaped the work in progress. And to Susan Thurston-Hamerski, my editor who is herself a novelist and poet, and Ian Graham Leask, teacher, writer and coach who knows far more about publishing than I do. Most of all, my deepest gratitude goes to my wife, Susan Stavig, who encouraged my writing and gave me the time and space to be AWOL for this preoccupation with imaginary people and places.

ABOUT THE AUTHOR

Newell Searle grew up on a southern Minnesota farm near the fictional Alton County among people whose parents or grandparents were Scandinavian and German immigrants. His vocational high school focused on agriculture, but he earned degrees in history from Macalester College and the University of Minnesota. Ditching an academic career, he worked in government affairs at Cargill, Inc, served as Minnesota's Deputy Commissioner of Agriculture and retired from Second Harvest Heartland as its public affairs officer. He published *Saving Quetico-Superior, A Land Set Apart* and received the Frederick Weyerhaeuser book award in forest history. He has also published articles about Minnesota's social and natural history. He began writing fiction in retirement and divides his time between Minnetonka and Finland, Minnesota, and Puebla, Mexico.